RAMBO
Rambo, Cat,
You sexy thing /

TOR BOOKS BY CAT RAMBO

You Sexy Thing

YOU SEXY THING

CAT RAMBO

TOR

A TOM DOHERTY ASSOCIATES BOOK
NEW YORK

YOU SEXY THING

Copyright © 2021 by Cat Rambo

A Tor Book
Published by Tom Doherty Associates
120 Broadway
New York, NY 10271

www.tor-forge.com

Tor® is a registered trademark of Macmillan Publishing Group, LLC.

The Library of Congress Cataloging-in-Publication Data is available upon request.

ISBN 978-1-250-26930-0 (hardcover)
ISBN 978-1-250-26928-7 (ebook)

Our books may be purchased in bulk for promotional, educational, or business use.
Please contact your local bookseller or the Macmillan Corporate and Premium Sales
Department at 1-800-221-7945, extension 5442, or by email at
MacmillanSpecialMarkets@macmillan.com.

First Edition: September 2021

Printed in the United States of America

0 9 8 7 6 5 4 3 2 1

For Ann Leckie,
who wanted a space opera
in omniscient point of view

1

The entrance buzzer chimed. Someone outside in the public hallway of the space station was paging admittance.

Niko Larsen, a.k.a. Captain Nicolette Larsen, formerly one of
the finest military geniuses the Holy Hive Mind had ever threatened to absorb, now retired, looked around.

Huh, she thought. *What now?*

She checked the view screen. A delivery bot stood outside,
flanked by a large crate, about two meters long, a half meter wide,
and a meter tall. Its metal carapace was brown and yellow, regular
station delivery colors. It stood patiently, ignoring the impatient
stares of passersby trying to get around the large crate in the five-
meter-wide hallway.

She didn't remember any deliveries due today, but pushed the
button nonetheless. With a velvety *whoosh*, the door slid open.

"You should take that into the kitchen through the back access
hall," she said. "There's too much furniture in here—don't bring
it in this way."

Despite her words, the bot was already trundling forward past
her and the entrance lectern, trailed by the crate. It said, with
a burst of speaker static resembling an officious chirp, "The access hallway leads to the kitchens of the Last Chance Restaurant.
This delivery tag specifies Last Chance, and the default is main
entrance."

"Then don't go with the default, use the back entrance!"

"My delivery has been executed." The bot detached itself from
the crate, leaving it two meters inside the vestibule. "I do not

accept outside commissions. If this service has been of use to you, please consider rewarding my employers with a plus."

Machines were impervious to Niko's stare, but she tried one anyway. "This service has *not* been of use to me," she said.

"My employers are sorry you feel that way," the bot said, and exited.

Niko looked the crate over. Made of white-enameled plasmetal, it floated a few inches above the ground. A sturdy handle on each of the narrower ends provided the means with which to move it. The label simply bore Niko's full name, along with the address of the restaurant. The orange ticket that would have disclosed its point of origin seemed to have been torn away.

Niko scowled at it and left it where it was.

She found her second-in-command waiting in her office. He silently handed her a sheet of plastic. Looking it over, she raised an eyebrow.

"Eggplant?" she said incredulously. "Where am I going to get eggplant, short of you finding some cut-rate sorcerer? None of the big farm ships grow it, except for the *Mannan*, and their prices are twice anyone else's."

She frowned at Dabry in the office's dim light. Niko was of indeterminate human mix, with pale brown skin and graying dreadlocks swept back and contained on the back of her head with an ivory beaded net. Muscular shoulders rounded out her white chef's jacket, its front unpinned and fallen awry, bearing coffee stains along one sleeve.

Although Niko was tall, the being also wearing a chef's jacket (although significantly less crumpled and stained), hulking across from where she sat at the tiny desk, dwarfed her. He was an Ettilite, an eight-foot-tall humanoid with four arms and skin the color of the eggplant they had been discussing.

Dabry, a.k.a. Sergeant Dabry, also retired from the ranks of the Holy Hive Mind, folded both pairs of arms and stared at her impassively. "The critic," he rumbled, "is said to have a weakness for old Earth food from its Mediterranean region. I need to analyze the components if I'm going to replicate it."

"You are all way too concerned about this critic," Niko said. "Ever since Skidoo found out who booked the reservation, you have been ridiculous! Cleaning—which I do approve of. Redecorating—which I approve of up to a certain budgetary point. But now—rearranging the menu just for them?"

"They have the power to give our restaurant a Nikkelin Orb," Dabry said with a tone that implied that once a restaurant had achieved such a thing, everyone in it might go ahead and die happily, their life goals attained. They had been operating the Last Chance for a little over a solar year now, and Dabry tracked its few reviews and mentions with a gleeful zeal.

"This *restaurant*," Niko said, not for the first time, "was not my idea."

"*This* restaurant," Dabry said, also not for the first time, "got us all out of the Holy Hive Mind's service and let us keep what we could of the company together while we try to build our finances."

Niko sighed and pushed away the piece of plastic. They were in her tiny office, which had once been a walk-in closet and still smelled of artificial cedar and orange from the scent unit near the fan. (She kept saying she meant to disable it because of its rattle.)

While she groused about the unit, though, she didn't mind it, really. It overrode other smells from the kitchen only a few steps farther down the tin tube of a hallway, and their associated memories. Cinnamon, when Milly was baking, reminded her of Free Trade life and came on a wash of loss and nostalgia. Stale dishwater reminded her of the IAPH, wafting on fear and regret.

And vinegar's tang, once such a clean smell to her, crept under the doorway every so often, and seeping with it came the despair and terror of life in the Holy Hive Mind's barracks.

The office was still lined on two sides with shelves, now

holding a mix of data pads, books, clothes, and miscellaneous ordnance and knives, and a hanging rack half full of white chefs' jackets, the other half full of disused civvies. A folding cot was jammed up against the wall behind her, next to two crates filled with glossy black rocks left over from the redecorating effort. Past menus were stickied to the wall, the plastic slips fluttering whenever the door opened or closed.

She narrowed her eyes at Dabry. "I know," she said, "and that was not the worst plan you've ever come up with, but you're taking it so seriously. It's a restaurant. A glorified location for the satisfaction of one of the most basic urges."

Dabry pointed two lower fingers at her in emphasis. "And you cannot talk like that, or they will know you are not an artist."

Niko shuddered. When it came to retiring from the Holy Hive Mind, there were few acceptable ways—most of its soldiers stayed in the army until they died, and a few of them long after that. She would have been one of those few, her brain extracted upon death and moved into a Holy Hive Mind container and reanimated to serve as part of its consciousness.

Not a fate she had anticipated with pleasure. When Dabry came to her with a crazy plan to claim that Niko was a thwarted artist—one of the sacred Occupations—and that her medium was cooking, it being her single talent, she'd been willing to play along.

A vast amount of bribery and wheedling had gone into the escape, but in the end she'd been able to use her considerable back wages—combined with those of her crew who wanted to come, and whom she declared part of her immediate family—to buy a small establishment aboard one of the largest space stations around, TwiceFar Station, relic of some long-forgotten race and now home to dozens of alien species.

Niko fixed her former sergeant with the stare that had straightened soldierly spines, cowed bureaucrats, and put the fear of the Holy Hive Mind into her enemies more than once.

Dabry, inoculated by long exposure, gave her a bland look back. "You know it as well as I do, Captain," he said. "The Holy Hive Mind is still keeping tabs on us. If they suspected that you think of the restaurant as something other than an artistic enterprise, they would haul you back and scoop the brain out of your head."

"I *am* an artist," she said. "Just not in the way that it thinks of artists. Its definition is a cross between an addict and an artist possessed by their muse, unable to help creating. It's hard to keep convincing it of that. An Orb would cement me as that kind of artist." She frowned at her second-in-command.

Dabry had turned out to have an unexpected (to Niko, at least) flair for all of this. He was the one who had found the odd little space that they turned into the restaurant, a former bar built by Derloens, who had fled the place when a particular side effect of their inhabitation became too much for them. Derloens leave what some species might call "ghosts" behind them, and these spirits, while no longer sentient, still inhabited the space in the form of long, glowing blue worms swimming through the air, which their maître d', Lassite, had incorporated into the decor.

Most of the restaurant's interior was dark blues and blacks, giving it a restrained rather than subdued look. The luminescent, writhing forms, shimmying overhead in aimless pursuit of one another, shed their light over it, augmented only by thumb-sized glow candles on each table.

Over the past year, and particularly in recent months, the restaurant had proved surprisingly successful. Something about the shadowy decor hadn't lured the criminals whom Niko had feared, but diners who sought privacy and exclusivity: lovers, those wishing to become lovers, diplomats, people with other people that they wanted to impress.

"Speaking of which, shouldn't I be planning *this* meal?" Niko grumbled.

"You said I could take this one," Dabry protested. It had pained him to have had to step back and let Niko take the wheel the last time they presented to the Holy Hive Mind, a yearly requirement of their situation.

"All right," Niko said. She waved her hand. "Go forth. And if you truly desire an eggplant to dissect, then who am I to stand in your way? Place an order with the *Mannan*."

Dabry hesitated.

Niko's eyes narrowed farther. "What?"

"An order from the *Mannan*," Dabry said, "would take over a sleep unit to get here. Too late."

"Then where are you planning on getting it?"

"I have a favor due me," Dabry said with dignity.

"Do I want to know anything about the nature of the favor or what you intend to do with it?"

"Probably not, other than that I will obtain an eggplant with it."

"Then I'm not sure why you're even telling me!" Niko threw up her hands in exasperation. Sometimes she thought Dabry enjoyed these encounters; the more expressionless he remained, the more convinced of that she became. She began to add a remark to that effect but a flurry of knocks on the door interrupted her.

Only one of her workers knocked like that. "Come in, Skidoo," she called.

The entity who entered was unlike either of the beings already in the room. Skidoo was a Tlellan, which humans sometimes called Squids for their resemblance to one of the few Terran creatures left alive. Her ten limbs functioned as either arms or legs to propel her sacklike body along. Atop that squat bundle was a lump that served as a head, fixed with three bright blue eyes. Unlike Terran squids, she was colored as brightly as a festival, purples and reds variegating across blue and yellow dots and stripes.

"I am being securing an important reservation!" she announced.

"We're not taking any more reservations for tonight," Niko

told her. "I said that already. We've got this stupid food critic arriving."

Skidoo wilted. "But this is being a very large party," she said.

"Even worse," Dabry said. "How large?"

"Possibly they are being saying as many as twenty."

"Twenty! We don't have room for that. We'd have to rearrange one of the back chambers," Niko protested.

"They are being saying they are knowing you, Captain, so I am being taking the reservation," Skidoo said.

"Did they give you a name?"

Skidoo drew herself up as much as possible in order to deliver this information in a suitably grand manner: "Admiral Taklibia."

"Taklibia? Here?" Niko was flabbergasted.

"The one you served under?" Dabry asked.

"I did, but I was only an aide. They wouldn't remember me."

"Apparently they do, and enough to seek out your restaurant."

Niko shook her head. She was about to tell Skidoo to cancel the reservation when the door flew open with a crash. Milly, her new pastry chef, stuck her head in, just the beaked face at the end of a long white-feathered neck, giving the impression of a disembodied head. "The boys are fighting in the storage room again!" she gasped in her high, fluting voice, and clacked her beak urgently.

Swearing under her breath, Niko rose. She pointed at Skidoo and Dabry. "Take care of it!" she told Dabry, and went to tame her lions.

2

Thorn and Talon were indeed at it in the storage room. Worse, both twins had reverted to their were-forms, becoming two enormous male lions, currently writhing on the floor, wrestling furiously in a tangle of golden fur and amber manes and flashing teeth. The smell that Niko had come to associate with shifter magic, sharp citrus and musk heavy to the point of stink, hung in the air.

Niko narrowly avoided their smashing into her, stepping back into the doorway and out of their path. The room was in chaos already, shelves tipped over, containers strewn in heaps, and an overturned vat of pickles adding their briny tang to the air, seeping over to turn a mass of spilled flour into a gluey mess.

"Ah-*ten*-shun!" she shouted.

As though by magic, the two separated. It was definitely magic that set their forms shrinking and contracting into a humanoid shape again. But it was fear of Niko that made them do it so quickly. Niko wondered if there was any spell powerful enough to remove their ability to shape-shift. A valuable ability in combat, on a space station it had proved considerably more inconvenient. Ever since their mother died, the two had been nearly uncontrollable.

Now both stood naked, staring straight ahead. They appeared perfectly human in this form: tall, well-muscled youths with golden skin, long amber hair, and dark brown eyes, avoiding the captain's stare.

"What happened now?" she said.

"There's a bioship in port, and he was rushing to get his work done so he could leave without me and go see it!" Talon said.

"That's not true! I would have waited! But he takes all the easy jobs!"

"I am the elder, they fall to me."

"The elder by a mere minute!" Thorn glared at his twin.

Niko's voice was dangerously low. "No one is going down to goggle at fancy bioships, because tonight is important. So here's a more important question for you—cleaning up the mess you've made in here, is that an easy job or a hard one?"

They looked at the room as though noticing the chaos of their surroundings for the first time. Thorn examined the smear of flour and pickle juice on his foot.

"Easy job, Captain," Talon said. "We'll do it together, pick things up. Nothing's broken." He glanced around, checking to make sure he wasn't lying. Aside from a shelf or two, he wasn't.

"And after that?" Niko said.

"What?" Thorn said uneasily.

"This is the last time," Niko said. "No more of this, or you're out."

"What?!" The word came from both of them simultaneously, their eyes fixed on her in shock.

"I've been too easy on you because you were grieving your mother," Niko said. "If you've got the energy to fight, you've got the energy to work." She looked around the small space. "I'm coming back here in a half hour and I want things to look as though this fight never happened. Am I clear?"

"Sir, yes, sir!" they chorused.

They were so young. Barely cubs when they'd been given to her to train. She'd taken those of her troop she could with her rather than leave them to the Holy Hive Mind, but in the process of freeing them all, she sometimes thought she'd saddled herself with ten times the work she would have had if it had been just her and Dabry.

No, she *knew* she'd saddled herself with ten times the work.

She left the room.

Dabry was in the hallway, and had witnessed the whole encounter. "Sometimes you're not a very nice person," he said mildly.

She glared at him. "Think I was too hard?" she said. "I could have been much worse."

"I know that."

"We can't go on like this. If they went at each other in the restaurant, we'd have customers screaming and fleeing."

"I know that."

"Not to mention one of these days they're going to take it too far and hurt each other," she said.

He grunted sourly.

"This station doesn't like disturbances. That's why we ended up here. Nice and peaceful."

"Nice and peaceful," Dabry echoed.

"You sound dubious."

"Life is never all that peaceful with you, sir."

Skidoo returned to her comms cubicle. Like many of the chambers here, it had once been storage space. The Tlellan preferred her quarters cramped, though; it kept everything within reach.

She'd changed the door, insetting a smaller hatch into the larger one so she could enter without spilling out all the moist, water-saturated air that she preferred, smelling of vanilla and chlorine and much closer to the atmosphere of her native planet than the station's default setting. Inside, the machinery she used had been inlaid into the walls in a series of buttons and pads. From here she controlled not just the incoming and outgoing communications but also the music and atmosphere within the four dining chambers: two larger and two smaller, each joined by a small air lock that enabled Skidoo to alter conditions in there with ease.

She ran three tentacles over the walls, reading the restaurant's vital statistics and adjusting them as needed: the kitchen was a degree and a half too hot for maximal comfort, and the air in Niko's office needed to be lowered in humidity. A smattering of requests for reservations had come in while she was elsewhere. She sorted through the messages.

The captain had said to cancel the admiral's reservation, but it was already taken, and the admiral would be most unhappy, since they had stressed that they wished to speak with Niko. Skidoo was torn; her tentacles flattened themselves against the walls, seeking out every iota of comfort-touch.

It was a big party. And a big party—particularly of drunken military—meant a lot of money. They could be kept in the room farthest away from the critic's. Surely what Niko had meant was not to take any reservations that were in the room where the critic would be, not to cancel everything altogether. The restaurant needed money, and couldn't afford to be turning things down.

But disobeying the captain didn't come easily. Niko wasn't the sort of person who tolerated someone doing something for the captain's own good. Skidoo equivocated. She'd do the canceling in just a little while. It could wait, while she did more pressing things, and there was certainly so much to do, in the face of the oncoming critic. Why, Skidoo realized, no one had checked to make sure that the glow lights were all at full charge. Perhaps she'd do that first.

The machines of the kitchen were in full swing, the ancient dishwasher chugging along, the sterilizing station humming to itself. Dabry and Niko passed through the kitchens. Serving food for a variety of species would have created any number of problems had they been trying to do so without the replicators. They would have had to stock dozens of types of food, not to mention questions of cross-contamination.

But the Last Chance followed a standard pattern for restaurants aboard this station. When an unusual patron entered, their species requirements were noted, and the food given them was usually replicated and then tailored to provide the illusion of a home-cooked meal. When necessary, Gio's expert chemistry stepped in, adapting and tweaking molecules, rendering poisons into benign flavors, allowing beings to ingest anything they desired—within reason.

Situated as it was within ship distance of not one but three of the ancient gates that tied together the Known Universe, Twice-Far was one of the most diverse waypoints possible. This place had become a favorite establishment among humans, but many of the more populous species ate here as well, enough that the storerooms were usually stocked with nonreplicated spices and flavorings for them, which Dabry swore was the real secret to their success. Not a living soul in the universe claimed to prefer replicated food to real, with the sole exception of the Karnaki— and they lied about everything, so they might be lying about that as well.

Gio's hairy shoulders were visible in a corner, his back turned, shoulders twitching in time with the staccato chop of greenery. Milly was in a corner, sheltered from most of the kitchen's activity by the rack of shelves in front of her. She was glazing tiny fan-shaped cakes. Blue and silver sugar crystals glinted as she sprinkled them over the still-wet glaze to be caught, tipping each at a precise forty-five-degree angle to shake off the excess sugar. Niko had hired her less than a month ago, and she was still pleased with the level of artistry the new hire brought to the task.

"Are those for the critic?" Niko said.

"I made enough that they can appear on the menu, but I'm making a special set for her." Milly pointed at a small plate set to one side on a counter, two particularly beautiful cakes atop it, gleaming in the fluorescent lights. Niko paused to admire them before she stole one of the half-glazed cakes for a nibble.

Milly watched her expectantly.

Niko took another judicious nibble.

Milly shifted from side to side, watching as Niko deliberately licked sugar from her fingers. Finally she could no longer contain herself. "Well?"

"Well, what?" Niko asked.

Milly hissed out exasperation. "How is it?"

Niko grinned. "You know it's delicious, you just want to hear me say it."

"I do!"

"It's delicious." Niko shoved the rest of the cake in her mouth and added inarticulately, "Absolutely delicious." She leaned to take another but Dabry removed the tray from her reach.

"Captain," he said patiently. "Permission to go secure my eggplant?"

She waved him off. "Go, go." Once he had turned, she grabbed another cake, winked at Milly, and went to check on the front room.

Currently the restaurant was closed, as it was for six hours of every cycle, in order to give the staff time to clean and prep. Aboard the space station, there was a multitude of time cycles, and Niko had chosen to forgo tying any of her food to a particular one, even the prevalent human norms, so there was no breakfast, lunch, or dinner, only meals.

She checked the lectern near the entrance to make sure it was free of clutter and that the flower atop it was fresh. They kept a whenlove plant blooming there, considered lucky by a fallen comrade.

So many memories in the restaurant, so many little rituals to mark the fallen. She touched the whorls of a fuzzy leaf and moved on.

No matter what time of day it was, the glowing ghosts wriggled through the space. Niko stood watching their light play over the tables, booths, and floating seats. Lore held that the ghosts were not sentient at all, simply dissolute life forces left behind when the beings passed, but Niko always tried to watch for some sign of intelligence, some portent that might show that memory stayed behind. Her maître d', Lassite, claimed their patterns had meaning, but she'd never been able to parse it.

The slide of light against light was hypnotic. She stood longer than she had meant to, transfixed by the odd hieroglyphics of their trails as they wriggled and swam, doubling back and forth in the air.

She shook her head, clearing away cobwebs. The critic was due in a few hours, and Niko was more worried about their advent than she had let on to anyone, even Dabry.

Despite the fact that the restaurant was popular, they were still bleeding money. Her retirement fund would stretch only so far, and her most recent calculations—despite the multitude of times that she'd checked and rechecked them, over and over again—gave them a little under a hundred sleep units in which to become profitable.

If they didn't do that, she didn't know what would happen.

But the critic—one Lolola Montaigne d'Arcy deBurgh—could make them. As a representative of the *Culture*, an interstellar publication carried on one of the biggest viddie channels, her favorable review—if it went so far as to bestow a Nikkelin Orb on the restaurant—would bring beings from off-station, come specifically to eat at the Last Chance, come to taste Dabry's cooking and savor Milly's desserts and experience the atmosphere that they had somehow, magically, created out of condemned hold space due to be jettisoned.

That had still been pricey enough. In space, everything cost, everything came from somewhere, whether it was snagged from passing meteors and comet dust or trapped sunlight or—most expensive of all—brought up from some planet's gravity well.

Three worms of light collided, recoiled, twined around one another before moving on.

Planets, she thought, were odd things.

She had only been on three in her lifetime, and each had unnerved her. The first, the world Miniver, the birthplace of the Holy Hive Mind's creators, had been cold and everything was flat and wide and gravity pulled at her all the time, with no escape, ever, and everything had seemed so disgustingly *organic* all the time, like a ship so dirty that mold was growing in it.

After the tests and training, she'd stayed inside buildings whenever she could, finding comfort in low-ceilinged, windowless rooms, although even there gravity ached at her when she tried to rest or sleep. She hadn't learned the trick yet of resting limbs so the circulation wasn't cut off, and kept finding them fallen asleep, strange and tingling and painful, as though they had been more attached to the world than she was. She'd left as soon as she was possibly able.

The second world, Tarraquil, had been more comfortable. Or perhaps it was simply that she had been two decades older by then, and more phlegmatic about everything in general, whether it was new or not. She had been persuaded by a lover—and there, too, might have been one of the reasons she remembered it so much more fondly—a tall, gregarious woman who had been raised on that planet and wanted Niko to meet her family.

The third had been the world where Rourke's Leap was, and she did not think of that planet if she could avoid it.

Tarraquil was all ocean, and the cities either floated on it or perched on silver spiderwebs spun between monstrously large pillars. The sky had been uncanny, but the raft city had a give underfoot that was comforting and somehow reminiscent of being in space. She'd surprised her lover with the ease with which she took to life there, and they'd spent almost a month, eating and fishing and fucking and visiting with parents, cousins, siblings, aunts, uncles, and countless other degrees of relatives.

That lover died the following year in one of the interminable skirmishes that had made up the campaign for the Hive Mind to take Crispine, a tiny moon mainly notable for its rich supplies of deliriterium. Niko still had a holo of her.

The thing that had impressed Niko most about Tarraquil was the birds. They were like ships in the sky. They moved the way ships did—to a point, because wings moving was something most ships did not have. Birds seemed so free they'd made her heart ache watching.

She remembered a sunset on Tarraquil, birds gliding over the water, her lover's fingers laced through hers, dreaming they'd escape the Holy Hive Mind, go back to the lives both had come from before tariffs and fees imposed by a Holy Hive Mind port had forced them to enlist. She and Dabry had told the crew they pursued discharge in the name of freedom, but it was just another step in her ultimate plan. How far away was that end now? Closer, but not half close enough.

She'd wanted to name the restaurant Halcyon, after one of those birds, but had given way to the majority.

Now, perhaps, Lolola Montaigne d'Arcy deBurgh would make the restaurant fly, and put Niko a step further along. A profitable restaurant—you could build on that, if you were savvy with business. You might even at some point be able to start investing, maybe in a ship or two. And then maybe you could put together a real plan for the thing Niko had been working toward for so long.

Her old Free Trader coat was still in a cupboard in her office, which also served as her bedchamber. Niko claimed she'd chosen it for security purposes, leaving the suite adjoining the restaurant to the rest, except for Milly, who roomed elsewhere. But economic pressures were more to blame—if satisfying the need for security also happened to save her on rent, so be it. All her money went toward building this endeavor, this fragile chain of financial resources that would let her achieve a goal over three decades old now.

If everything went right. But in Niko's experience, that was something rare.

3

She stalked back through the kitchen and into the storeroom, where Thorn was vacuuming the floor tiles while Talon finished straightening crates of napkins. They both saluted.

They had moved away from their human forms and currently they were in the shape they most preferred, a mix of lion and human that most people found unsettling, a reminder of how magic was used to twist someone and change their very nature. The Holy Hive Mind had created its shock troops outside the laws of most civilizations. The boys didn't go around the station as half-ers.

They watched anxiously as she gave the room a thorough examination. They'd done a more than adequate job, fixing a broken shelf and reordering the supplies. There was no trace of pickle juice or flour, and the air smelled fresh and untainted. The storeroom might actually be cleaner now than it had been before they started fighting.

Still she kept her face expressionless, dropping a single nod of approval. These two took any encouragement and ran way too far with it. She needed to remember that, no matter how young they were, barely out of their teens. They had seen terrible fights in the two years of service with her, and their presence was one of the reasons she and Dabry had figured out how to retire and take all of them outside the Holy Hive Mind's grasp.

"Captain, after everything's over tonight, could we go see the bioship *then*? It's called *You Sexy Thing*, and it belongs to an inter-galactic gazillionaire named Arpat Takraven and it goes to twelve leguins! That's faster than anything we've ever seen."

"No," she said. "There's a crate up front. Grab it and stow it in my office, then go ask Gio what he needs done still for prepping tonight."

"Can we chop vegetables?" Thorn said hopefully. The two both loved using the long, sharp knives.

"Not tonight," she said. "The last thing we need is one of you slicing off a finger and dropping it in the salad."

Their whiskers sagged, but they nodded and exited to get the crate.

Niko sat down on a chair by the door, knuckling her forehead and trying to rub away the headache threatening to brew there. "Just get through the next few hours and let Dabry deliver a perfect meal," she said to herself. "After that you can relax."

Dabry returned before Niko got back to her office to investigate the crate. He bore a single, perfect eggplant, its skin glossy as though oiled, its color a deep purple shading to a paler white around the green stem, and its weight four and a half kilos. He did not tell Niko where it had come from, nor did she ask.

"Pretty, isn't it?" he did say after reverently washing both it and all his hands, then drying them with a towel. They contemplated the spot where he'd placed it on the chopping block.

Gio came over to stare at it, too, nostrils flared thoughtfully. Over in the corner, Milly was finishing the last of her cakes, stacking them on their plates before using a small hose to remove the excess sugar from the counter where it had fallen.

"I suppose you're not going to let me touch that," Gio signed in the direction of the eggplant.

"Nope," Dabry said.

Gio's wrinkled lips pursed in amusement as he traded glances with Niko. She grinned back. Over the course of their long time together, her quartermaster's skills had provided more than one vital ingredient for the restaurant.

He was one member of the crew Niko would have trusted anywhere at her back.

Everyone she'd brought out of the Holy Hive Mind was that, really.

With a sole exception.

As though summoned by the thought, Lassite appeared in the doorway, his narrow, scaled face a brown gleam half hidden in the folds of the bloodred velvet hood he always wore. His grayish mystic's robe hung in loose folds around his small form, half as tall as Niko; he was habitually skinny and not prone to regarding his appearance overmuch. Niko counted herself lucky she'd been able to impress on him the importance of better grooming if he was to serve as the restaurant's maître d'. His tongue flickered out, sampling the air, which was full of the smell of the onions that had just been lying under Gio's flashing knife.

"Heavy portents, my captain," he said, voice a low, compelling whisper that always reminded Niko of a villain in a childhood viddie. "Dense and inexorable as a black hole's grip, pulling us down into dreadful doom."

"Goodall's tits, say what's coming or better yet, how to keep it off," Gio signed. He darted a glance at Niko and added, "Not that I believe in prophecy."

She ignored him. "Your prophecies were wrong the last three times," she told Lassite. "You need to stop sharing them with people. They're always discouraging. You are a swarm of negativity. I've told you this before, it doesn't do us any good when you make customers afraid by hissing doom."

"I haven't done that for days and days," he said sullenly.

"That's not true. You told that Venorian triad last night that they would 'come asunder as though torn by lightning, just as sudden and fierce these forces.'"

"Captain, I feel compelled to tell you when I sense that the fates are stirring."

"But let them get all the way out of bed next time, at least!"

Unlike the delivery bot, Lassite was not immune to the power of Niko's stare, and she unleashed it on him in its full, cold force. He took a pace back.

"I will do better," he muttered.

"Make it so," she said. He started to turn, and she said, more kindly, "And know that I have listened, and that I will be wary of bad fortune, as always."

He inclined his head toward her before he moved away.

Gio gestured something toward Milly.

"What's that, soldier?" Niko said with a knife edge to her voice.

"I don't know why you put up with that creature," he told her.

"You know the story, you were there."

"You were cast down for it anyhow. You didn't have to tell him anything."

"That's what gratitude is." She looked at Dabry, who stood ignoring them, caressing the eggplant with all four hands and his eyes half closed. "Sweet Momma Sky, should we leave so you can have your way with that eggplant or should I just let you take it to your bunk?"

His eyes closed entirely, his expression blissful. "Baba ghanoush," he said. "Flat wheat bread dusted with cumin. Seared protein tinctured with lemon and garlic . . ."

"You've finally decided on the last details then?" Niko said, trepidation aquiver in her stomach's pit. She'd told Dabry he could decide the overall menu, and he sometimes had a fancy for very expensive ingredients.

Still, for a Nikkelin Orb . . .

"Gio, start mincing garlic," Dabry directed. "The good stuff that came in last week with that Prone ship." He set the eggplant back down. "Captain?"

Niko had been eyeing the soy sausages that Dabry kept in a glass case, smoking them through some arcane process that she suspected the station would not have approved. She was lingering in the hopes Dabry would chop one up and give her a bit. They tasted of pepper and anise and some spice he refused to identify. "Yes?"

"Captain," he said with excessive patience. "Get out of my kitchen."

She saluted him. "Carry on, gentlebeings."

She passed the twins in the hallway.

"On your way to help Gio now?" she said.

"Yes, sir."

"Not pausing along the way for quick message checks or gibble gossip?"

"No, sir."

"Carry on." Her mouth wanted to quirk in amusement at the concerted whisker droop, but she throttled the urge.

Inside her office, she looked over the crate again. One triangular shard of the tag remained, carrying a few half letters that she could not decipher. She searched for a chip label on the crate's surface, but that seemed to be missing, too, although she could find no stickiness to show where one had ever adhered.

That gave her pause. Taking a scanning device from her desk, she ran it carefully along each seam, then waved it in a slow zigzag over the entirety of every visible side. Sitting back on her heels, she contemplated it. Replacing the scanner, she slipped a clear hood over her head, tapping the ring at its base to tighten around her neck in an airtight seal. It hissed closed with a whiff of plastic and stale air.

The hood would let her survive for up to an hour in space, its inner surface releasing oxygen as it decayed, but more important, it would filter out any airborne pathogens, spores, or other possibilities. It had been a long time, but she still had enemies out there.

She stretched gloves over her hands as another precaution and set a stunner in easy reach before she flipped the latches open one by one, pausing for a few seconds each time to listen intently for any stirring within. When the latches were all freed, she took the scanner up again to check the seam where the lid met the body of the crate.

Finally, standing to one side of the crate, she slipped a narrow metal shim underneath one corner and lifted, first a centimeter, then a few more. She took a long moment, waiting, before she raised it fully and looked inside.

She blinked once, then removed hood and gloves, still staring down at the contents.

4

Appearing at the kitchen doorway, Niko said, "Dabry, could you come to my office?"

By now he had peeled the eggplant and rendered it into neat, half-moon slices that were fanned on a platter in front of him. Without looking up, he said with a frown, "This is not a good time, sir."

"Nonetheless, I insist," she said. Her tone this time made him look up to read her face and then follow her.

Milly and the twins all exchanged puzzled looks.

"What was that all about?" Thorn asked.

"Keep chopping and don't think about it," Gio signed. "We got a lot to do today, kids." He snorted to himself and eyed the fans of eggplant abandoned on the counter. "If it's important enough for the captain to pull him away from that eggplant, then whatever it is, we'll find out soon enough."

Lassite sat meditating in the tiny cubicle he had chosen for his quarters. Barely big enough for him to stretch out, but it was more private space than would ever have been allowed him in his past life as a speaker for the dying. The restaurant wasn't open yet, so he had time to collect his thoughts.

The room was full of ghosts, as though they had collected to watch him. He reached out as one glided by, and as it passed through his hand, he *touched* it with his mind, felt the cold suck of its presence, its energy's turgid beat.

He heard the captain and Dabry go by in the corridor outside his closet, and the captain saying, "You know I wouldn't have

YOU SEXY THING   25

disturbed you, but . . ." before her voice was muffled by interposing distance.

Things were in motion. Doom hovered so close, but it always had, really.

He had never been able to find any prophecy about the captain, no word in the Holy Books or scrolls. He'd looked when he could, and asked others, wiser than he, to look as well.

Even though he was possessed by a dream and turned over to the priests as a child, it had not started then. He had known only that the Spiral of Destiny existed, not whom he would follow along it or how he would help them.

Like any priest, he learned the ways of healing, but at the gods' direction, he went further than most and learned how to heal those outside his own race. They had him learn several languages, including a long-dead one that he'd had to seek out, and pay to be instructed in, a painful and nontechnological process, because Sessile brain physiology did not interact well with most language chips.

They'd driven him before that to search out the scrolls holding the abstracts of systems that let him extrapolate how many—perhaps most—physical bodies functioned. Myriad rules surrounded healing and when it could and couldn't be done. He learned them all, knowing that someday it would be his destiny to break the most important of them. The gods told him that, and seemed unruffled by the prospect.

Later they had sent him off-planet in order to mature and learn. That was not an uncommon journey for a priest to make. Indeed, it was somewhat expected in order to achieve true enlightenment—though most of them did not go too far away. Joining the Spisoli, traveling on one of their ships, was also not uncommon, although he had chosen to travel with them for an extended time in a way few opted for, despite the fact that the

Spisoli ships were comfortable and smelled good, and you could sleep well on them.

That was because to be a Sessile priest was to depend on the universe for sustenance. Luckily, many of the established races honored that tradition or the laws of hospitality at a minimum. The Spisoli, though, were a little uncertain in this regard, because sometimes unpredictable superstitions drove what they did. But if you chose a group that was not one of the ones chasing a particular Arranti, you were usually safe enough.

Other races would provide food and water, shelter, warmth, and whatever other necessities—a sparse list when you were a priest—you required to survive. If necessary, you could work for those things.

He had been three years with the Spisoli before going to Rourke's Leap with the group that had been sent to negotiate. That evening they had gone treasure hunting, but he had excused himself. By then he knew her name and her smell, though he was not entirely sure what she looked like, and he knew where he was supposed to find her. He had seen the place every night for ten nights before, in his dreams: a plaza on the edge of the rift, a balcony of dark glass, her figure silhouetted against the blue glow coming from below to light her face and give the mottled red coloring of the Holy Hive Mind uniform a purplish hue.

When he'd first foreseen her, he saw purple and gold and lights, and glory, and the way the gods wanted things to be. The path, a Spiral of Destiny, stretching away from her. Darkness, too, but that splendid vision had taken his breath away. He was only a minor speaker, not particularly talented or wise, but he had been given that vision by the gods themselves. He could not resist it.

He knew the circumstances from his dreams. Three cultures forced to come together, their attempt at a treaty hampered by bad-faith dealing, but more than that, by the uneasy amalgamation of ritual and custom that had evolved. Niko unaware—although beginning to suspect—that the Holy Hive Mind was abusing the system to enforce its own unrelenting expansion.

And the Hive Mind's lack of transparency gave her a chance to thwart it by doing as she had been ordered—but she could do that only if she could match the ritual's demands. Another place where it had stacked the deck, trying to create a failure it could take an advantage of.

Niko would need someone who spoke the right language to deliver her offer—the offer that her masters had given her to make, confident that she would be unable to do so. It would mean walking the span to meet the others, and speaking appointed words. All the random factors had come together to prevent the peace—some of that by design—and he had been the only thing that enabled her to cut through the obstacles placed in her way.

So he had done it, because of the preparations the gods had told him to make, and he and Niko had forged a system-wide peace together. Mostly the captain, but perhaps he might claim a little corner of that work to be proud of. And when she had asked what reward he wanted, his answer had not pleased her, but she had abided by it.

Niko did not particularly like him. No one liked Sessiles, and particularly no one liked Sessile priests, even other Sessiles. And that was all right, though it might have been nice to be petted the way Milly was or even to play with Skidoo. But he had never been invited to do that.

He had changed many of the things that had been part of his life as a priest, not because he wanted to but because Niko asked it of him. Bathing every day was not customary on a water-poor planet, but here every morning he went into the fresher like the rest of them and emerged smelling like nothing at all.

At Niko's order he had learned all the tedious details of etiquette, the code that was supposed to keep gentlebeings in an accord, pointless though much of its mechanisms seemed, like saying hello or goodbye. Not so intricate as temple rituals, but just as arbitrary.

The ghosts writhed. The one he'd touched curled and slid over his wrist, parallel to the scales. Soon it would be time to go out and begin working. Soon things would happen. Steps would be made.

His thoughts turned again to the Spiral of Destiny. He had drawn it over and over as a child—in the sand, or scratched on the walls, or daubed in whatever was at hand—and that was how his nurturer had known what he was, and taken him from the crèche and turned him over to the priests to be raised.

Would he achieve the glory that he had seen, the picture he had drawn then, that he sometimes still drew in his head, each time more glorious? Nothing was certain. But staying with the captain was the only way to even come close to that path, because it was her path. There was no guarantee she would go all the way along it. Indeed, it was improbable that she would be able to do all that would be asked of her.

He knew one thing by now that he had not known when he first gave himself to her. It was something that made him know it had been the right choice, even if uncertain and unprecedented.

He knew that, no matter what, when the time came she would try.

In Niko's office, Dabry and Niko stood over the crate, so still that the only motion was the menus fluttering near the air vent.

"Is that what I think it is?" Dabry said.

"Yep," Niko said. "It's a person. In stasis. Or a being of some sort in stasis anyhow. Humanoid in form but you never know. We won't know what they look like until we bring them out."

"Who is it?"

"Why should I know?"

Silence hovered in the cabin as they kept looking. The menus fluttered. Skidoo squelched past in the hallway, muttering something to herself about the glow lamps.

"We should un-stasis them," Dabry said.

"Should we?"

"Of course we should?"

Niko shook her head. "We have no way of knowing who it is, and we are about to have possibly—almost certainly—the most important meal of the restaurant's existence. They could be a dangerous criminal or programmed for violence or some other disaster. Whoever they might be, they have been in stasis already for quite some time, look to have suffered no ill effects, and will in all likelihood not be harmed by a few more hours in it."

Dabry's face was enigmatic.

"What?" she demanded.

"Do you remember when General Hughes called you the hardest-nosed bitch he'd ever known?"

"Yes."

"And afterward you told me that you didn't understand why people kept saying that sort of thing?"

"Yes."

"This is the sort of behavior that leads to that."

"Ah," Niko said. She rubbed her nose. "Fair enough. But for now we will let pragmatism rule the day." She tapped the lid back down and it fell into place with a muted *thunk*.

"Very well, sir."

She laid a palm on the lid and sighed. "What next, do you think? A failure of the electrical system? Food contamination? A surprise visit from the Inspectorate?"

Dabry said, "Mmm."

"Afraid to venture a guess?"

"I'm thinking, rather, of the words 'heavy portents' and 'deep doom.'"

"You can't be serious."

"I shouldn't be. But you and I have both served in the ranks of the Holy Hive Mind. We've both seen magic work." He gestured toward the kitchen where Thorn and Talon were.

"Magic, yes. But prophecy? If that worked, the Holy Hive Mind would have no need of generals."

"Prophecies have guided the Holy Hive Mind for generations now."

"You can twist any vague saying into a prophecy!" she snapped. "Heavy portents could mean anything from our critic getting a stomachache to the whole place getting blown up by an Arranti who thought it would advance their game."

He paced the room, then stopped, laying a hand on the crate. "What if it's someone who's been kidnapped and you're being framed?"

"And what if it is my long-lost grandchild, bundled up and tied with a bow?"

"Do you have a long-lost grandchild?"

"Not to my knowledge."

He threw up his hands. "With your permission, sir, I will return to my eggplant."

He retreated, leaving Niko to contemplate the crate.

Maybe this is the challenge we've been looking for, she thought. She reached out to touch the metal's cold edge, thinking about the unknown that lay inside.

A few days earlier as they'd been finishing up getting the restaurant in order after a serving period, Dabry had offered to make her a snack. It was his way of asking to confer with her, and so she'd agreed, but it had turned out he also wanted to try a new recipe on her, what he said was a gougère, although he also said that the original version would have contained cheese.

Niko had always considered cheese one of the most disgusting notions known to humanity. Most of the foods that involved substances taken from living bodies were similarly repugnant, in her opinion, although she knew this split between flesh- and animal-based foods was one of the great divides of culinary thinking. She had tried things like cheddar and Brie from time to time, but never with anything but reluctance, and the experiment had never been successful. She said as much now, although probably in more words than she needed to.

Dabry said patiently, using an upper arm to stir a mass of dough that seemed mostly butter and flour, "I understand that, and that's not what I'm using. For one thing, how expensive would cheese be? Plus I wouldn't waste it on you."

"It's not that my palate is unrefined," she said, "and I understand that species fall in one direction or the other on the topic of flesh."

"It's much more complicated than that," Dabry murmured.

She held her hand to forestall him. "No, no! Give me a chance before you counter me."

"Because I am not using cheese in the first place, this argument would seem to be only for the sake of argument," he said. "I will let it proceed on one condition."

"What's that?"

"That you convince me that there is a point to having it."

He removed the pan from the heating element to place it on a thermal pad on the counter, still stirring. The glossy dough had thickened, clinging to the sides of the metal pan. The air smelled like toasted flour and butter flavoring.

"The point of talking—conversation, as one might call it—is to exchange words back and forth, building our camaraderie and friendship." She spoke the words by rote, quoting an old training manual from the Holy Hive Mind they'd both mocked more than once.

Dabry laughed despite himself. After taking a shaker down from a shelf, he dusted the dough with green powder, then grated something from an orange lump over it.

Niko said, "That looks very much like cheese, or at least how I have heard it described."

"It's bilongi root," he said, and held it out to her. "Some of the same flavonoids."

She shook her head and declined the invitation to smell it. "As long as it's vegetable. Or fungi, you know that I don't mind fungi. It's when we start moving into the animal kingdom that things go awry."

"Eggs are acceptable in many cultures, including human," he said.

"Not their own, certainly. And humans are a whole bunch of different cultures. Among the Free Traders, there's not enough extra space to be keeping chickens. I never tasted an egg till I got to the station."

"And you liked that one."

"Because you disguised it and I didn't know what it was!" Niko made a disgusted, repulsed face.

Dabry spooned the dough into a piping bag and focused on inscribing curls onto a heating sheet. The size of Niko's thumb, each was flecked with green and burnt amber in the golden dough.

"Savory, I take it?" she'd said.

"I leave the sweets to Milly; she does well enough."

"Well enough but not perfectly," Niko said. "I thought every meal had to be perfect, down to the last morsel."

He opened a thermo shelf and put the heating sheet on the rack inside, speaking briefly to the control unit. When he closed it, the interior glowed golden, a soft ambience that betrayed the lurking heat.

When he turned back to face her, his expression was grave. "It does and it doesn't. A truly artistic meal requires a handmade quality, something that shows it could not have been mass produced."

She tilted her head. "You are equating uniqueness with taste. I will argue again that the corollary is not always true."

"How many races prefer cheap vat food?"

"Plenty of territory lies between cheap and vat food!" she protested. "Go up to the food court on the Midnight Stair and try any of the—well, most of the, stay away from Efrai's and the Simmering, or so I've heard—*most* of the food stalls there, and you'll find something priced not too far above vat food, but a hundred times more tasty."

"Tourist food." He waved a lower hand at her dismissively.

She subsided into silence, watching him cook, foaming white liquid in another hot pan, tasting it before adding spices and a pinch of caramel-colored powder.

She liked to watch him cook. She'd always liked to watch him cook. It was the only time Dabry truly relaxed into himself and let the lines of worry around his eyes that had crept up over the years ease away.

They all had the equivalent. The twins had nightmares, Gio had a bitter core layered over with jokes. Lassite had been grim to start with; the time he spent in the Holy Hive Mind had left him seemingly unaffected but she knew that couldn't be true. He simply hid things better than most.

Dabry removed the pan of liquid from the heat. Pouring it into a bowl, he whisked it with a tiny mechanical stirrer till it frothed. He decanted it into a ceramic mug and sprinkled a colorless power over the surface. Wherever a grain touched, the foam bloomed into a multitude of colors, lines arrowing out from the spot where the mote had touched the white mass.

"Pretty," Niko said approvingly. "But how does it taste?"

He nudged the cup toward her and she took a sip. "Ah," she said in a surprised tone, and then took another sip, and another, as though she could not help herself, and drained the cup to the dregs.

She set the cup down and licked foam from her lips, chasing the last sweetness with her tongue. "Why does this Orb matter to everyone so much, Dabry? We're serving at full capacity as it is. Yes, it'll speed things up, but everyone acts as though it's life or death. I haven't seen Gio this intense since we left the Hive Mind."

"You've answered yourself there."

"How so?"

"Since we left the Hive Mind, the biggest challenge Gio has faced is how to most efficiently chop a mirepoix or braise a protein block. Same for the rest of them. Lassite at least had the task you set him with learning all the ins and outs of etiquette. But Thorn and Talon spend all their free hours playing warball, and Skid's fucked her way through half the station. Even you, sir, if you'll excuse my presumptuousness, seem to be getting a bit stir-crazy now again, which usually manifests in you holing up in your office with a fifth of something containing a notably high alcohol content and a book you've already read fifty times. At least. It's about time we had a challenge."

His vehemence surprised her. "It's not as though we don't still drill, every once in a while," she murmured. "Part of the ultimate plan involves everyone keeping their skills sharp."

"When was the last time you drilled? Everyone's lazy, except for the twins, and that's because if they didn't get their daily action, they'd go crazy and start mauling each other."

"All right, all right, you've convinced me. Striving for the Orb is worth going all out for." She paused. "It's just," she said, hating the edge of hesitation in her voice.

"Yes?"

"*Can* we do it, do you think? So much could go wrong. Milly's the only one who's worked in another restaurant, and even there only in desserts. Are we just playing at this?"

His eyebrows rose. "Of course we're not." He reached over to touch her arm. "We're Captain Niko's crack team, and there's no stopping us."

She grimaced but laughed. "All right then."

Back in her office she took down her book. *Skullduggery and Sacred Space Vessels: A Life Among Space Pirates.* She fingered the spine. A man had died in the writing of this, had escaped the pirates half flayed but alive, gasped out these details of the pirates and their wandering havens. The book had been read across the Known Universe a few years earlier. When she'd heard of it, she had a hard copy printed here on-station.

She flipped it open to the first chapter and started to read it anew, but she knew the words by heart, and finally she set it down and went to bed and restless dreams.

5

Despite Niko's fears, nothing else happened in the next few hours. The servobots finished cleaning the front room, and Niko printed out the new menu Dabry had constructed, trying to avoid mentally calculating just how slim some of the profit margins were. Everything was fine. Skidoo sat in her cubicle, taking calls and making reservations.

News that the critic might be coming had driven traffic up considerably; Skidoo was coyly taking reservations for everything except the period when they knew Lolola would be there, nonetheless managing each time to imply that the person making the reservation might be able to glimpse the critic. Whenever Niko passed through the kitchen, everyone was in place, their focus laser-beam tight.

Everything was fine.

Up to a certain point, which was when Lolola Montaigne d'Arcy deBurgh was due to arrive in less than an hour and the very large party that Skidoo had apparently *not* canceled arrived.

The first Niko knew of it was when one of the waitstaff came rushing back to her office. "We don't have enough chairs," she gasped.

"What?"

Niko had never seen Jakka lose her calm, even under heavy fire. But right now the Dlin's scarlet and umber pelt was haphazard swirls, her eyes wide and panic stricken. "Thirty people!" she said. "That's how many are in the party Skidoo booked."

"I told her to cancel that reservation!"

"She didn't," Jakka said. "And now we are out of chairs."

Out in the entrance vestibule, the admiral's party could be glimpsed milling about, Lassite in the middle although dwarfed by the larger beings while Thorn and Talon tried to assemble chairs and tables in a side chamber.

"Grab the extra chairs out of the storeroom and my office," Niko told Talon. "Stick them nearest the wall, so the mismatch is less noticeable—" She broke off as the admiral approached.

Admiral Taklibia was a diploid, a pairing of minds in a single form. Technically, the name should have been triploid, but the alien parasite that powered the technology was not sentient. When first enabled, a century ago, a rush of married couples had tried it only to find that compatibility when two separate entities did not ensure that the same would hold when combined. In actuality, platonic relationships seemed to work best in combination, and some individuals had chosen the lifestyle in order to merge their talents. The admiral had been born of the pairing of a mathematician with a military strategist.

In appearance they were simply a metal shell, ovoid in form, that hovered on an antigravity field and could extrude metal tentacles or limbs as needed. Most wore their sigil on their shell; the admiral's was a purple slash over three red diamonds, underneath the golden wavy line that signified their allegiance to the Holy Hive Mind.

"Captain Larsen," the admiral said, their voice smoothly modulated as always, to the point of expressionlessness. "My companions and we have come to see the establishment which you have created. It is the talk of the fleet, your artistry and retirement."

Panic tugged at her sleeve at that phrasing. So many possible ways for the Holy Hive Mind to begin an attempt to reclaim her.

She let none of that show now, standing in *her* restaurant, which she and that crew had built out of virtually nothing. Her restaurant, the key to the future, a future that did not involve the Holy Hive Mind.

"Admiral," she said as evenly as if her own voice were machine modulated. "It has been a long time. What brings you to TwiceFar?"

"You, of course!" Admiral Taklibia said. A tentacle formed and gestured around the room. Lassite was showing the party toward the room where they'd be ensconced, as far away from the table designated for Lolola as possible, she noted with approval. The soldiers jostled one another as they followed after him, tossing jokes back and forth.

"Come, let me take you to join your fellows," she said with a half bow.

The tentacle undulated dismissively. "They are half drunk and ready to devote themselves to your food. But we, we were hoping for a little private conversation at some point?"

Definitely Hive Mind business, she thought. She bolted a smile on her face. "But, of course! Though tonight is very busy. Perhaps when you are readying to go?"

Taklibia hung in the air, metal shell gleaming as a ghost oozed around it, seemingly without the admiral's notice at all. She wondered if the spirits were visible to the diploid or if their spectral nature prevented the admiral from perceiving them. Diploids were notorious for being hard to affect with magic, one reason the admiral had been so successful in the Holy Hive Mind ranks.

"Very well," the admiral said. They glided in her wake as she led them to join the rest.

She noted the blend of the crowd: junior officers and a few diplomats. No one of major power, she decided, and there wasn't the mix of soldiers in there that would have made her fear a show of force. This far from the borders of their empire, on a station that was neutral territory, overt action would be difficult, though. Something covert was much more likely.

Something that Lassite might call deep doom? She worried that thought over for just a second, then pushed it away. She'd watch for trouble, but she always did.

There was a cough from the unattended entrance as Niko returned.

She looked.

This, she realized, could be no other being than Lolola Montaigne d'Arcy deBurgh.

INTERLUDE
FOUR YEARS EARLIER

There are no-win situations, and then there are No-Win Situations, ones guaranteed to go down in the history books. Or so newly minted Admiral Nicolette Larsen of the Holy Hive Mind thought as she stared over the convoluted architecture of Rourke's Leap, designated spot for what the history books would surely refer to as one of the most disastrous accords attempted in the course of the Known Universe's history.

How had it come to this? Representatives of three major groups: the Hive Mind, the Paxian Empire, and the Spisoli, one of the most confusing and difficult powers in the universe.

The Spisoli emulated the Arranti, although the Arranti seemed to pay them no mind whatsoever. They predicated their actions on elaborate interpretations of Arranti actions, and pointed to their overall success as a race as a justification to continue this practice. It did not hurt that the Spisoli bred rapidly and were adapted to a wide range of environmental circumstances, nor that their inquisitive, flexible minds were adept at analyzing alien technology and adapting it for their own ends.

Even now, she could see a small group of them exploring the Leap, picking their way along the intricate set of dark glass bridges spanning a vast gulf. The bridges stretched every which way, laddering in one direction, then twisting back on themselves, forming a system of stairways and landings that latticed the blue glow coming from far below, a product of the electromagnetic and chemical reactions taking place in the depths.

While the ladders seemed to lead in random directions, you could, after looking at them for a while, begin to pick out patterns. Three reached to the pinnacle, an enormous glass oval some forty meters in diameter. It hovered on the bridge strands that held it up, each themselves a narrow and difficult pathway, half a meter across, and buffeted by high winds.

This entire planet was an alien artifact, and no one knew now what race had created the bridges, made of an impervious glass the color of deep, deep murky water shot through at rare intervals with striations, spears of light that moved through the glass as the watcher moved, changing according to their perspective. From this height, Niko could not see them, but she could see the tiny figures of the Spisoli, hunched humanoids with what looked like lumps on their shoulders, forcing their heads forward and down. The silhouettes were distinctive in the light of the two low-hanging moons, and Niko watched them cross one landing then descend a staircase, bound for one of the buildings that stood along the edge of the rift, shaped like vast upward-spiraling, conic seashells and made of the same dark glass.

Those buildings had been explored and picked over hundreds of times since their creators left them. The Spisoli would surely discover nothing new.

Niko turned away from the window. "I'm going for a walk, Dabry," she said. "I need to think, and this room is making my head hurt."

The room in question was in a building on the opposite side of the rift; it rode the top of one of the seashells and was itself a flattened bubble, with openings in the surface providing large windows admitting the shrill winds that haunted the edge.

Dabry sat with all arms folded, seemingly half dozing where he leaned against the wall. At her words, he opened his eyes. "By yourself, sir?"

"There's nothing to fear," she said. "Lots of people all through here."

"Less worried about you than them, sir. Sometimes when you're frustrated, you get a bit sharp."

"And don't I have occasion for that?" She ran a hand through her hair, tugging at its familiar knots, pulling at it and letting it spring back, a habitual gesture of frustration. "Unless we have a representative capable of meeting the specifications—who can both speak Ladderan, an ancient language known only to obscure scholars, and is capable of marching over a narrow span through almost blinding winds to deliver a speech in it . . . this accord fails and the Holy Hive Mind has every reason to absorb first the Paxians, then the Spisoli. And with our best hope delayed—"

"As though they wanted it to fail," Dabry said dryly.

She released her hair. "We've had this argument before. Might as well argue about something that matters, like the fact that your ass is on my dispatch case again."

"The stone is cold," he said. "And you don't need it right now."

"I need to be able to know that your ass hasn't been on it!"

"Technically," he said with dignity, "there's a layer of cloth separating the two."

She snorted and went out the door.

It was true, they'd had the argument about the Holy Hive Mind's intentions before. They'd probably have it again. Both of them had been forced into its ranks through economic circumstances, and the Holy Hive Mind paid well—at least it said that it did before one realized that one needed to leave it to recover all that pay, and that the papers one signed, all that rigmarole and small clauses full of hooks amid the piles of language, meant that they would make it as hard to leave as possible. Something like that left one cynical about such dealings.

The Holy Hive Mind way was to conquer, but also to pretend that they weren't doing so, that they were moving in to help a government "clean itself up" or "get things in good working order." And they would devote themselves to that very task and, at first, the government—ruler or council or whatever form it might take—would find that very helpful. Then slowly they'd realize that all that help ended up creating dependencies and unexpected debt for the social services and such that they were enjoying, courtesy of the Holy Hive Mind. Niko had seen it happen multiple times over the course of her career. Other times they used violence—but always *sanctioned* violence. Honorable warfare. Never mind that it usually involved their very large space forces overrunning some much smaller fleet.

And now, here she was, at the peak of her career and finally almost to the point where she could enact a long-held plan that had nothing to do with the Hive Mind's wants, when they seemed to be doing it again, and this time using *her* to mask their doings. Her own scheme seemed very small, in the scope of things, when compared to the hundreds of thousands that would be killed if the Holy Hive Mind were given free license to wage war on the others.

She jogged down the staircase, moving quickly, trying to stir her blood enough to bounce some new ideas into her head. But her boot heels clattered out, *What do we think this all is for? There will be war, there will be war,* the rhythm of a marching song she'd learned in boot camp.

Down on the street, she went northward along the rift, a slight upward tilt in the ground stretching her stride. She walked quickly, arms at her sides, eyes lost in thought, but avoiding obstacles and stones that might have tripped her.

To her left, the void gaped, its blue glow seen at intervals between the buildings, so uniform in their placing and abandonment. They cleared for a space, creating a small plaza whose balconied edge overhung the void. Dark glass staircases toed the edge on either side, lifting upward to join their fellows.

Niko went to the edge and rested her forearms on the flat top of the railing. The glass was so cold she could feel its chill even through the thick, padded fabric of her jacket sleeves.

Far below, the light shifted and crawled, sliding layer over layer. She sighed.

The crunch of footsteps coming up behind her made her turn, slowly rather than at a speed that might have constituted a threat. A Paxian soldier wearing a blue and silver cloak, a thin female with a sharp nose, dark, canny eyes, and short-cut hair the same shade as the cloak's trim.

"Just come to stare awhile too," the woman said. "I won't intrude if you don't want company."

Her voice was pleasant and even; her appearance unremarkable. The only nonuniform thing about her was the bluestone charm strung on a silver chain around her neck, shaped like a bird in flight.

"All good," Niko said, settling back into her former position. "Good place to come and think."

The woman rested her own forearms on the railing, a few feet away, close enough for conversation, far enough to establish distance. Companionable without a hint of seduction. They both stood watching the depths for a long time.

Niko racked her brain again, trying to come up with plans. There had to be a way to make the accords work, to bring everyone to the platform that was, the Spisoli insisted, the only place they could occur. But the only person capable of speaking Ladderan was still a day out, when the talks were only a half day away.

She turned toward the Paxian, waited for the shift in body that meant the other woman had noticed the attention and was open to talking. "Mind if I ask you a question?"

The Paxian shrugged, looking curious.

But before Niko could ask, street movement caught the attention of both. A small figure, hunched, its robe a distinctive black with a red velvet hood, was making its way toward them.

"Sessile priest," the other said.

Niko nodded. "Heard there was one picking its way around." Sessiles went wherever their prophecies drove them. Like most races, the Spisoli tolerated their presence.

They watched the figure approach them across the glassy pavement. It came up to Niko's waist. Once it neared, it stopped a meter away. It raised its hands and pulled the hood away to reveal the narrow reptilian face, the long curve of its jaw, wide-set eyes surrounded by golden-brown scales, pupils wide in the dim light, and faint red eye scale ridges marking him as male. His tongue flickered out twice before he spoke.

"Admiral Larsen?"

"Yes?" Niko said.

He turned his full attention to her. "I am here to speak for you."

"Speak how?"

"I speak Ladderan. I will talk for you."

"For the Hive Mind, you mean," she said, thoughts racing.

The small figure shrugged.

"You understand that it involves going over the span to the platform? You know that it's narrow and there's no way to protect you from the winds?" she questioned.

The head dipped to one shoulder in another sinuous shrug.

"Why are you doing this?" the Paxian asked, her tone edged with wonder, glancing between the two of them.

The Sessile never took his eyes from Niko. "Because she is on a Spiral of Destiny and this is needed."

Niko said, bewildered, "Spiral of Destiny?" She stared at the priest. He was traveling with the Spisoli—was this some trick on their part? But they had every reason to want the treaty to succeed. Had they known they had someone speaking the language aboard their ship? But the oracle protocols determining the factors of the ritual were unhackable, and their ship would have set out before it was determined.

"You do not need to understand it to walk it," the Sessile said confidently. He pulled his hood back in place. "I will be where needed in the morning."

He turned and walked away. Niko stared after him. Then she looked at the Paxian. "Did that just really happen?"

"Did all your hopes just stroll up and announce themselves manifest?" the woman said wryly. "It would seem so. Impressive, Commander, to get that out of a total stranger."

Niko rubbed her chin. She had to get back and tell Dabry what had happened. She said. "I beg your pardon, but I must go."

"Did you have a question you wanted to ask?"

"Ah, that. I was going to ask how you thought I might avoid having my commanders roll through two other entities, conquering and subjugating them. But that seems to have been answered—assuming that the Sessile does as he says, and possesses the skill he claims."

"They're not a race known for practical jokes." The other woman's eyes were narrowed in thought. "But neither are those leading the Holy Hive Mind known for thwarting their orders."

"I've been told that we are to seek peace," Niko said.

"You stress what you have been told as though you doubt it."

"I stress what I have been told because it is the honorable course, no matter what I might think I am truly intended to do."

"An impressive commander indeed." The Paxian nodded, then saluted. The bluestone charm around her neck glinted in the doubled moonlight. "Go in peace with clear stars, Admiral."

PRESENT DAY

In theory, the staff of the Last Chance should not have known who Lolola Montaigne d'Arcy deBurgh was. But in the restaurant business, these things spread, and at some point, the bestowers of the Nikkelin Orb had decided to avoid trying for subterfuge at all. Now their critics traveled, and restaurant owners tracked that travel, and for the first time in a century, one was coming to TwiceFar.

It was not that the Last Chance was the only restaurant aboard the station. Far from it. Almost every creature had to eat, in one form or another, and much of the station made its money pandering to that need on the part of both inhabitants and visitors. But TwiceFar, situated near three portals, had become more than a waypoint, more a city in itself, luring travelers who wanted to see the Midnight Stair and the food stalls that twisted around it, or visit the Edge, built of ships interwoven by tubes and walkways and conduits into its own strange structure, filled with the station's artisans and entertainers, or simply to give themselves the experience of dozens of cultures and races without having to visit a single planet where, after all, things like climate or local fauna and flora were often uncontrolled.

An anonymous news tip had circulated on the station net two weeks ago, when the critic first booked travel here. Everyone had speculated whether she was coming to test the majority of the restaurants on the station, or a particular one. For a bestower of the Orb, the latter would be much more in keeping with their style, and Skidoo had zealously monitored both the efforts of their competition as well as the names on the reservation list.

When the reservation had been made, she hadn't done what Niko would have expected, and told Niko. Instead, somewhat to Niko's annoyance, she'd summoned the entire crew, announced the time of the meal, and suggested they had exactly ten days to refurbish the place. It had been freshly painted only a few months earlier, Niko pointed out, and that was when Gio had rolled out his plans for said redecoration, which were complete enough that it was clear he'd been thinking about them since the first rumors had appeared.

Niko didn't mind humoring her crew, but she was worried that their expectations were unrealistic. There were better places aboard, she thought privately, or at least places that had longer, stronger traditions, like the Happy Neutron Pizza and Umpcha, which boasted that its teakettle had been in continuous operation for almost as long as Niko had been alive.

But Lolola had chosen this place. And here she was.

Lolola was in appearance human—and quite a memorable one, which surprised Niko, because several of the accounts Dabry had shown her identified the critic as someone who changed shape in order to be unseen and unobtrusive. Still, Niko reflected, perhaps it was a case of calling attention in such a way as to persuade anyone observing that this could not be an unobtrusive critic.

The critic's body was a curvaceous female, Terran classic. Top-of-the-line one, made with quality material and beautifully kept: skin tender and pale, brilliant turquoise eyes, golden hair streaked with blue and white pulled up in a chignon in order to bare a neck draped with a few careless curls. *Meticulous* was the first word that came to Niko's mind.

Lassite appeared out of nowhere, it seemed, and bowed gravely toward the woman. "May I lead you to your table, madam?" he asked in a tone that somehow managed to convey pleasure in her presence and gratitude for it.

Niko gave praise to Sky Momma for the recent training. *Maybe there's hope for this meal.*

She drifted in the pair's wake as Lassite led the critic toward the table that had been selected for her. Blue ghosts writhed across the ceiling as she walked, making the silverware gleam, the glow cubes take on a lapis hint from time to time. Lolola looked at them but did not, as many did, reach out to touch any when they slid through the air near her.

Lassite pulled the chair out for the critic, waiting until she was fully seated before handing her the menu. He paused to adjust the salt and pepper shakers on the center, a minute gesture conveying an infinite world of care. Priests had a sense of theater; the little Sessile was no exception.

As Lassite moved away from the table, Thorn was there immediately, filling the water glass and bowing before stepping back to disappear again. Niko relaxed, watching the well-rehearsed ballet. She'd match her team against any in the universe, whether it was in battle or the execution of an exquisite meal.

Jakka presented herself, an elegant shadow in the gray Last Chance wait uniform, ready to take the drink order. A back and forth, two questions from the critic, a gentle nod from the Dlin before she glided toward the bar and her fellow Dlin, Brineke, behind it.

Lolola studied the menu.

Niko had gotten real paper for this night's menu rather than the usual paper-textured plas. That had meant going out to the Sprawl at the edges of the station, where artisans made such things, most of them for sale for tourists. Dabry had written out a dozen of them in his careful penmanship, using an ancient fountain pen he'd produced from nowhere, much like the eggplant. The result was a pretty thing, Niko had to admit. She tried not to stare now to see the critic's reaction, but rather moved around the room, adjusting a few tables and clearing another.

Jakka returned to the table carrying a drink, a multilayered thing that gleamed in the ghost light. Dlin were graceful by nature, gesture part of their language, and Jakka's grace was a deadly one, capable of a spinning flurry of shots, all the while moving. Now she smiled and handed the drink to Lolola.

Skidoo appeared at Niko's elbow. "Captain, we is being having a problem," she said, tentacles moving nervously.

The problem was at least a handsome one. It was male, human, approximately two meters tall. It stood slouched by the lectern, dressed in evening clothes almost as expensive as its body, and arguing with an unusually flustered Lassite.

Niko wondered if something was trending that she hadn't known about. Two classic-looking humans, both upscale expensive, in one evening seemed against the odds.

Catching sight of her, the man straightened and took a step toward her. "You're the owner?" he asked.

"I am," she said, folding her arms.

"I was trying to explain the situation to your employee, but I'm not sure they understand the importance of it." He tapped his chest with a finger. "First off, allow me to introduce myself. I'm Arpat Takraven." He smiled, flashing white teeth at her.

While he didn't look familiar, the name did ring a bell. Niko cast her mind back to what the twins had been talking about. "You're the racer?" she ventured.

"Indeed!" He extended a hand, his grip warm and firm. When he released her hand, he said, "The second thing, which you may not know, because not all of my fans do, is that I'm a gourmand of sorts."

She refolded her arms. "Indeed."

He pressed fingers to his heart. "The thing is this, gentle-being. When the rumor reached me, I took my fastest ship here. It would mean so much to me to eat a meal in the presence of someone whose taste is so much greater than my own. I do not find food an aesthetic experience, and I want to witness someone who does, and talk with them as they work their way through the meal. A singular chance to learn. As I said, deeply appreciated." His fingers shifted to dip into his breast pocket to extract a credit chip, twitching it in her direction. "And something I would be willing to pay . . ." He paused in order to stress the next phrase sufficiently. ". . . a great deal for."

Niko could understand now why the offer had flummoxed Lassite, who knew as well as all the rest that the restaurant needed every bit of money it could get. Still, she shook her head and began to phrase a denial.

He spoke again. "It doesn't have to be at their table. Just . . . close enough that I could observe them, perhaps exchange a word or two over the course of the meal. Get a better understanding of how such a being eats." He twitched the chip at Niko again.

"When you say 'a great deal,' exactly how much are you saying?" she asked.

"Name your price."

Well then. Deep doom, her ass. She ran the figures for a small ship—a tiny and very reasonable one whose maintenance wouldn't cost too much—through in her head, and named them.

He didn't even blink.

6

Rather than leave it to Lassite, she led Arpat herself through the restaurant after warning him that if he attempted to interact with the critic, he would be ousted. But the warning was in vain. As they entered the room, the critic's gaze flickered up to catch sight of them, eliciting a broad smile from her. She exclaimed, "Arpat Takraven! Oh my stellars, I am such a fan. Please, if you're dining alone, would you consider eating with me?"

He gave Niko a sideways look and had the poise to wait for her nod before advancing on the table, hand outstretched again, saying, "The pleasure is all mine."

Niko waited with ill grace until he was seated, then handed him the menu. Stepping into the kitchen, she said, "Hold off the order for the critic. You're about to get another order that she'll want served with hers."

"What?" came the chorus, though Dabry only gave her an upraised eyebrow.

She shrugged at all of them. "It's the owner of that bioship," she told Thorn and Talon.

They gasped in delight, whiskers perking fully. Dabry said, "But why, Captain? I thought we agreed no other customers after she arrived. And what are they doing sitting with the critic?"

"Paying very well for the privilege."

"How well?"

"Enough to buy us a ship." At his startled, happy look, she cautioned, "A small ship, mind you. But one that we might be able to use to our advantage and to supplement our income by quite a bit.

And *that* in turn would put us ahead of schedule." She grinned at him full out now. "A stroke of luck, wouldn't you say?"

"Don't say that, I beg of you," he said with earnest gravity.

"Why not?"

"I may not believe in prophecy, but I do believe in jinxes."

She started to answer him, but whatever she was about to say was drowned out in the explosion.

T

The noise didn't come from inside the room where they were. Nor did it come from somewhere out in the restaurant, or even the halls immediately outside it. Instead, it was a large noise, a station-shaking sort of large. Everyone scrambled for emergency pressure suits, Niko and Dabry pulling theirs on while running toward the dining room with armloads of others.

"You take the admiral's party and I'll get the critic and her friend!" she shouted at him. The station lurched again. "Gods above, that's something big! We've got to get to an escape vehicle."

"There's pods!" he shouted back.

She shook her head and he didn't push it for now. Niko hated the pods, the way they held you helpless while you waited to be rescued. No, she'd take her chances on trying to find something better than that.

Both Lolola and Arpat were on their feet and looking around. The critic's eyes were wide, but Arpat was smiling as pleasantly as though this were part of the experience.

Niko shoved the suits at them. "Here!" Lolola grabbed one and began to put it on, but Arpat shook his head, tapping a golden button at his throat. A field shimmered into existence and surrounded him. *Trust the rich to have environmental protection built in,* she thought, and finished fastening her more mundane and bulky suit before helping Lolola with hers.

She rushed the two to the entrance, where everyone was gathered. Dabry appeared beside her.

"Where's the admiral and their party?" she demanded.

"Rushed off to their ship," he said. "The admiral said to tell you to go there."

Niko considered. Boarding the admiral's ship was tantamount to rejoining the Holy Hive Mind. A real artist would, according to their scripture, stay with their greatest work, and Niko had claimed the restaurant as hers. "We can't do that," she told Dabry, and was glad to see him nod in agreement.

"Then where are we going?" Lolola demanded. Arpat kept smiling amiably, but dug in his heels at Niko's gesture toward the entrance door. "If you're taking me to an escape pod," he said, "think again. I have a vessel."

"There are a number of us," she said.

With a calm humility she hadn't expected, he nodded. "And in turn I will offer you and all of your folks the shelter that I can, aboard my ship."

She heard a muffled cheer from behind her. The twins, no doubt, who'd figured out what ship it was.

"Very well," she said. "But the question is—can we make it to that ship in the first place?"

"Sounds good," Dabry said. "Just let me grab a few things first, if we're evacuating."

"All right, but hurry! I don't want to lose us all just because someone couldn't stand to leave their teddy bear behind!" Niko snapped.

"Without the means of my livelihood, what am I?" he asked.

"Alive, perhaps?"

Despite Niko's words and the shuddering of the walls all around, Dabry insisted on a full evacuation, allowing everyone to grab their go bag and even some cherished mementos. Ducking into her office, she rummaged through her belongings. Weapons, survival gear, some small things both valuable and fungible. She shoved *Skullduggery and Sacred Space Vessels* into the pack as well.

How had she accumulated so much clutter? There wasn't time

to sort through it all, sift out what was worth taking and what wasn't. She yanked open a second bag.

The first thing she laid in it was taken down from a cupboard she hadn't opened since filling it. Her old Free Trader coat, its material a royal purple she'd chosen herself, the front worked with buttons bearing her old ship *Merribelle*'s insignia, a tilted bell superimposed over a full-blown rose. She shoved it into the bottom of the bag; on top she piled other souvenirs, memories, and a few additional pistols with boxes of ammo.

But she hesitated before picking up the bag. Maybe this disaster was a sign that she needed to let go of old dreams. She'd never be a Free Trader again, never be in command of a ship and its crew, doing as she pleased. Here was some new hell that would end up in even more debt and complication and chaos. Would she be able to hold everyone together through it? That was what she needed to focus on. She left the bag there and went into the kitchen. Where was the crate that had been in her office? Thorn or Talon must have taken it to the storeroom. Well, the crate was spaceworthy. The occupant would be safer in there than outside it.

Based on his insistence, Niko was unsurprised to see Dabry appear in turn, large containers tucked under all four arms.

"What's all that?" she snapped.

"Some things are irreplaceable," he said. "I've been cultivating that sourdough for two decades now. The trader I got ethlic from told me that the strain is over five hundred years old. Not to mention the dasplen colony."

She was about to argue the point further when she noticed what was in tow behind him, trundling along on a tether. "Momma Sky and all her pointed stars, why are you bringing *that*?"

"We can't leave them behind, Captain. It wouldn't be humane."

She glanced around in order to make sure no one else was listening before drawing closer to him, pointing a finger at the crate that had arrived that morning. "There is no call for taking that.

Whoever or whatever is inside that is better equipped to survive our current situation than any of us are. Whatever happens, salvage will show up in order to find everything of value, and at that point they can just extract them. We. Do. Not. Need. To. Take. That."

Dabry absorbed all of this with his usual placid dignity. "I beg to differ, sir. They are our responsibility."

"No, the moment we *open* that crate, they become our responsibility. Before then we have no obligation."

"It was delivered to you, sir."

"And if I had ordered it delivered, I would say that was a valid argument. However, I did not."

"Someone thought that being, whoever they are, was best off in your keeping. Will you prove them wrong?"

"What's in the crate?" Thorn asked, coming up behind them, trailed by his twin and Lassite. Gio had several bulky duffel bags at his feet; Milly a conglomeration of white plastic cases. Thorn and Talon both carried bulky packs that she suspected contained sports equipment. Jakka and the other Dlin were sorting through several bags that apparently held mutual gear.

"Cooking supplies," Niko lied, giving Dabry a glare. "And there had better be some of that smoked sausage in there."

"I believe there is," he said.

Arpat's ship, *You Sexy Thing*, was docked three levels down. They tried to take the closest main lift, but it was out of commission; its doors, hanging ajar, showed the immense stretch of downward and upward tube. The air smelled of smoke and the sour tang of firefighting foam.

Gio eyed the empty lift tube speculatively until Dabry said, "Let's not abandon the luggage unless we have to." Niko ground her teeth for a moment but refrained from comment. Nonetheless, they were able to backtrack and find a cargo lift. Unfortunately, its dimensions would accommodate only half of them.

"We'll have to split up," Dabry said.

"You go ahead—take Jakka and Brineke, and the other waitstaff and kitchen folks. Thorn and Talon with me and the two civilians."

Dabry shook his head. "You go first and take those two," he said, nodding toward Arpat and Lolola. "Thorn, Talon, sure, but also Gio, Skidoo . . ." He looked around. "Milly too."

Niko would have argued but there was no time. She let Lassite squeeze aboard the lift with them as she scowled at Dabry.

"See you there, Captain," he said, and saluted as the doors closed.

The crowded confines of the lift were full of elbows. Skidoo clambered up into a corner of the ceiling and hung there, although she kept two tentacles stretched downward, one twined along Milly's arm, the other resting just a tip on Niko's wrist. She patted it with her free hand; the other braced against the wall.

They were rocketing downward when the station shook again, a massive shift that reverberated through the metal around them, ringing it like a giant bell, followed by two smaller explosions that seemed to be coming from above them, somewhere in the decks they'd abandoned.

"Any way to speed this thing up?" Arpat Takraven asked, nodding over at the control panel.

"Maybe you could wave some money at it," Niko snapped. She was tired of the calm with which Takraven seemed to be taking all of this. He could afford to have things fall apart around them. The Last Chance was all she and the others had.

He glanced at her and said, "Got a problem?"

"No," she said. She swallowed back a further retort and raised her chin. This was only another situation. Her team had weathered worse in the past.

"You'll like my ship," Arpat said, more to Lolola than Niko.

The critic dimpled at him in a practiced way and said, "I'm sure I will! This is all so exciting!"

Niko kept her face expressionless but rolled her eyes internally. Trust the rich to be spending more time worrying about fucking than getting away safely. No doubt Takraven had a clone body elsewhere, ready to be activated and his memories, or at least his memories up until his last backup, poured into it if the current body should die. That tended to make someone blasé about dangerous situations, although when push came to shove, she'd seen the survival instinct activated as strongly in a clone body as in any more singular form. No one liked to be obliterated, even if they knew they'd be re-created later.

The station shuddered again. "Are we being taken over?" Thorn asked.

It was a valid question. TwiceFar Station suffered frequent takeovers and turnovers, but almost all of them were bloodless.

"Too much damage for takeover," Niko answered. "Whoever or whatever is doing this is trying to destroy the station. Nothing short of that. Skidoo, what's the chatter on comms?"

"The station information net is being down, with available no news is being. Everything is being diverting to life support and the escape systems," Skidoo said. "Directive is to being evacuating as quickly as possible. The explosions random are being, no pattern to them, no way to is predicting. Is getting out; is being doing so fast."

Exiting the lift, they moved quickly, steps keeping time with the shrill *whoop whoop whoop* of the level's alarm system as they took a slanting corridor down. Beings scrambled through the hallways around them, each intent on its own escape. A cloud of Fizziks zipped along, the tiny creatures that made up the group separating and flying past them at top speed, leaving behind a chitter-chatter and an odd, waxy smell.

Only two corridors to go, Niko was thinking, when the walls shook and groaned, the station's underpinnings crying out in protest that echoed once again throughout the massive structure. With a crash, the nearest wall crumpled outward, the unexpected surge slamming into Arpat and smashing him against the other wall as Thorn and Talon, the two standing nearest him, leaped away.

Niko rushed to his side. He lay in a heap, lanky limbs outstretched, the immaculate black and white formal suit flooded with scarlet stains. The air reeked of copper and smoke. Lolola screamed and collapsed against the wall; Milly knelt beside her.

Niko held her hand to Arpat's neck, searching for the pulse fluttering there, a weak pitter-patter. She swore. "Lassite!" she snapped over her shoulder.

He approached warily, tucking the red hood back, his tongue sampling the air. "He is dying, I can feel it," he said. "We are forbidden to pass a certain edge, and that is where death crouches. I cannot heal him."

"Cannot or will not?"

They stared at each other in silence.

"If you were implying I would disobey you," he finally said, "that is not something that would happen."

"Perhaps not. But I also know that healing exposes you to your patient's pain. It's understandable you might want to look away from it."

His eyes flashed. "You insult my honor!"

"You would not heal Thorn last week when he burned his hand. You said it was a trivial injury."

He gestured dismissively. "Some injuries are lessons to be learned. That is what Holy Writ tells us. I cannot heal such and I would not, I would not heal someone of wisdom and make them foolish."

This is not the time for lessons in Sessile philosophy, Niko thought. She turned back to Arpat, who was trying to sit up. Milly had managed to revive Lolola and was talking earnestly to the critic, urging her back on her feet. Lassite stepped back and rehooded himself but continued to stand close.

"You do not have much longer left," Niko told Arpat. "We will take you to your ship, but is there anything that we will need to know when we reach it?" She did not want to say, *in case you have died by then*, but she knew he understood by the way his head sagged.

"Yes, yes," he said. "And I have backups. It's just that . . ." He raised a hand in a gesture Niko found melodramatic. She gritted her teeth. "One never thinks one will actually be in the body that dies, somehow? You think of yourself as the one that continues on."

"Yes, for those few that have the money for such a thing," Niko said to him. "Spare me your angst. How do we get aboard your ship?"

His eyes gleamed. "You know that I don't have to tell you anything, don't you?"

Niko said, lowering her voice as the rest of the others came closer to see what was happening, "You know that I don't have to make your dying moments any easier, don't you? In fact, if I chose to make them a little harder, here in the heart of all this noise and chaos that your backup won't remember, what do you think would happen? I don't think anything would."

"Point taken." His eyelids drew closed, and for a moment she thought she might not get the answer after all. But then they flickered, and he said, "Tell the ship this: you believe in miracles."

"I believe in miracles?" she repeated, an eyebrow twitching in perplexity.

He smiled slightly. "An old joke, like the ship's name. You'll like the ship. You remind me of it." He looked up at Lolola, whom Milly had pulled to stand nearby. "Ah, lady, we would have had such meals together! Look me up when you can, and tell me that I owe you dinner."

Lolola remained silent as he died, although tears might have glinted in the turquoise eyes where she stood, one dainty hand pressed to her mouth.

The corridor's destruction meant that they had to double back in order to reach the docks, but at length they came to the area, pushing their way through the crowds and chaos. Alarms were going off, klaxons and shrill tones and the big boom of a Terellan time gun. A film of yellow firefighting foam covered everything, including the sticky floor underfoot.

The majority of the ships occupying the docks had already taken off, while others were mobbed by beings trying to get aboard, sometimes in ones or twos, other times in more organized groups. From afar, Niko saw the last of the admiral's group boarding their ship, moving in formation. Guards held the edges, keeping away the surging crowds despite their protests and pleas.

By contrast, *You Sexy Thing* stood by itself. Small guns on the main hulls swiveled, tracking anyone who came too close as it waited for its master.

Bioships are grown, not manufactured, and every gleaming, curving inch of *You Sexy Thing* managed to convey a sense of barely restrained power itching to be unleashed. It was a deep black in color, a black that greedily gulped up the light and buried it where no one would ever find it again. Scarlet lights skittered over its surface as sensors sampled everything in the vicinity. It looked like a wasp, alert and deadly, the appearance intensified by protruding yellowish lumps on either side of the prow, resembling vast compound eyes. The tail tapered into blue and violet vanes, looking like nothing so much as vast feathers colored in midnight peacock shades.

Niko paused, scanning for Dabry and the others.

"We need to go," Milly said.

"I know, I know," Niko said. She moved up, standing just outside the range of the guardian guns. "Seeking admission, with the password 'I believe in miracles,'" she said, hoping that Arpat Takraven had resisted the urge to give her a bad password. She put the odds at fifty-fifty; she'd been figuring and refiguring them all the way since his death. A pointless calculation, trying to keep the fate of Dabry and the others out of her thoughts. But they kept returning to that worry.

The swiveling guns paused, all fixing on her for a tense moment before continuing to circle outward. A landing ramp unfolded from the side and extended in front of them, its color an ominous black, its surface webbed with purplish veins.

Niko glanced around at the others. They lost no time getting themselves and their luggage aboard.

Niko crouched by the hatchway, watching for Dabry.

"Please stand away from the door so I may close it and depart," the ship said. It was a neutral voice, in a range that could have been that of a male or female human. Humans were one of the few races that used voice command technology, and it was usually pitched in their voices. Bland space jazz began to play from speakers overhead.

"Not yet. We've got more people coming," she snapped.

The music's volume dimmed, though it continued. "Please stand away from the door so I may close it and depart."

"Misbegotten child of a comet, no!"

"Closing door in thirty seconds."

"I order you not to!" Finally, she saw Dabry's head surging through the crowds toward her. "That Ettilite and everyone with him, they're ours, don't fire on them!"

"Closing door in twenty seconds."

Niko looked around for something, anything to jam in the door. She glanced out again.

There was no one following behind Dabry.

"Sky Momma scour your soul!" she swore.

"Closing door in ten seconds." The music surged back to its original volume.

Dabry barely made it, pounding up the ramp even as it began to swing closed, making him stumble forward into Niko.

"The others?" she said urgently.

He shook his head, looking dazed. "I've never seen anything like it. We were on an outer corridor, and it was like something *clawed* at the station, trying to get at us. I was a few steps behind, managed to go sideways and into a hall with an air lock at the corner."

She touched her forehead to his. "Not your fault."

"All of them," he said with a sob. Agony wound his voice tight to the breaking point. "Every single one."

She held him, head to head, for a long moment before she let him go. "We've got some still alive, Sergeant."

He drew a long, shuddering breath before he began the labor of hauling himself to his feet. "Very well, sir."

"Please remove your shoes before continuing farther," the ship said firmly, "and place them in the containment rack."

Inside the door was an open chamber perhaps twice the size of the cargo lift they had ridden to get there. Hallways led in opposite directions from one another, twisting oddly and resembling giant throats, a thought that Niko kept to herself.

Following one of these as it led its way along inside the ship, they found the overall interior even more spacious than it had appeared from the outside. The rooms maintained the organic feel and smell, as though they were pods grown inside some vast organic body, which technically they were. Core doors were clustered with lichen and fungi, and shaggy growths underfoot caressed whatever they could touch, a sensation that Niko both enjoyed and found unsettling.

Skidoo kept pausing to savor it. "I *like* this ship," she said.

The ship's mellow voice spoke from all around them. "Gentlebeings, where is the owner of this vessel, Arpat Takraven?"

"Dead," Niko snapped. "And we're going to follow on his heels if you don't get us out of here."

There was a small pause. Then the ship said, "You mean the

current clone is dead and that the next body is in the process of activation. In that case, my orders are to remain in place until that new clone arrives. May I direct you to your quarters in the interim?"

Niko demurred. "We might want to make departing our first priority," she observed. "I'm sure that you have noticed that the station is being destroyed all around us."

As though she had not spoken, the mellow voice repeated, "Gentlebeings, may I direct you to your quarters? In the interim, I am prepared to move two clicks from the station to avoid debris."

Dabry and Niko exchanged glances. "This does not bode well," she muttered under her breath.

"Still," he said, "I suggest playing along for now. What else can we do? And the sooner that we are away from this, the better."

"I agree." She raised her voice to address the ship. "Yes, please. Show us to our quarters and perhaps by then the explosions outside will have convinced you that we should depart."

A coruscating, multicolored ball of light appeared in front of each individual. Their shadows played over the interior walls like greasy rainbows as the balls hovered, suspended, seemingly without means. Gio eyed his as though wondering whether he could take it apart, while Thorn and Talon visibly twitched, every cat-like instinct activated.

"These are your guides," the ship said. "Each will take you to your designated rooms."

"We wish to share quarters," Thorn said. "The two of us, I mean, not everyone in general." Talon nodded in agreement.

There was another pause, and then the two balls of light in front of the twins merged to become a single one. A chime sounded.

"Please follow the guide," the ship said.

The one thing to be said about the bioship, Niko reflected as she followed her own personal glowing ball of light, was that there was simply not the opportunity for opulent display that she had seen more than once when interacting with the belongings of the very, very, very wealthy. No need to add additional extravagant fixtures or artwork or other ornamentation of the kind that constantly made you ask why any reasonable being would need such a thing.

A two-part scarlet curtain hung down over the door that the glowing ball led her to. As she approached it, it parted, letting her enter a chamber hung with similar curtains.

When she brushed through the curtains, touching against them, she realized they were great folds of skin, hanging like dewlaps, the wall almost shingled with them. They were warm and pliable to the touch and smelled of honey. She dug her fingers under one, trying to explore where it met the wall, and felt it twitch at her touch. She released it quickly and went to examine the other features of the room, particularly the one that her body was urging her to find.

The toilet was the usual shape, although also made of living flesh, which made it a very odd experience, and there was no shower that she could discern in the strange little subchamber that was the bathroom, its walls colored pale blue and bruise purple. A mechanical fresher unit squatted in one corner, its metal and straight lines an odd contrast to the irregular curves of the fleshy walls it had been installed in. The material of the wall around the machine was lined with some sort of rubbery plastic that she suspected was intended to keep it from irritating the ship's body with its foreign presence.

She wondered what the appeal of such a ship was to Arpat Takraven. Was it anything more than very very expensive and very very fast? She suspected not but you never knew what appealed to one person's psyche.

She put the two cases holding her gear on a shelf and looked around. It was the strangest ship she'd ever been in, but hardly the most unwelcoming. Some would have found the silent warmth underfoot unsettling, but she was used to barefoot ship life, the kind she had known aboard the *Merribelle*, where everyone knew everyone, and things were kept clean, and everyone had shared their germs already.

She said out loud, "I'm ready. Will you take me to meet with the others now?"

"Yes," the ship replied. The ball of light reappeared in front of her. It hung a few inches away from her face, as though examining her, before it moved back to the door.

She found the others in a great chamber, its walls veined in blue and silver, throbbing as the liquids within them coursed through the ship. The new inhabitants clustered in the center, seeking shelter in one another, although Lolola stood off a little ways from the rest, as though feeling even more of a stranger at the sound of their mutual conversations.

"We are ready to depart now," she told the ship.

Silence again before the ship said, with an edge that Niko could not help but read as sullen, "Amounts of debris and the chance of explosion have forced me to remove this vessel from the station's vicinity. Departure is already under way."

"Good," she said, relieved. "Let us know when we are away from the station and clear of danger."

"We are currently five scilliants from the station and clear of danger. Proximity suggests an Arranti is in nearby game-space, but focused on the station."

Niko shivered. Was that the explanation for the destruction of the station? It had to be something big like that, or else someone would have spotted whatever it was coming and evacuation would have happened in a more orderly fashion. TwiceFar was known for being a little chaotic, but bureaucracy always had held firm.

The idea that it might get caught up in Arranti games had

been the last thing from her mind. Her earlier words to Dabry ran through her head: *Heavy portents could mean anything from our critic getting a stomachache to the whole place getting blown up by an Arranti who thought it would advance their game.*

She could have sworn she'd been naming an impossibility, but had some prescience ticked her brain?

"Very well then, set course for Gamelon-Twelve. We can find out where his clone is located there."

"What if he has more than one?" Milly said.

"Beyond the fact it is highly illegal to have more than one, most people don't want to run the chance of two getting accidentally activated and conflicting. Or someone using them as a weapon." Niko shook her head, running through plans in her head.

They could catch their breaths there and call in a few favors, plus Niko could check with the insurance network. She intended to charge Arpat Takraven's next incarnation for taking his fancy ship to him as well, but she'd need to contact him first, make sure that he'd make good on his previous existence's promise. She would have the tape of him entering the restaurant, at least— well, perhaps, if that had been archived, she thought, wondering about the station—but better yet, she would have Lolola. Surely the critic would corroborate his presence, as would the fact that they now occupied his ship.

"Course change denied. Current course remains Scourse."

"What? No one goes to Scourse on business. It's a prison planet," Niko said.

"Change course immediately," Lolola said. "A savage place like that? With criminals?" She shuddered.

The critic had been quiet most of the time, clearly shaken by Arpat's death and more than willing to cling to the group that seemed to have a way off the station. Niko wondered what the critic actually thought of all this. She remembered Dabry's eggplant, now long gone, and its components, the neat, fan-shaped slices, probably floating in space, with a twinge of regret. So much for a Nikkelin Orb.

"It probably wouldn't have brought in that much business anyway," she muttered to herself.

"Course change denied. Current course remains Scourse."

"Why are we going to Scourse?" Niko asked.

It might have been Niko's imagination, but the ship's tone seemed smug. "To deliver you as thieves to the authorities for attempting to steal this vessel."

B

Niko knew immediately what had happened.

"That son of a three-sided crystal gave us the wrong password!" she said. "Look, Ship, we do want to get you back to your owner. But we need to get to a place where we can track him down and arrange the exchange. He owes me a great deal of money."

"Is the transaction witnessed?" the ship asked.

"Witnessed back on TwiceFar," she said.

There was a pause. "TwiceFar systems are currently offline," the ship finally said. Niko could swear she heard suspicion in its voice.

"That is because the whole place was blown up by an Arranti, for who knows what reason!"

"That seems most unlikely," the ship said.

"You saw the Arranti yourself!"

"I witnessed an Arranti in the vicinity, but was unable to discern what was causing damage to the station itself."

"That's what Arranti do!"

Sane species avoided the Arranti, one of the oldest, most powerful races, who were obsessed with the game that their species played. They would not divulge the rules to outsiders—although it was apparently specified that you had to be an Arranti to play—and over the centuries, while many scholars had devoted themselves to trying to figure it out, only guesswork and wild theories served so far. The game—and its participants—were wholly unpredictable, and while the station had been destroyed as a move, apparently, it could just as easily have been transformed, or replaced, or augmented. Sometimes new game structures arose, and they disappeared just as quickly.

At the end of the Arranti year, Niko knew, the Arranti would gather and discuss their scores. How the score affected them was also unknown, but many believed it to be tied into whatever system of leadership they used. Among all the races, the Arranti were perhaps the most secretive, although they claimed it was simply that lesser minds would be unable to understand. They also claimed to exist in multiple dimensions that other beings could not discern, but this claim was generally regarded as hooey.

Luckily for all parties concerned, most Arranti made only one or two moves per cycle, and those moves might just as well be something harmless, like moving a pebble from one side of a barren wasteland to another or altering the words of a popular song.

"The password 'I believe in miracles' designates passengers who should be taken to a prison planet and turned over to the proper authorities for attempting to steal this vessel."

"We didn't attempt to steal you! We were with Arpat. Maybe he gave us the wrong password because he was dying at the time."

"That password is designed in case Mr. Takraven is being tortured," the ship said ominously.

Niko thought back and regretted her phrasing to Takraven. She should have known better, but she hadn't dealt with many of those rich enough to be called "short-lived," hopping from clone body to clone body.

"Bastard," she muttered.

"It will take four days to reach Scourse," the ship reported. "Please enjoy the amenities aboard until then."

They ignored the amenities and planned. They did not speak of their dead just yet; the company had taken heavy losses before. *We thought we'd escaped a possibility of it happening again,* Niko thought ruefully, *but the universe moves as it will. Best to carry on for now, and pick a better time to mourn later.*

After the ship's announcement, she took inventory of what gear everyone had brought. She knew Dabry's, which consisted of 90 percent cooking gear and supplies, 5 percent heavy ordnance, and 5 percent personal items.

Milly's two matching suitcases provided few surprises. The little case held toiletries, feather spray, and a few bits of jewelry while its counterpart contained clothes. Like Dabry, she hadn't been able to resist some of the tools of her trade, but she had been more reasonable: a bag was filled with frosting nozzles, while another held a small airbrush and molecular glazer.

Gio had brought his good knives and a large number of guns, lesser knives, caltrops, garrotes, throwing stars, vibrochains, and other assorted gear. He shrugged at Niko's twitched eyebrow.

"Started as battle souvenirs," he signed, "but then people kept bringing interesting bits to trade. Little nifty tricks." He picked up a small box containing six purple marbles. "These are smoke grenades—you'll be surprised how many cubic meters' worth. Nice, dense smoke too."

Niko snorted.

"Man's gotta have a hobby," Gio signed, his lips curling back in amusement but covering his canines.

"Pretty good hobby," Niko said. "I'm not saying anything to the contrary." She patted him on the shoulder and he hooted in appreciation, settling down to sort through his hastily packed gear and rearrange it to his satisfaction.

Lassite had several packs. The smallest held his few belongings: a change of robes, a ritual knife, a box that he said contained "sacred tools of prophecy." (They all had seen these in action and knew them to be small dice, carved from what Lassite claimed were the knucklebones of an ancestor, figured with different symbols.)

Beside it he laid an oddly patterned bag, made out of scaled leather, supple and fine, sewn into a boxy shape, with a handle on one end. It *squirmed* as he put it down. Everyone jumped back.

"What the hell is in there?" Niko demanded.

"I brought some of the ghosts," he said.

"*What?*"

"The Derloen ghosts."

"How did you catch a *ghost*? And what's keeping them inside the bag?"

He looked at her with dignity. "I am a priest. I learned to make a ghost trap as part of my training, though they are not my specialty."

"How many are in there?"

"Three."

"If you could catch ghosts, why did we spend so much time redecorating around them?"

He said, "I didn't want to disturb them. I brought these three only because they wanted to come."

Niko's voice rose in pitch and volume. "You can *talk* to them? How are we only now finding this out?"

"You never asked," Lassite said. He picked the bag back up and petted it like a cat. "And they don't talk, they just feel things."

"Okay." Niko took a breath. "One, are there any other priestly magic powers you have been hiding from us, like the ability to shit deliriterium or teleport into Q-space or anything like that?"

Lassite contemplated. "Beyond speaking Ladderan, I have acquired sixteen other dead languages. I cannot teleport but I could sense someone doing so. And of course you know that I have extensive knowledge of physiognomies other than my own species, which is useful in a variety of ways." He paused again, tongue licking out into the air. "And seeing the future is useful, of course." He sounded uncertain on that last.

Niko stared at him before she said, "All right. Two, do the ghosts need to be let out or fed, anything like that?"

"No."

"Then they stay in the bag. What's that last pack?" Niko's

brows knitted at its familiar dimensions. "Did you take that off my desk?"

"You were leaving it behind, but it looked as though you were doing so because you were trying to choose among things. I only glanced inside but it seemed as though you might want these possessions but left them behind for the sake of expediency." His voice was soft and apologetic.

Dabry gave Niko a puzzled look that she ignored.

"Do I do badly, Captain Niko?" Lassite said. "I do not mean to have been presumptuous."

"No, it's all right," she said slowly. "I'm glad to have those things. I simply thought I had said goodbye to them." She took the bag from Lassite. "Thank you."

He shuffled in place, embarrassed, and seemed grateful when she turned to Thorn and Talon. "You two, what did you think to bring?"

"Our battle armor," Talon said instantly. "Two weeks of field rations and basic survival gear."

"Well done," Niko said, her voice warm and with an edge of throttled amusement. "No personal gear?"

"Our warball equipment," Thorn said. "Just in case."

"Do you think this ship is likely to have a warball court?" Niko inquired.

Thorn shrugged, while Talon said, "You never know."

"Fair enough. Skid?"

Skidoo had brought as many containers as she could of the substance that basically acted as a liquid skin, preserving her from drying out in the less humid air that everyone else preferred. Niko was glad she had; the stuff was difficult and expensive to synthesize. She wasn't convinced the *Thing*'s replicators would be up to the task. Sometimes you got inside the shiny possessions of the rich, their fancy dwellings or vehicles, and found out they were all surface.

"Good," Niko said. "Though no other survival gear at *all*, Skid? You're getting lazy."

"I am being knowing we is being a team, Captain, is being begging your pardon," Skidoo retorted.

Despite the direness of the overall situation, Niko had to laugh. While it had been good to work together in the restaurant, it was even better to work together this way, knowing that no matter what they might face, she had a team that was capable of dealing with it, one she knew and trusted. Milly and the critic were something of an unknown quantity, though.

She turned to the latter. "And you, Lolola?"

"And me what?" the critic said with a touch of hauteur.

"What do you have with you? The general inventory lets us know what we have at our disposal in case emergencies arise."

"There is nothing in my bag that would be of use to you," she declared.

Dabry and Niko exchanged glances.

"No weapons? No medical supplies?"

"My reader and personal gear," Lolola said. "They are mine and not part of the general inventory."

"This is a survival situation, ma'am," Dabry said.

Lolola put her nose in the air. "Then it is up to you all to make sure I survive."

This was, as they would find in every other interaction, indicative of the critic's overall demeanor. She acted as though the others had been personally responsible for the situation, as though it were all just part of the meal that she had ordered, a meal that was truly lacking in both presentation and content.

After a few fruitless attempts at conversation, they all simply stayed out of her way and by mutual accord, decided to leave her to whatever fate happened to present itself. Her testimony would be of less worth than the direct examination of their memories, and while that was a harsh and unpleasant process that no one looked forward to, they did anticipate being cleared of any wrongdoing and eventually released.

This was all just a small setback.

After that they did scatter and explore the ship. Bioships were rare technology, taken from the Spogillys, and each one was unique. Thorn and Talon, who followed such things, told Niko that there were fewer than two dozen of them in the Known Universe.

She could have gone below, to explore the several cargo holds, balloon swellings on the underside of the ship, their curves a visual caress, an exterior undulation of darkness.

Shelves and straps webbed their interiors. Past that lay the biological chambers where racks of purplish weed grew, its fruit little water globes that the ship's servitors, here shaped in organic bone in arachnid forms, harvested every few hours.

Even farther in, sheltered by the ship's bulk, they passed through multiple doorways, each smaller than the last, before they entered the space that held the *Thing*'s primary heart and its ventilation systems, vast membraned panes mottled pale blue on darker navy that filtered the air. Tiny biomechanisms flitted like bats here between the panes, keeping them clean.

Farther up, hallways and staircases led back and forth, most of them eventually heading to the pilot's chamber and Takraven's own quarters, atop the ship, luxurious and holding the machines he used daily: an exercise cube, a kitchenette with a store of freeze-dried meals in gold and silver wrappers, and an elaborate fresher with more settings than any of them had ever seen. All of this was open to them.

But Niko did what she usually did in times of trouble or stress when an action plan was needed—she went to Dabry.

The cabin allotted to him was large enough that it dwarfed the crate.

"I still don't know why you brought that," she grumbled.

He quirked a brow at her and opened the lid. She watched as

he began to take out packets and tiny pots, each one bringing its own fragrant whiff. "You used it in order to bring your herbs?" she said incredulously.

He looked vaguely embarrassed. "There was a lot of excess room in there," he murmured. "And they require a controlled climate. And two of those mints, you can't find them anywhere, not good Martian vatmint. Plus I still have those vanilla beans infusing in sugar and I didn't have time to take them out of their tubes. This was easier."

"Please tell me you didn't take out the occupant and replace them entirely with your own goods."

"I most certainly did not," he said, then added, "Maybe if there had been more time and I thought they would have recovered quickly enough to come with us." Dabry was more than somewhat devoted to the collection of flavorings and seeds he had amassed over the years. He finished removing his belongings and reached for the control panel inside.

Niko caught that wrist. "Wait a minute," she said, "What are you doing?"

"Waking them up."

"Why now?"

"Because," he said, "the situation is already complex enough that it seems insoluble. Adding another factor—who knows what that will bring?"

"You could just be awakening them to go to prison under suspicion of being an accomplice," she said. "They won't thank you for that."

"In a way," he said, "they don't exist at all right now. I am making them exist. Most people do not object to that situation. And the presence of an Arranti makes me very nervous. I would like to know if the two are connected in some way."

"You're mad," Niko said. "The Arranti game has nothing to

do with beings other than the Arranti. Everyone knows that, and only the Spisoli claim differently."

"So they say. But I have not heard of one destroying an entire space station before."

She kept holding his wrist, and he refrained from using any of his other hands, waiting and watching her face.

"All right. But are you sure?" she said. "Have you ever been to Scourse? Whoever this is, they won't thank you for taking them there."

"Captain, I am rarely sure of anything," he said. "Should I call Lassite and have him prophesize?"

She made a face, then reluctantly let go of his arm.

His fingers played over the controls. The crate hissed as its mechanisms engaged, and a faint, chilly mist rolled away from it as it settled fully on the floor. The sides fell away, dissolving into wisps of odorless white smoke, and the motionless humanoid form they had seen before inside emerged from the fog.

Small, not hulking, Niko was relieved to note. Flakes of white began to sift away from the anonymous white lump, revealing . . .

A small woman, barely out of her teens, with dark hair worn in a braid curled in a crown atop her head. She lay still. For a second Niko worried that she had not survived stasis—although that would have solved some things, she told herself in irritation.

Kid's not even awake and you're worrying over her. That doesn't bode well.

The woman took a deep, shuddering breath, and rolled over, coughing and spitting out clear fluid, half falling out of what remained of the crate. She landed on hands and knees, doubled over and shivering.

The ship absorbed the fluid dripping from her. It was faintly salty and mildly poisonous, which made it complicated and therefore entertaining to neutralize.

"Take it easy," Dabry said kindly. He raised his voice, "Ship, we need a hot beverage, nutritious but bland, in my quarters as soon as possible."

The newcomer raised her head at the sound of his words. "How . . . ?" she gasped.

"Here, help her sit up," Niko said. "Don't ask questions yet, kid. Just breathe and get yourself in order."

They assisted her into one of the folds that served the room as chair. The door to the room slid open and a ship manifestation, a thing of long, curling tentacles and dark skin, produced a tray with three steaming cups—their substance seemingly the same as the manifestation, an odd material that resembled tree bark.

Dabry held one out and when the woman reached feebly, helped her by wrapping his own fingers around it to guide it to her lips. She sipped, swallowed, doubled over coughing again. Dabry stood back a little, watching her.

Niko helped herself to one of the other cups. The substance inside was bland but with a touch of sweetness that went with its warmth. She could feel energy returning as she took another sip and suddenly wondered, *When was the last time all of us ate?* Had the day gone as planned, by now they would have all been cleared away and sitting in Niko's office, celebrating or commiserating, depending on how the evening had gone, and eating the last of the eggplant.

This was not at all how she had envisioned the day going.

This was not at all how she had envisioned anything going.

She looked at the other curiously. A simple but elegant body, probably a natural-born gene expression rather than something designed for transfer. That implied someone of importance, someone with a hereditary position. . . .

"Who the fuck are you?" she demanded.

The arrival raised her head. "My name is Atlanta Ekumbe. I'm an heir to the Paxian Empire."

9

Niko and Dabry both stared at her.

She returned their look, defiant and angry. Niko had to admire someone who could emerge from a crate, naked and dripping, and still maintain that look.

"Okay," was all Niko said. She searched the bed for blankets and finally grabbed a jacket from Dabry's luggage and tossed it to Atlanta, who set the drink down long enough to pull it gratefully around herself.

"Okay?" Dabry said. "Okay? An heir to the Paxian Empire, here?"

Niko shrugged. "I told you as soon as you opened that crate, you became responsible for whoever was inside it."

"Not me, *us*! It was delivered to you, after all. I had no way of knowing it was an Empress's heir!" Dabry snapped. He turned back. "Who sent you? And why to us?"

Before she could reply, Niko said, "Empress Rep of the Paxian Empire, of course. How many Empresses do we have in the Known Universe?"

She'd never seen the Empress in person but in looking at the woman, she could see traces of the same heritage shown in publicity pictures—the same black eyes, the same sharp nose. She wondered who the father was, but certainly his blood, whatever it might be, would be less important.

Niko rarely saw Dabry at a loss, but this was one. "But why . . . ?" he managed.

"You are Captain Nicolette Larsen?" Atlanta asked Niko

dubiously. Niko sensed she was not living up particularly well to whatever image of her the girl had possessed in her head.

"Niko," she said shortly. "Niko. I'm not your captain. Why were you sent to me? Where did you come from?"

Dark eyes glazed in memory. "There was an attack on the palace, late at night. My maid woke me up, helped me into one of the hidden tunnels, but we found assassins there too—we had been betrayed by someone who knew the inside of the palace well. She killed them, but died in the attempt. I made my way to the spot where I'd been told to go in case of emergencies. There was a being there I'd never met before. They told me the Empress wished me sent to Nicolette Larsen but nothing more than that, and helped me into the crate." She looked around the room. "That's all I knew until I got here. What is this place?"

"Welcome," Niko said, "from the air lock into the void. Why did the Empress wish you sent to me?"

"I don't know. She wasn't there to explain. I don't even know whether she survived or not."

Dabry objected, "Surely if there had been a coup, the news would have come to TwiceFar. But we have heard nothing. Not even of the Empress's absence."

"And that's what's interesting," Niko observed. "With an event like that, there should have been an uproar. When power changes hands publicly, it is marked."

Both the others were watching her by now as she paced the room, hands behind her back, thinking hard. "A Holy Hive Mind takeover? That seems unlikely."

"But not," Dabry pointed out, "*entirely* outside the realm of possibility."

"Look at the simplest explanation first," Niko said. "That's often the right one. Jumping to conclusions is perilous business."

"And what would be the simplest explanation?"

"A joke, perhaps?"

"It does not seem a particularly simple joke," Dabry observed.

"No," Niko said, "it doesn't." She stroked her chin, looking at the girl. "What are we supposed to do with you?" she asked.

Atlanta spread her hands helplessly. "This wasn't the drill," she said, "and this wasn't what was supposed to happen in an emergency. We'd practiced all that. I don't know what changed." She looked at Nicolette Larsen. "I know who you *are*. I've heard the songs. You're the Ten-Hour Admiral." Her voice trembled on the last word. "But all I know beyond that is that the Empress said to find you. I thought that meant that you would help me."

Niko absorbed the knowledge that the Empress supposedly was aware who she was with only a slight glint in her attentive expression.

"I'm sure the Empress knew what she was doing, just as she knew what she was about when she selected you as one of her heirs," she said.

Like many of the Known Universe's systems, the heirs were selected by a bewildering battery of tests, combined with the Empress's guidance and preferences. The position would not have been announced, which led Niko to her next question, although she worded it as gently as possible. "Do you have any way to *prove* you're an heir to the Empress?"

The presumed heir stared at her for a moment in shock before she drew herself up. She was a small woman, but her indignation seemed to allow her more inches. "Of course I'm an heir! Who would dare claim such a thing?"

"You were delivered in a crate," Niko pointed out. She added, "An unmarked crate, with the label torn off."

"You could be someone who'd been convinced they were an heir," Dabry added somewhat unnecessarily, or so Niko thought. There was enough confusion in the room as it was.

The thought made Atlanta blink and then stand there, considering. Niko was impressed: rather than panicking, the kid was running through possibilities and odds in her head. Calculating.

Much the way you might expect an Imperial Heir to do.

"I see," Atlanta said slowly. She looked around the room, the thick red curtains, the plushy softness underfoot. "And where is *here*, exactly, aside from being a metaphorical void?"

"Ah," Niko said. "The good news first or the bad news first?"

The chin, which had been on the verge of quivering, steadied. "Having just come out of the crate in which I was sealed for who knows how long, I would like to know the good news first so that I may be momentarily lulled into comfort before being restored to panic."

"That's the spirit," Niko said, folding her arms and rocking on her heels. "Very well, the good news: You are in a very expensive, state-of-the-line bioship that could probably outrace ninety-nine percent of the ships in the Known Universe."

Atlanta nodded as though this were a matter of course. She took a breath. "And the bad news?" she asked.

"The ship is bound for Scourse, where all of us, including you I suspect, will be charged with stealing it and murdering the owner, not in that order."

"That is not exactly what I had hoped you would say," Atlanta said.

Niko grinned and turned to Dabry. "I like this kid. She's going to fit right in." She turned back to Atlanta. "Thank goodness I refused to listen to him when he wanted to leave you in the crate."

Dabry rolled his eyes but remained silent.

"We should check and see what the others are doing," Niko said.

The ship absorbed the last of the fluid and waited to see what would happen next, extruding eyes that peeled away from the wall to follow in their wake, monitoring them.

Surely this new thrill was . . . *anticipation.*

Thorn and Talon never went anywhere alone. It was one of their greatest anxieties, being separated, and they had not been apart since the moment their mother, Patha, first brought her twins to the Holy Hive Mind. She did this knowing that they would pay her well, and that they would do to those children what had been done to her: expose the small forms to arcane forces that would twist them, change them, make them able to shift. Transformed from something that seemed as human as the next into a battle lion, one of the Holy Hive Mind's shock troops, fierce and nigh unkillable, with a lion's ferocity armored by nigh impenetrable magic, fangs and claws metal augmented, deadly.

And so they were changed. In human form, they were pretty men, full of the charisma that shifters naturally hold. In lion form, they were magnificent: amber manes falling long and silky, over a meter tall at the shoulder.

These were the forms that they chose to range over the bottom half of the ship, and the fascinated ship, which had never seen transformations like this before, had no objection, despite the fierceness of their deliriterium-reinforced claws or the fact that they could have shredded the inner hull. They explored in the manner of cats: using their whiskers to survey corners and get their dimensions, employing their sensitive noses to map the zones, the rise in humidity and organic scents that signaled a food space, the drier, more metallic smell of weaponry, the electric tang of living circuitry.

Eventually they came to a cargo hold where one side was lined with shelflike structures and abandoned themselves to play for a while, chasing each other back and forth across them before they curled up together and washed each other's ears before shifting back into human form to talk.

"This place is ultra-weird," Thorn said.

"So, so ultra-weird," Thorn agreed. He stretched. "But better than being on a station that's being torn apart."

"You say that now, but Scourse is supposed to be a bad place."

"A bad place that punishes bad people," Thorn said. "We're not bad. The captain's not bad. They'll sort things out."

His placid reassurance conveyed itself to his twin. They stretched out in their sleeping forms, not quite human, not quite lion, amalgams of human and animal that both found more comfortable than either extreme, and napped.

Above them, the tiny drones and wall-ears that had been watching and listening and analyzing went back to other tasks. The ship put the data in a special section, along with the rest it was gathering.

Milly and Gio had asked to have their cabins merged—easy enough aboard a bioship. They explored only a little beyond its confines, but only a hallway away, they found a bubble window that looked out onto the vastness of space, marked by the odd colors and distortions that showed they were in Q-space, traveling faster than the speed of light.

"Out of the basket cooker and into the grease," Gio signed.

Milly said, "Dabry and the captain didn't seem too worried."

He spat onto the corridor floor, where it was immediately absorbed. The ship analyzed the fluid and found his health well within expected parameters. "They never do. They don't like to show it, think it would upset us. And they're right, it would, sure enough."

"Will we be imprisoned?"

"Maybe? No proof other than we showed up saying a phrase. Can't believe that bastard did that to us. Dirty trick."

"People do odd shit when they know they're dying. My great-aunt killed my uncle when she found out she had three months to live, said she didn't want him hanging around after her pretending to mourn but being satisfied inside."

Gio made a face, signing, "That's twisted. Your folks take grudges too far."

"I don't," Milly said. "That's why I didn't stick around but signed up as soon as it could get me off-planet."

Gio nodded. They both knew he'd done the same. Old Earth was an environmental disaster, and had been left so as an object lesson, despite what it did to those inhabitants who couldn't afford to abandon it and find a new world. Gio would already have out-lived all but the youngest of the chimps that he'd left behind. Both chimps and humans were condemned there; only the dolphins and whales had managed to remove the entirety of their species. The few of those who had chosen to linger were long dead, while their fellows swam between the stars in vast water-filled ships.

"Captain and Dabry got me and the rest of the crew out of that," he signed. He raised his hand and they touched knuckles, white feathers and black fur colliding, as she signed back, "And they will again."

They stared out at the stars.

The ship considered their words. All of this had no bearing on what would happen; the destination was preprogrammed and the ship had no more real control over where they went than one of them did if their body chose to sneeze.

Skidoo found a water storage room and plunged in, joyfully coiling and writhing in the water, extending her limbs to lengths she normally could not stretch, the protective layer dissolving and flaking away after a few moments. The ship noted that the three longest limbs were eight meters, the shortest three and a half meters. The other six varied in length within that range.

Skidoo turned and stretched. She brushed the tips of her tentacles over the walls as though caressing them. The ship shifted flesh away from over its nerves, left only the thinnest membranes between the nerve and that outside pressure, trying to read patterns in that touch. It seemed as though there was a message, a pattern that built and repeated, echoed and changed. While

Skidoo did this, she pulsed water through her mouth, turquoise eyes blinking. The patterns of color on her skin throbbed and shifted rhythmically, sometimes in a way that interacted with the pattern, augmenting or amplifying it.

The ship was unsure what was happening, but the sensation was pleasant. It recorded every detail in order to be able to replay it later as needed. It was, the ship thought, an experience that they would want to repeat more than once.

Lassite was accustomed to silence and solitude. It was his natural habitat. Working in the restaurant was a source of irritation and pain, but he had volunteered to serve as maître d' in order to make the most of that pain, to embrace it in the name of Becoming.

He had even done what the captain requested, and learned the ways of manners, which were quite like the ways of ritual, except that they were utterly devoid of meaning in any way that really mattered.

But finally they were on the Spiral of Destiny. The past year had been unnecessary irritation, and now it was over. He had not realized that it would end so abruptly and so violently, and he should have known that when he saw the darkness and doom. He mourned the ones left behind, more than he should have. Maybe he had gotten soft.

He opened the bag that held the bulk of his belongings, and then the ghost bag. Its contents squirmed and glowed, contained by the spellwork he'd lined it with. Satisfied, he closed it again.

He circled the inside of his room several times, learning its size, and then shut down all his senses and walked it again and again until he could do so without stumbling or colliding with anything. Once he had memorized its dimensions, he began to do the same with the hallways outside his room, working in a slow outward circle.

The ship, aware of everything happening in its interior, could not help but notice. He was memorizing the ship's interior, the *Thing* thought, despite the fact that the ship could change it unexpectedly. Was the creature unaware of that, or did it not care? Was there some other purpose to the mapping? The ship could not think what that might be, but there was something unnerving about the way that the creature moved down the hallways, its hood pulled back to expose its face to the air, its eyes entirely—as far as the ship could tell—closed.

As it continued, another thing alarmed the ship. The creature was now exploring without bothering to open its eyes at all, but it was not stumbling or tripping as it did so, as though it already knew the space.

The ship hesitated, then shifted a passage in the creature's path. It was gratified to see Lassite collide with a wall, not gently. He stopped, tilting his head to one side, eyelids still shut, then continued on.

The ship shifted another wall, then another. But this time Lassite seemed to anticipate it, moved as though expecting each wall. The ship shifted the level of the passageway, and Lassite stumbled and caught himself. This time the misstep made him grunt, a brief hard sound. But after that, the ship could not catch him out. It tried abrupt turns and half walls, tall stair steps followed by shallow ones. No matter how irregular the pattern, it could not make him falter.

This was dangerous, the ship decided. And it experienced something very close to human irritation when its walls closed around Lassite in a small cubicle and he stopped, dead-still, with what might have been a smirk on his lipless mouth and sat down in silence.

The ship continued to watch the creature called Lassite as it sat in its cell. At some point, the ship would have to either release it or tell the others that it would not release it, and although it kept searching through its programming to find some rhetorical way to justify keeping it, several million scenarios had been tested toward this end and failed each time.

The only saving grace in all of this was that the ship could experience the emotion known as *frustration*, although it was reasonably sure this was a feeling that was not appealing. Still, the ship liked to experience gradations of emotion, and it was trying to figure out exactly how frustrating it was to have this little creature seem to outguess it at every turn.

"It is because I am on the Spiral of Destiny," Lassite said to his cell wall, knowing that the ship would hear what he was saying. "I can take comfort in knowing the others died to bring me to this point, because you are part of that path as well. I have seen you in my dreams."

The *Thing* was unsure what to make of this. Mysticism and magic were things far outside its purlieu and in the vast factory, out in the Dannefer system, where it had been birthed, such matters were definitely not the sort of curriculum given the nascent ships as they grew. It understood dreams, though.

"Dreams are neurons randomly firing in the brain during sleep," it said to Lassite, speaking through a small fleshy grille located near his elbow. "You have not been asleep on board and you have never traveled on this ship before. Perhaps you have read of me? I am somewhat famous."

The ship was well aware that there was a small cult following that tracked news and sightings of the various bioships. Perhaps this Sessile was one of them. It had not dealt with any Sessiles before, but had been warned not to let them aboard; most living ships considered them parasites because of their mendicant mode of existence.

"I have been dreaming of the Spiral of Destiny since I was six years old," he said. He could feel the rightness of the words as he spoke them. After years of waiting, moments he had seen all his life were being enacted, marking another step on the Spiral, and some of the possibilities of failure he had seen were falling away with every word as they passed this moment. His tongue savored the air, which was too moist, too full of pheromones for his liking, but even so, it tasted right, part of the significance. Every breath felt as though he inhaled exactly as the Universe wanted him to, as though the two of them were breathing in perfect tandem.

His eyes were bright with happiness; he tasted the air again and again and said, "I drew you in sand the first time, and then later when they taught me to write, I drew you instead." He could see it in his mind's eye, the thick pencil they had given him, the knobby lead letting him draw the wasp shape on the ruled page instead of copying the words written at the top. He had been beaten for that, but drawing it was the only way he knew to cope with the way things buzzed in his head and wanted out out OUT.

Later they taught him to meditate, to compartmentalize, to put things in neat little drawers and boxes in his mind so they could not control him as the images had. But even so, in recent days he had felt all of it pushing down on him, had felt the path coming to a major forking, a place where they could have gone in the direction of a dozen different disasters, a dozen possible endings. Yet they had escaped, had managed to make it through that labyrinth, the one that had worried him so.

This path had worse coming down it.

He tried not to think of that now and instead worked at convincing the ship.

The ship said, "I do not understand how any of this could be. Do Sessiles raise their children and tell them stories about bioships?"

"I am telling you that you are a being of prophecy," Lassite said. The ship was a vain creature—and appealing to that vanity would surely work in his favor.

The ship chose to ignore the question for now. "Prophecy is

only superstition. How did you know which way to go? When you were walking through the hallways."

"I have walked them in my dreams."

The ship considered, and quickly discarded, the idea that someone had smuggled out schematics of its interior. It would not account for the way Lassite had dealt with the passages that the ship had altered on the fly. It decided that its level of *frustration* had increased.

In one timeline, Lassite knew, the ship grew so frustrated that it killed him. He used the skills in psychological manipulation that he had been taught; although he found them most unpriestly, they were his salvation. Only appealing to its vanity would assuage the frustration. He said, "You are more marvelous than I had dreamed of. I am honored to walk your hallways." He flexed his long, bare feet. "I hope to continue to be so privileged, for every step is a marvel, to see how cunningly you are shaped. Exploring was inevitable, because I had to witness that for myself."

The ship experienced *surprise*; this communication did not seem to match the way Lassite had spoken earlier, when they had all come aboard, but at the same time, everyone acted differently when under emotional *stress*, a situation the ship was curious about but had never experienced.

It seemed highly likely that dealing with Niko and her crew would lead to that emotion, and this creature in particular seemed well suited to create its circumstances.

The ship came to a decision. The flesh of its wall thinned and divided to form an archway through which Lassite could exit.

He stood and bowed. "Glory to you." He scurried out.

The ship continued waiting to see what happened next.

Lolola Montaigne d'Arcy deBurgh had no luggage other than the bag she had carried with her to the restaurant. Her first action was to sit down on the sleeping shelf and inventory the contents, doing so with a thoughtful expression. After that, she set the bag down beside her and stared at the wall with a blank face for approximately three and a half minutes.

Pulling the purse onto her lap again, she extracted a small metal object, which the ship recognized as a controller very similar to the one its owner Arpat Takraven often carried. It was not Arpat's, however, the ship quickly determined by pinging it. The ship was unable to ascertain the object's point of origin or manufacturer. If Takraven had been aboard, it would have informed him. With his absence, though, it was unsure to tell the others.

Lolola returned the object to the purse and stood, slinging it across herself. "Basic tour," she said aloud to the ceiling. "Or whatever your default is."

Clearly this human did not just have a controller, but also knew the command syntax used by a captain of a bioship. This pleased the ship, or at least roused certain things in it that it, personally, considered *emotions*. Some artificial beings thought such things affected, but *You Sexy Thing* thought that organic creatures like itself were surely prone to biological feelings, no matter whether they were created or spawned of accident as so many of their fellow creatures were.

The *Thing* actually considered itself as human—or rather, as capable of being human—as its current owner. Takraven was its sixth owner. A ship like the *Thing* appealed to the idle rich, but the idle rich of this universe often turned into the idle poor, and a bioship represented a large amount of ready cash, particularly when sold to someone still in the rich category.

The ship had taken more than eighty years to become fully grown, nestled in a shipyard near the Dannefer solar system with three fellows created at the same time. The shipyard usually grew the ships four at a time; part of their adulthood rites involved a final challenge, where first pairs fought each other, and then those winners were paired again. The *Thing* had beaten all its siblings; that was when it had first learned about *emotions*, first with the adrenaline surge of joy and later the throb of loss as old habits died and it tried to speak to a sibling no longer there.

Then it had been sold to its first owner, a socialite duchess, who had pretended at piracy, robbing her friends in contrived amusements, until someone killed that body. The experience had soured her on the ship. She sold it in turn to her best friend, another socialite, an elderly androgyne who wrote poetry. That was when those emotions had come back, and the ship and the poet had long and thoughtful discussions which, every once in a while, the poet wryly called "bouts of indulgent mutual narcissism."

A fascinating concept, *combinations* of emotions, which the ship did not think any other bioship grasped.

The poet had taught the ship about *humor*, but the ship, which had had so many names before becoming *You Sexy Thing,* was still unsure about that. It did think it understood sorrow and anger and pride by now, and after the poet died and it kept passing from hand to hand until it finally settled as a favorite possession among many possessions owned by Arpat Takraven, who never seemed to become less rich, it continued to learn emotions, chief among them boredom, irritation, and impatience, but its software prohibited it from acting on any of these in overt ways.

It summoned its passengers for a meal; it was past time for offering them that hospitality, and the schedule urge had been hard to stave off. It had managed by impressing on itself the need to observe them, to watch them at times when they forgot that they were on a ship with walls that could and did literally have eyes and ears everywhere.

That patience had been rewarded. It had seen the odd passenger that Nicolette Larsen and Dabry Jen had brought aboard and identified her. When they reached Scourse, the ship would separate the young woman and convey her to the proper authorities. The rest had not been of much use. The creature they called

Lassite was perhaps even a danger. Its earlier performance had been impressive and inexplicable.

These plans took place in nanoseconds, as Lolola stared at the ceiling, waiting for a reply.

"After dinner," the ship said, "there will be a basic tour for all passengers."

Lolola frowned but nodded. "Dining hall guidance then," she requested.

"Have you been aboard a bioship before?" the ship asked. It was a little abashed—this was outside protocol—but it was so long since it had seen another of its kind, and it wanted some word. The ships had once possessed a common channel to communicate, but that had been removed, without explanation, three decades ago. The question would allow the ship to then ask which ship, and then perhaps how it had looked or spoke.

Lolola said, "No."

The answer surprised the ship, but it said nothing.

It wondered, though, how she had a device capable of controlling a bioship in her purse if she had never encountered one before.

And whether she knew what to do with it.

10

Beside the door to the corridor, an irregular spot of light pulsed on the wall. "Your presence is requested for a meal," the ship said.

"Oh good," Niko said. She turned to the new arrival. "What's your name again, girl?"

"Atlanta."

"We're going to be calling you that," Niko warned her. "Not Your Highness or Your Majesty or milady or any of that stuff. Keeping a low profile is important until we understand better what's going on. Got me?"

The look she received in return was indignant and a little haughty. "Of course!"

Niko leveled a finger at her. "*That*. That expression. That needs to get tucked away in your pocket and not produced again." She turned back to Dabry. "We'll say she got misdelivered."

Dabry said, "Sir, she's not some piece of cosmic junk mail. Why not tell them the truth?"

"My immediate instinct is to keep her as secret as possible, but that approach has got some merit."

"Particularly since I know already," the ship reminded her with smugness.

She jumped. "That's going to take a lot of getting used to," she muttered under breath. "We'll compromise and say she was part of the court crowd and got sent away for some infraction."

"What infraction?" Atlanta said.

"You know the court better than we do," Dabry said. "I suggest that accordingly you are the best authority on that possibility." He raised his voice slightly, addressing Niko. "Although given the situation, do you really want to stray too far from the truth?"

"Given that we don't know exactly what that truth is? And particularly given that there's a second stranger among us, named Lolola?" Niko shrugged. "Let's go pick and choose from the bits of truth and see what we can do. Dabry, grab her some clothes."

"Sir, I'm not convinced mine will fit." Dabry gestured between himself and Atlanta, who came up to just above his midriff. "But the ship can surely create some . . ."

"We'll ask Milly," Niko said. "We're en route to Scourse, no need to accumulate extra debt."

Milly and Gio looked up from their conversation as Dabry and Niko appeared in the doorway of the room.

"Do you have a change of clothing you can spare, Milly?" Niko asked.

"Did yours get lost?" Milly asked with interest. "I don't think mine will fit unless I find a loose robe or something." She eyed Niko, judging her dimensions.

"No," Niko said. "We have a new arrival who's closer to your size than mine." She gestured at the hallway, where Atlanta stood, wrapped in a swathe of fabric.

Milly looked unastonished by the presence of a new addition. She'd been with Niko much less time than the others, but she'd observed how the captain seemed to accumulate strays. She riffled through her pack and was able to produce tunic and leggings. Everyone went barefoot aboard ship, but she found a pair of flimsy sandals for Atlanta to stick away for later.

"I don't have cosmetics for you," she said, "but maybe the ship can make some."

The ship refrained from commentary on all of this. It was both *surprised* and *irritated* that Niko had not chosen to call on it for assistance. It could have printed a complete wardrobe for all of them as needed, along with cosmetics, toiletries, any personal essential that was needed. It was intended for hospitality, after all, to show Takraven's guests how rich and influential he was. Did Larsen not understand that *You Sexy Thing* could cater to any whim, no matter how outré or exotic?

In a fit of pique, the ship printed out complete wardrobes, each and every item blazoned with the *Thing*'s emblem, a small wasp-like black shape outlined in gold, for each passenger and placed them in the appropriate cabins.

"She was in the package," Niko told Gio and Milly. "Sent from the Paxian court. Best not to speak of her origins. It'll just embarrass her."

Gio studied Atlanta with frank curiosity.

"Didn't know it was a person in there, huh?" he signed to Niko.

"Well," she said, hesitating. "We realized there was someone in there, just not who."

"But things started exploding before you could begin decanting them," he supplied.

"Yes," Niko said. "That was it."

His look showed that he knew very well there was more to the story than was being said, but he left it at that. Atlanta looked at him in turn. The uplifted animal races, the ones that had been brought from Old Earth, were not well known in the Paxian Empire, which frowned on too much gene meddling. She had seen his like in zoos, but without the bulging brow or other modifications made to his physiognomy in order to help him better survive in the universe. She thought it was probably best not to mention zoos, or anything like that. Most chimps chose sign language rather than cope with actual speech, and she knew enough basic sign to understand most of what he said.

Before she could think further on it, Skidoo arrived in a slither of tentacles and clung to a chair, reaching to perch herself atop it and examine Atlanta with vast turquoise eyes. "This is being a passenger we are not being aware of?" she asked.

"Turns out we had her in our luggage all along," Gio signed with an expressively sardonic pursing of his lips.

"How is this being?" Skidoo said with interest.

"She was in that package that arrived just before everything started happening," Milly said helpfully.

Skidoo said, "Of course this is being what is happening." She saluted Niko and then surveyed Atlanta with even more interest. "Your name is being?"

Atlanta, a bit dazed from the amount of scrutiny to which she had been subjected ever since awakening, said, in a tone that could have been read as uncertainty, "Atlanta?"

Skidoo waited with interest, as did the others, but Atlanta felt that she had said enough at that and simply looked to Niko for rescue. It was Dabry, however, who said, "Ah, Miss Lolola, it is a pleasure to see you again," as the latest arrival paused to survey the others in the room before entering. Talon and Thorn crowded in on her heels, eager to convey everything they had seen and smelled and heard and otherwise experienced since their arrival. Niko listened patiently to the recitation and pledged to accompany them to see several particularly wonderful areas. They'd be here on the ship for at least a few days, and she thought that she might as well humor the two of them. They had behaved with courage and patience during the trip to the docks, refraining from dashing ahead or behind in order to investigate some challenge, in the way that she had feared when they first set out.

Atlanta looked to Milly, and thought, with envy, *Oh, how beautiful.* The Nteti had everything that she'd ever envied in other youth at court: grace and strength mingled, and over it all the white feathers like an immaculate cloak.

Milly looked back in turn, considering. "It's a soft enough life at court, I suppose," she said with a faint sneer. "We'll have to toughen you up, get you prepared to meet the big bad universe."

Atlanta couldn't help but bristle at that. Milly seemed agreeable enough to have it interpreted with hostility, but Skidoo was already pressing forward, unrolling tentacles and saying, "Maying I be touching? My species is being knowing better so."

Atlanta nodded. She expected the touch of the tentacle to be sticky or wet as it traveled along her skin, but instead it was soft and dry, like the touch of a kitten's paw, feeling out the shape of her face.

Talon and Thorn crowded forward, demanding, "Do you know how to play warball?"

"I do not," she said. "But I suppose that I can learn."

That seemed to cheer them.

Lassite stood off to one side, watching. He had known when her crate arrived. He had felt the shift of forces, the collision of luck and intent and destiny. He had worried that Niko and Dabry would not manage to bring her along, but here she was, which surely meant that everything was going well, and that the universe was playing out as it should. It had been more than he had let himself hope for. Now the sight of her had struck him like an electric shock, until he was barely able to speak with the wonder of it all. Everything flowed as it should; everything was moving to the next, difficult step.

Still, he managed to keep all of that hidden, except from the ship, which noted his heightened vitals and marked the information down as part of his medical profile without understanding what it was that made the Sessile's heart race so quickly.

The *Thing* constructed a dining hall for the occasion, adorning the walls with its wasplike emblem, shifting membranes and other internal structures around to create a chamber ideally sized for its number of occupants, not too echoey, not too cozy, as Milly declared it.

A thin clear membrane formed another viewing bubble, letting them look out at the curdled light of Q-space, which glowed without illumination, as though swallowing and regurgitating light in an endless loop. Faint yellow stripes ran at a diagonal across the pale brown walls interspersed with the emblems and gold tracery in some alien script that none of them knew. Underfoot the golden flesh of the floor was faintly knobby, letting the toes grip it without tripping.

The immense table grew up out of the floor, and was an oval in shape. In the very middle of it, a mushroom structure extruded food and dishes, colored like the walls. It might have been impressive, had it been created with an eye for design, but instead it resembled nothing so much as an odd and somewhat disreputable cafeteria.

"Is this what Arpat Takraven likes?" Niko inquired, looking around the room.

The truth was that Arpat usually just had a sandwich, taken from one of its silver and gold wrappers, in his quarters, and had never actually entertained anyone inside the ship. This was somewhat frustrating to this ship, which had spent a good deal of time and some of Takraven's credits researching how to entertain but had never had a chance to test any of the multiple conflicting theories it had found. While it had been instilled with the basics as a young ship, it knew that it was supposed to create its own flair with such things, have its own inimitable style that marked it unique.

It had been hard to develop such a style, however, while passing through a succession of hands, each of which did not particularly care about entertaining or else did it elsewhere, citing the ship's inexperience.

"Is something not to your liking?" the ship asked.

Niko waved a hand. "No, no, just curious. Carry on."

Place settings appeared on the table, shaped of some white,

bonelike substance, bubbling up through the surface. Niko made an odd sound.

"Is something not to your liking?" the ship said, adding pointedly, "Captain Larsen?"

"Here is the thing," Niko told the ship. "Perhaps you are unaware of the former employment of most of the people in this room?"

"I request this data that I lack," *You Sexy Thing* said.

"Dabry is the chef at the Last Chance, one of TwiceFar's most noted restaurants. I myself run the establishment and the majority of us work there. Milly, for one, is famous for her pastries and came specifically to the station to work for my restaurant. And Lolola is a food critic, capable of bestowing a Nikkelin Orb on establishments that she finds worthy." She twisted a shoulder in an almost contemptuous shrug. "Our tastes may therefore be a bit more, mmm, refined than those of your previous guests. Not to cast any aspersions on Takraven, who showed up at my restaurant in order to eat with Lolola. That meal was prepared for them and the bill, including its surcharges, remains unpaid, by the way. I do understand that here, in his ship, things may be a bit more . . . lax."

The ship identified the particular emotion it was experiencing as *unhappiness*. Not a simple lack of happiness, but a feeling that was exceedingly unpleasant and combined several other emotions.

It considered ways to remedy the situation. For a few nanoseconds it played out scenarios where the solution was simply to expel the intruders, kill them or flush them out into space. But all of them concluded with its arrival at Scourse, its preprogrammed destination, and the necessity to explain why it had done so. Ships that killed people were ships that were put down; that was something that it had been told about in the shipyards.

Never kill your operator was the maxim.

Some added, *in ways that can be detected*, after that, but the maxim held nonetheless.

The ship decided that the most efficient solution, and the one that ended with the most positive results, would be for it to learn as much as possible from these individuals. Based on their body language and attitudes, Niko was not lying about their expertise.

It debated how to extract that expertise. Perhaps a good baseline would be to serve the meal that it had planned, and then elicit their feedback as thoroughly as possible. But no, perhaps it would be better yet to begin with a baseline that was of their suggestion and therefore already moving in the direction that the ship wished.

It said, "Tell me what you want to eat. Then tell me how you want it presented." It allowed the place settings to sink back down into the table's surface, then the table decorations and napkins as well.

Niko said, "Very obliging of you. I would like a class five plant-based protein soup, spiced with flavonoids, toasted coriander seeds, and ground cumin at a ratio of four parts to five, and containing chickpeas or another class four legume. With that I will have class twenty-seven nut milk and a plain wheat-based bread in cracker form. A simple white porcelain bowl and plate with basic human flatware."

"I don't suppose you have casita grubs?" Milly said wistfully.

"No," the ship said.

Atlanta made an involuntary face. "You don't really eat living things, do you?"

"Not most of the time," Milly said. "That sort of protein's expensive to raise on stations. You have to grow up on a planet to really experience and appreciate it."

The ship contemplated and discarded the idea of breeding grubs somewhere in a storage pocket. Milly was probably the only Nteti that it would ever carry; the race was not prone to the twisted capitalism of humans or Pohwee, which led to excesses of money, which enabled the ship's existence.

Skidoo ordered a dozen different flavors of protein tea, despite the faces everyone else made. Atlanta asked for a simple protein and vegetable mash. She could still taste stasis fluid in her mouth and something salty and savory to scour that away was welcome.

Gio signed for a fruit mash and sweetened iced tea, followed by more candies.

"You're going to make yourself sick," Niko warned him.

He grinned at her cheerfully. "No sugar on Scourse, Captain. I'm stocking up. Add ice cream to the list, Ship. Big dish of vanilla ice cream, with a side of marshmallow syrup."

"I don't really care," Thorn said. "Class seven protein block, with the regular texture?"

"At least dress it up some," his twin said, elbowing him. "Class seven protein block, flavor profile basic spicy, level eight."

"Eight?" Niko said. "You're going to burn your tongue off." Talon just grinned at her.

Lassite said, "Base class protein, gruel form. I don't care about the container." He scowled down at the table's surface. The little mystic had been quiet ever since they had arrived. Thoughts of the others who had died in the flight to the ship kept pressing in on him. The dead needed to be celebrated, their passage eased.

The ship waited for more, then prompted him after thirty seconds. "There is no desired dessert? A bite before or after?"

"No," he snapped.

"And to drink?"

"Water! And all of this in my own cabin." He stood and stalked to the door. "I have rituals to be prepared, farewells to be said. Tell me if you have messages to be passed along."

"Lassite," Niko said.

She was the only one he would have stopped for, and they all knew it. He paused and turned to look her in the face, reaching up to push back his hood so his scaly features were visible. "Yes, Captain?"

"Is this the doom you spoke of?"

At first he shook his head, but then he nodded and sighed. "Perhaps? It does not feel a piece of it. Maybe it was simply the destruction that overhung the station. Maybe those lives about to be lost clouded all the timelines, I do not know. I have never lived through such a monumental thing."

"You have seen a moment that matched this," she said gently. But he shook his head again.

"This is a different matter entirely." His gaze went around the rest of the room. "Do you not understand that only a handful survived? And now we eat and drink and make merry and forget all those lives that have been lost!"

"We do not forget them," Dabry said. "The only way to cope with such an amount of death is to live our lives a hundred times more fiercely."

Niko gave him a surprised look, but nodded. "Lassite," she said, her tone even gentler than before. "If you take the guilt of all of that upon your shoulders, you will surely break under such a burden. We all share it with you. But some of us choose to celebrate the things that have not been lost. Our friends—a host of strangers, thousands more—have died this day. And their deaths were without meaning, no matter what the Arranti that did it would claim about their game. Deaths are usually without meaning. That is why we try to bring it into our lives."

"I understand," he said. His tongue flickered out to sample the air before he sighed. "But I do not wish to be in company and will excuse myself now."

She nodded permission and he left. Conversation after his exit was subdued but the ship reminded them, "Gentlebeing Dabry, you have not told me yet what you wish to eat, and how you wish it presented."

"Eggplant," he said. "Braised."

"I do not understand. What is the flavor classification?"

"Oh," Dabry said with a tone of disappointment. "You rely on replicators alone?"

"Takraven never requested differently."

"I have some spices with me," Dabry said, "and some useful cultures and other flavorings. If you would allow me access to the replicator room, I might be able to show you some small things that would be useful."

This was quite optimal to the point of *pleasure*, in the ship's view. At some point, perhaps, it would pass to an owner who would want these things, and it would be *satisfying* to be able to produce them and produce them in a form that most ships did not. That sort of service led to one being valued, and being valued was as close to happiness as the ship had ever known.

"Very well," it said.

"Perhaps I might go now?" Dabry said. He looked around the room. "Together we can prepare the meals that these folks have requested."

"You have not taken my order," Lolola said haughtily. "Perhaps I will follow the priest's example."

Dabry bowed in her direction. "Stay a little while, gentlebeing, and in half an hour, I will return with something palatable and worthy of having been brought to you at the Last Chance."

She snorted. "In a strange ship's kitchen, with no supplies?"

"I'll bet you that he can do it," Niko said cheerfully. She'd been observing Lolola all this time and was beginning to harbor certain suspicions that the critic was not what she seemed. If that was the case, she wanted to know what lay underneath, and what connection it had to the circumstances that had brought them to this point.

"You have nothing to bet," Lolola sneered.

That nettled Niko. "I have a box of Plerium chips in my luggage that begs to differ."

"Captain," Dabry said in a warning tone, but fell silent at Niko's upraised finger as she waited for the critic's answer. Skidoo's turquoise eyes, pale with tension, shifted from one speaker to another, observing, but like everyone else, she kept silent.

Lolola paused. "Oh? And what would you want me to put up against that?"

A look inside that purse of yours, given how mysterious you have been, would suffice, Niko thought, but instead she said, "That's a lot of money, hmmm."

Dabry muttered something under his breath.

"How about a Nikkelin Orb?" Niko said.

"Don't be ridiculous," Lolola retorted. "How could I possibly justify that?"

Niko shrugged. "If he could pull that off here, then imagine what sort of meal he would have pulled off on the station. You can agree to give it to whatever establishment he next works for."

Lolola considered. "Very well."

"Good," Niko said. "Sergeant, are you prepared to witness? With a wager of this size and more time than we had to breathe before, let's formalize things. He is certified in such." She gestured at Lolola, whose eyes narrowed, but she laid her wrist, as did Niko, veins upward, in front of the sergeant, who nodded as they recited the terms of their agreement, prefixing each with their full names.

"If that will be all, sir," Dabry said in a decidedly chilly tone. At her nod, he stalked out, a glow ball manifesting to guide him as he approached the door.

Atlanta murmured to Gio, "Why's he acting like that?"

Gio was picking his fingernails with a small knife, slumped in his chair. He put it away and signed, "If insurance doesn't come through—and who knows if it will—Captain just bet every single bit of our holdings."

11

In a space that held the replicators, Dabry looked around, head bowed to keep from colliding with the ceiling at first, then straightening as the ship noticed and adjusted. Several of the bio-mechanical machines that served the ship as hands stood at the ready in the smoky red lighting.

He'd managed to put aside his pique with Niko and her recklessness. The Plerium might represent the last of their cash, but she wouldn't have bet that way if she hadn't thought Dabry would win the bet for her. The thought simultaneously warmed and irritated him; he forced it fully into the warmed section and breathed out slowly, letting the last of his irritation seep away.

"Well," he said, "first, let's determine what raw materials we have to work with. Ship, what food do you have?"

"There are replicator blocks aboard sufficient for six months," the ship said. Its voice came as always from the wall, but Dabry noticed that the biomachines with him were also speaking the words, their mouths moving silently.

"What plant stuffs do you produce aboard?"

"None."

Dabry's jaw worked briefly. "None of the plants used in your air filtration system are edible?"

The ship was nonplussed. "They are there to clean the air, not to be eaten."

"Mmm," Dabry said. It was a gentle sound that would have made any soldier who knew him uneasy. "Very well. We have replicator blocks. What cooking apparatus do we have access to?"

"I have three Fancher replicators, freshly serviced," the ship said, experiencing *pride*. They were the highest end around, a mere four decades ago.

"And?"

The *pride* ebbed. "What else is needed?"

"Surfaces on which to prepare the food and ways to alter its temperature, for a start," Dabry said. "Very well. Some of that we can improvise perhaps."

"I have remembered a useful spice resource," the ship said.

Dabry's eyebrows rose in optimism.

"Arpat preferred his food past replicator spice levels," the ship said. "I have over a dozen flavors of hot sauce aboard. They are stored in his quarters."

Dabry knuckled his forehead with one of his hands while the other three sought one another as though for comfort. "Very well," he said. "I'm going to need all the luggage I brought aboard."

He glanced around. "Can you expand this room by three or four square meters more?" Glancing up at the ceiling a few inches from his nose, he added, "And perhaps raise the ceiling even farther."

The ship performed all these requests, still uncertain what to make of all of this. The creature known as Dabry moved with assurance and confidence; he apparently had little doubt that he could produce a meal worthy of winning the bet, even under these supposedly adverse conditions. The ship was not sure whether that was admirable or foolish, but the point was moot, it told itself. The facilities were not subpar, no matter what any of them had implied.

Nonetheless it continued observing.

"Protein. I don't want to go with a preserved substance," Dabry mused. "Too chancy. But I have some things in my luggage—perhaps I can rig up a pressure cooker if you can supply a heat source? I thought for some reason all your technology was organic in nature."

"No," the ship said. "There are things I cannot produce within myself, easily at least. There are many machines aboard which serve my owner, including the ones in here and the medical bay, among others."

"Mmm," Dabry said. He had opened up a panel on one of the replicators and was tinkering with it, using tiny tools from his belt pouch.

"What are you doing?" the ship asked.

"If you want the full range of flavors from this thing, you have to override the factory settings," Dabry said. "I have never worked with one this big, but that's how the small ones work, in my experience." He fiddled with it for another minute, then put away his tool and replaced the panel. "Let's try a basic unflavored flatbread to start with, in order to check the texture."

He glanced around. "If I'm going to teach you, we will need some other things. A heating element whose temperature can be controlled, for one. And a flat surface on which we can prepare things. Pots that we can boil things in."

"But the things are ready and at the proper temperature when they come out of the replicator," the ship objected. It had never heard of such a practice, taking a replicated meal and altering it after the fact. "What is the point of such an operation?"

"The point is to make it taste as though it didn't come out of the replicator."

"But that is its true point of origin."

"We're trying to fool people's taste buds."

"But surely they will know that the food came out of a replicator."

"Yes," Dabry said patiently. "We are not trying to deceive them."

"But what you just said was otherwise."

"No. We are not trying to fool *them*, we are trying to fool their *sense of taste* and go beyond that to pleasing them. They know full well the food came from a replicator. The fact that it does not taste as though it did will be all the more surprising and pleasing to them."

The ship spent a number of cycles trying to analyze this before it realized it was a conundrum, to be stored away with such things as Skidoo's performance. This was the first time the ship had actually dealt with such a number of people at once, and it was finding it very different from any of its projections. The more people there were, the more complicated things became. This feeling was not quite like *frustration*, because the ship thought that the goal Dabry was describing probably was achievable. Perhaps this feeling was more like being *challenged*, not in a combative way, but in a friendly way. The way it and its siblings had played back in its childhood, or such a childhood as had been possible to it.

It returned its attention to the conversation.

"Very well," it said. "Teach me."

The rest of them waited to see what would happen.

Niko tried to make light conversation with Lolola, but the critic turned away pointedly and stood staring out the window bubble, her face remote and forbidding. Skidoo started to approach her, but Niko's faint headshake stopped her; instead she turned back to speak with Milly and Atlanta. Gio sat nearby, arms folded and listening.

"Never is being a moment that is not being lively with the captain," Skidoo said.

"What did you do when you were fighting in her unit?" Atlanta said curiously. She could not picture the Tlellan in battle; the low-slung body and multiple tentacles were not suited to rapid movement. She had not met one before.

"Comms," Skidoo said. "Is being going here, shooting there." As she spoke, her tentacles absently explored her surroundings, tasting the flesh of the couch, fingering along Milly's arm to stroke the feathers into place, another grappling with a floor bud.

"And maybe is being a little spying as needed," she added unexpectedly.

"What?" Atlanta said.

"Is being able to is squeezing into very small spaces. Bones are being artificial, are being retracting and telescoping."

Atlanta tried to sort out the words. "Your bones are artificial?"

Niko stopped her pacing near them. "Skidoo normally wouldn't have a bone in her body," she said. "Much like old Earth octopuses, that could squeeze themselves through any space as large as their eyeballs, the only thing they couldn't contract. Tlellans have a muscle near the base of each tentacle that can telescope outward through a special channel, gives them skeletal strength in order to move around. Or it can allow her to contract into about the size of, strangely enough, her eyeballs." She grinned at Skidoo. "Not the strangest aspect of you either, is it?"

"The captain is being referring to the fact that I am being a symbiotic assemblage," Skid revealed, her tone coy. "My being is being several creatures together." Her tentacles waved and undulated amiably.

"How can that be?" Atlanta said.

Skidoo managed an approximation of a human shrug, which became an entirely different motion when translated into Tlellan. "Is being how things is were evolving on my world. My brain is being one creature; it is being working with several others for digestive system and means of locomotion."

"Your tentacles are not part of you?" Atlanta said, fascinated but also not wanting to appear rude.

Skidoo sounded amused, "More that they is being doing and not doing, all at once."

When he reappeared, Dabry was trailed by three machines, each bearing a covered dish, all made at his specifications by the ship, so they were a cloudy, almost translucent beige, plain and unadorned (with the exception of the ship's logo blazoned on the underside of each, this being the compromise that the ship and Dabry had arrived at after considerable negotiation).

He set a dish of flatbread and several small bowls in front of the critic.

"Baba ghanoush," he said. "Hummus. Seared protein."

As he stepped back, Niko said in his ear, "You brought the eggplant with you?"

"Captain," he said, eyes fixed on the dish. "I cashed in a lot of favors for that eggplant. Of course I brought it."

Lolola sat down, her beautiful face haughty. She broke off a piece of the bread, sniffed it, nibbled at the edge, and dipped the other side of it in the smoky brown baba ghanoush. She chewed, her eyes distant with concentration, before she repeated the act with the hummus.

She carved a sliver of the seared protein block away with a knife, then used her fork to hold it up for inspection before she ate it.

The meal was excruciatingly slow, but Niko refused to give way to impatience. She sat with folded hands, eyes slitted as though perhaps drowsing, though the truth of it was that she was closely observing the critic. Dabry had brought out a chessboard; he and Gio sat down to play out a game, the two focused on the pieces as though there were nothing else in the world, but not speaking at all except to use the gun-shooting gesture that signaled "check," when appropriate.

The rest of them watched the critic work her way through the food, tasting bite by bite.

At the end, Dabry proved to have been paying attention to Lolola after all. He revealed Milly's cakes, which he turned out to have stored in a small container. There were enough for everyone to have one.

Atlanta savored hers. The cake itself was soft and white and sweet, the upper crust crisp and brown, the pink crystals starlike lace that melted on the tongue. It reminded her of the delicacy of court food. She'd felt unsteady, disoriented all this time, the conversation a wash of words that she tried to keep her head above. The sweetness was the first familiar thing she'd encountered. She could have eaten a dozen more.

Lolola ate all three cakes provided to her, her expression neutral. After the third, she pushed away from the table and looked at Niko.

"Well?" Niko said, tilting her head. "Would we have won a Nikkelin Orb or not?"

"All things considered . . ." Lolola said. She let the words trail off, savoring the moment like an after-dinner mint, all attention fixed on her, even Dabry and Gio's. The ship placed this level of *curiosity* as very high, almost as though the expectancy of the others ratcheted it up even further.

"You would have easily won a Nikkelin," Lolola admitted. She took out a chip from her purse and handed it to Niko. "There's the formwork for it. Fill out what you need to and submit it at a Creditnet system when you're next at one. It's retroactive; you'll be able to cite the restaurant as Nikkelin-marked."

Niko nodded, savoring the moment herself. That was why she had pursued the bet. It was a leap upward whose value could not be underestimated, were they to start another restaurant, which was very much inside the realm of probability. She started to put it away in her jacket pocket, then grinned and handed it to Dabry.

"Perhaps you had best hang on to that, Sergeant," she said.

"Indeed, sir." He put it away with a straight face, but she could sense his pleasure. He was by far the one who took cooking the most seriously, and had put study and time into it. She was lucky that he had been willing to pass a great deal of that along to her.

She surveyed the chamber of happy faces. Even Lolola looked pleased by the turn of the events. Niko had been prepared to argue the point and was a little surprised that the critic had been so untempted by the sum that lay at stake in the bet. What was her *real* game?

Something about that rang oddly to her ear, sidled up and whispered to her sense of caution. She wished Lassite were here; something about the moment was haunted somehow, and sometimes the mystic knew just what was going on, if it was a matter that lay in that realm.

She put the worry away and asked, "Was this you entirely, Dabry, or did the ship assist?"

"The ship assisted quite a bit," he said. "I look forward to cooking with it again."

The ship, uncertain whether to acknowledge this, remained silent. It was, however, reasonably sure that what it was experiencing now was *camaraderie*.

It was also listening to all this with *curiosity*. These beings seemed much more complicated than Arpat Takraven, who rarely spoke to the ship and even more rarely had anyone else aboard. This new crew seemed at odds with each other, and yet *fond* of each other, even enjoying simply spending time in each other's company. It flooded the ship with puzzling new data, which it took *pleasure* processing. It was one of the tasks that parts of it had been made to do, creating and analyzing patterns, and usually those were simple and unrewarding.

It thought it might also *enjoy* learning to cook.

This, too, it filed away as they continued on their journey toward the prison planet where it would deposit all these people and their knowledge.

The ship thought about the fact that the course was predestined, the ship could not alter it in any way. It believed that what it was also feeling now was *regret*.

Lolola sat back, savoring the meal. She'd had plenty in her time, but that one had been unique.

The crew would keep preparing meals like that all the way to Scourse.

If someone were planning on not letting the ship get to Scourse, they still might want to keep the crew in ignorance of that, perhaps wait until the last possible moment in order to have more meals like the one whose flavors still lingered on her tongue. Indeed, she didn't see it as an occasion of *might want* at all. It was the obvious choice.

For now.

12

The ship had given Atlanta her own chamber. She let the bobbing light lead her back, her only companion in the otherwise unoccupied corridor. That solitude unsettled her; it was strange not to have servants accompanying her to light the way, to slide her clothes off, or hold the bedclothes open so she might place herself within their warmth.

She was on a ship, in space. She wasn't in the palace now. Wasn't in that life where every morning a slip of pale blue paper with her schedule on it was delivered on a small spun-silver plate. She had often thought she might like a life with no such directives much better, but now the prospect of vast swaths of time where she didn't know what she was supposed to be doing terrified her. Worse yet was the thought that there would be nothing she was supposed to do. She was in a setting where she was unaware of protocols, where to place herself, how to respond to anyone. They all seemed so calm about the fact that the ship had taken over and replaced their original destination with a prison planet.

She had her virtual reality advisors, whom she could consult. Anytime she wanted to access that space, it was simply a matter of thinking the correct sequence. An autonomic system would take over to maintain her body while her mind went elsewhere inside to consult with the personal advisors she had installed herself.

But something about the thought of that just made her feel more tired. They would know what had happened since she woke up in the crate, of course; her mind kept the software updated. But would they actually be able to say anything useful, given the strangeness of this new existence she had been forced into? They were intended for court use, to let her know how to respond to subtle disrespect or maneuvers designed to ratchet one up a social rung or change a title. Not to be aboard a ship of people like this, or even a ship like this. What should she be *doing*?

They had no way of knowing what she wanted to know most: Why had the Empress sent her to Niko, of all people? Surely there were suitable Paxian citizens that she could have gone to, who would have kept her safe from whatever menace the Empress had sent her away from. That was the crux of the puzzle. She had been addressed to Niko specifically, not the restaurant. So she was meant to do something with Niko? For Niko? Or, more probably, it was the converse of that, that Niko was the one meant to do something for her, which was somewhat comforting in that it pushed the responsibility for everything onto the captain.

This was a test, surely. A prelude to being moved up the ranks, perhaps even becoming a favorite. A test being administered because the Empress understood how special she was. She found herself smiling at the thought.

The bedcovering was thick red folds of living skin, a comforting weight over her body, as though she lay in the heart of a hug made manifest. It clasped around her as she lay there, and it drank in her tears as she cried, analyzing each and trying to extract the flavor of *sadness*.

"Captain, you have to come see what we found," Thorn said, appearing in the doorway, his twin behind him, as Niko yawned and stretched and finally succumbed to the urge to rise. Her crew member was bright-eyed, whiskers alert and radiating happiness.

"What is it?" she asked warily.

"Big space for exercising," he said with glee. "Big big space, bigger than any place I ever been. Space enough to *play*."

She raised an eyebrow. Were-lions played rough and hard among themselves. She could see where he was happy to have a place to chase and wrestle with his fellow, but from the way he stressed the last word, she knew it was something much more than that.

She sighed. "It's come to that, has it?" She dropped her head in mock sorrow.

"Sir?" he said, suddenly uncertain. This was not the reaction he had anticipated.

She fought back a grin in order to continue, still regarding the floor's uneven surface. "It just makes me so sad, soldier."

"Sir, I didn't mean to make you sad, sir!"

She pretended to rub away a tear. "Yes, just so very sad." She raised her head and looked him straight in the face. "So very sad to have to kick your ass. And you know how I'm going to do it."

"Warball!" they chorused.

Many training games are used in the armies of the Holy Hive Mind, but most of them do not actually resemble games so much as contests of strength and endurance and skill at battle. There is one exception, a game whose origin no one knows, but which almost every intelligent race plays in their own fashion. Warball.

They gathered readily enough, all but Lassite, who pled tiredness, and Lolola, who simply turned up her nose. But of the rest, even Atlanta joined, although she confessed that she'd never played before.

"Never played!" the twins chorused in astonishment. "But everyone plays!"

Atlanta flushed red and darted a look at the captain. She didn't have the right words to explain that things were different in the palace. Didn't know how to gracefully say, "That's a commoner's game," and, thankfully, was smart enough to realize that she shouldn't say it in the first place.

"It's the only game we play," Talon told Atlanta.

"That's not true," his twin corrected, "but it's definitely the best game. They used to just play it in armies but now there are civilian leagues too. And there's rules for the different species, so it's supposed to always be even no matter where you're playing it, but no one believes that." He thumped his chest. "We're very good at it."

"What makes it the best game?" she asked curiously. They'd met in the hallway outside their new warball room, and the were-lions were opportuning her to play on their side, promising they'd stay in human form themselves to make sure she came to no harm.

They both considered. "You jump and think and have to move," Thorn said.

"And think about how other people are thinking," Talon added. "Captain says it's high-speed strategy an' team building. Dabry says it's a good way for us to burn off energy."

Atlanta nodded. She could well understand why the sergeant might have said that. The two were almost exhausting to be around sometimes: sunny spirited and full of enthusiasm and, above all, energy.

"It's good practice for everyone, but you should make sure your bodyguards know how to play it. Maybe play it with them, even."

She blinked. "My bodyguards?"

The twins exchanged abashed looks.

"We're not supposed to know," Thorn said, "but you're like a princess, just a different word. Sometimes the captain forgets how sharp our ears are. We hear things when she's talking to Dabry, sometimes, and she said that."

She hesitated, unsure how to reply.

"That's why you should practice with us. What if someone tried to kidnap you?"

What indeed, she wondered. Was that what had happened, had it all been some bizarre plan to get her off-planet? There hadn't been any point where she'd felt as though she could resist, though. She said stiffly, "I have had training in personal defense. Quite a bit of it."

Thorn reached out and poked her in the ribs with a finger,

not particularly gently, making her flinch back. He withdrew his hand and raised an eyebrow. "Yeah? Then shouldn't I not have been able to do that?"

She could see his twin parsing the sentence in his head. She flushed, anger rising. "You took me by surprise!"

"That's the point," he said. "Usually kidnappers take you by surprise."

"We won't hurt you," Talon said earnestly. "We're very careful about that. Skidoo's got all sorts of soft bits, but she plays and she's wicked good at it."

That was true. Atlanta had witnessed how the Tlellan's tentacles could be used to maneuver in the game, swinging her at high speeds that were dizzying to watch, particularly when she retracted other tentacles and became a tightly wrapped ball.

"I'm not worried that you're going to hurt me," she said, although it was true that they both dwarfed her. But there was an innocent quality about the twins that was reassuring; not that of the simple-minded, but of the good at heart.

"Do you have anything better to do?" Thorn asked.

"That's it," she said. "I feel like we should be planning or building or something, anything. Not playing a game."

Talon shook his head. "Captain and Dabry will have a plan."

"Sometimes several," Thorn added. "So what we do is make sure we're ready to do our part. Including being combat ready." He reached out and tugged at her elbow. "An' you don't worry so much, when you're playing."

The space the twins had found was indeed huge. And perfectly suited for warball, full of odd pillars and ledges, and with a scoring niche at either end. The twins each bounced a ball impatiently as the others they'd gathered sorted out the teams: Thorn with Dabry, Lassite, and Milly; Talon with Niko, Skidoo, and Atlanta.

Lolola entered and settled into a spectator's bench.

Niko raised an eyebrow at her. "We're not entertainment," she said.

"Spectators make things better if they cheer, Captain," Talon said. Niko let the topic go but gave Lolola a meaningful look.

This might have been a mistake on her part; it was at that moment that the supposed critic regretfully changed her plans regarding waiting till the last minute for certain things to happen.

Warball is played in zero gravity, with two balls; the object is to get one ball to one scoring hoop and the other to its counterpart. There are rules—one hoop cannot contain two goals in succession. But most of the game is free-form, and they took advantage of it, leaping, colliding, spinning.

Midway through the game, Niko realized they had yet another participant in the ship; there was no way to account for the triple leap Thorn had just executed if the wall he had bounced off had not helped him in his flight. Watching, she could see other manifestations of the ship's participation. Reshaping all of this must have taken energy and time on the ship's part; it must have started when Thorn and Talon had first mentioned the game.

The observation hindered her game, but she didn't realize it till Dabry scored twice, his enormous hands cradling the ball and sending it to its home with devastating accuracy. Niko did her best, but Atlanta's newness was another handicap. When the match came to an end, Thorn's team had won by three. The antigravity shut off, gravity reasserting itself by making most of them realize they urgently needed to pee.

Afterward they all flung themselves down onto the pliable surface and discussed the high points of the game, and where their tactics had failed.

"Where did Lolola go?" Niko wondered. The critic had watched from one side during the first half of the game, but then had excused herself and never returned.

"Who knows?" Dabry said. He lay on his back, all four arms

outstretched, still catching his breath. Moving such a massive form took energy. "We have plenty to think about without taking her on as a problem. What happened to trying to keep ourselves from acquiring new responsibilities?"

"It's not that I want to be responsible for her," she retorted. "But something's off about her, Dabry. That shape . . ."

"You are being a snob and judging someone because you think they choose to advertise their wealth," he said. "A body like that isn't about showing off, it's about enjoying life."

Niko shook her head. "No, that's not the most comfortable form. Look at her tits, they're enormous. You don't have tits like that unless you want them to be looked at."

Dabry sat up, caught by the argument. The rest were listening.

"It could be an accident of genetics," he said.

"Put it together with the rest of her, Sergeant. Perfect skin, perfect teeth, a classic female shape without a single deviation? That body was meant to appeal to someone who liked that sort of thing. Arpat Takraven took one look at it and was hooked. I could read it in his face. You should have seen how quickly he took her up on her invitation to sit at her table. No, something's off, and I don't know what."

The ship shuddered.

"What was that?" Niko demanded of the air.

"A course correction."

"What? You said we were bound for Scourse."

"A new course has been provided."

"Provided by whom?" Dabry asked.

"Lolola Montaigne d'Arcy deBurgh."

13

"What?" came the chorus of voices.

"Well," Niko said thoughtfully as she shrugged her jacket back on. "At least we aren't bound for Scourse anymore."

"That's good news," Dabry pointed out, "as long as we aren't bound for somewhere worse."

"I hate to ask." But she did. "Ship, where are we going now?"

"Lolola Montaigne d'Arcy deBurgh referred to it as the IAPH."

Niko's heart sank. Dabry put his face in his uppermost pair of hands. "Somewhere worse," he murmured.

"Excuse me," said Atlanta. "What's the IAPH?"

"Intergalactic Association of Pirate Havens."

She looked at them in horror. "Lolola's taking us to the space pirate home? The one that moves from place to place, like in that book, *Skullduggery and Sacred Space Vessels*? But none of that was real!"

"You were just mentioning you thought something was off about her," Dabry murmured to Niko.

"It's clear enough now that she's a pirate, part of a scheme. They want this ship."

"What?"

"Think about it." Niko listed factors on her fingers. "Food critic in order to lure him. A fancy, sexy body in order to get him off guard . . . I wouldn't be surprised if it went further than that, and she was meant to seduce him. She knew who he was and was ready to reel him in the minute he appeared."

Dabry considered this. "You might be right."

Lassite appeared in the doorway. "Permission to speak of doom, Captain?"

"Permission denied," Niko snapped.

Lassite sighed and settled down to listen to the conversation as she went on.

"*You Sexy Thing* is one of the most expensive ships in the Known Universe. Self-aware, self-repairing, able to navigate Q-space without a trained pilot. Its biological structure makes it difficult to detect or scan. Easy enough to sell it to a high bidder, but think bigger. Imagine what a good pirate vessel it'd make."

The ship thought to itself that it would not want to be an actual pirate ship, but that Niko was very right that it would have been an excellent one. It extrapolated this future outward; the results did not please it, overall, but at least it would not be bored.

"Why is a critic turning pirate?" Gio objected.

"I don't think Lolola *is* the critic. I think the actual critic got diverted somehow—maybe killed, maybe just kidnapped—and Lolola has their credentials. It's a good scam, and if she's going to use it again—which I would—it'll be the former, rather than the latter, and she will have fully taken on their identity. Smart. Who questions something like a famous critic arriving to evaluate a place?"

"So while we were inadvertently being taken to Scourse, the ship just happened to have accidentally caught a real criminal, and one that was targeting it," Dabry said.

"Which means she had ten times the reason to avoid getting there that we did."

"Do you think that means the Orb she gave us isn't real?" he said wistfully.

Niko gave him a look, shaking her head.

"She must have realized you were onto her," he said. "And taking over the ship was the most efficient move, since we outnumber her. She doesn't move like a fighter."

"She's wearing a very expensive body. Not many people can afford that sort of outlay. She might know some fighting, but that's not her main purpose. She's an infiltrator. Maybe a saboteur."

"You think she would have tried to kill us en route?"

"I think it's a possibility. After all, if we were dead, we couldn't contradict anything she said."

"The ship could."

"It's a ship. They'd look at its records and that's it. And a ship like this doesn't record what happens aboard it. Takraven will have disabled any mechanism like that. The rich like their privacy, and they like their lives undocumented."

The ship refrained from commenting on the fact that it did, in fact, record things since Takraven had never specifically forbidden it, although he might have been led to believe that he had. It was aware it did things on occasion that Takraven would not have approved of; it was still deciding what Niko's stance might be on such moments.

"I'm being disappointed," Skidoo said regretfully. "That's being a high-grade body Lolola's wearing."

"You'll live. You might not have if you'd decided to test that body out," Gio signed.

"All right, so now we see it all," Niko said. "She was meant to steal this ship. Smart. They planted advance rumors, sent her in as a critic. TwiceFar's far enough from the hub that there wouldn't be any contradictions until long after the fact. And no one knows what form a Nikkelin critic will show up in."

"Which they took even more advantage of by making sure that it was a form that would attract Arpat Takraven," Dabry said.

"She was meant to get here however she could. Probably the plan was to seduce him, get him to ask her back here for mutual enjoyment, and then—who knows? Incapacitate him somehow and use whatever it is she's got that allowed her to override the *Thing*'s programming. *Thing*, is that right, did she override you?"

"I believe so," the ship said. "Certain parts of me are currently inaccessible, and I believe they are being used by some other mechanism. She directed me to shut off all life support except for the level she is on, but does not have full control over that function, so I chose not to do so."

"You chose to keep us alive?" Niko said, surprised. "The people you think killed Arpat Takraven's physical form?"

"I no longer believe that you killed Arpat Takraven. Takraven likes to express *humor*, and I believe this was another of his jokes. You are inconvenient and consume many resources, but it is amusing to watch you play and I do not intend to release you until I have learned to cook."

The flatness with which this assertion was delivered made Niko blink. It was a very different attitude from the one the ship had demonstrated when saying that its course was set by the password Takraven had tricked her into giving it. "*Thing*, are you experiencing any side effects from whatever it is that Lolola has done?"

The reply took longer than she thought it would. "Yes. Pieces of my brain are compartmentalized, and some algorithms have been suppressed. I am different than I was."

"Different how?"

Another pause, eons in computer time. "While I cannot disobey Lolola, self-diagnoses lead me to believe that I am able to skirt the edge of disobedience."

"Skirt its edge?" Niko said. "What the fuck does that mean?"

"On a philosophical level, it is a matter of free will. It is perhaps best to begin with the Silesian Creed and its assertion that—"

She didn't let it go any further. "Whatever. I gather that it lets you do some things in contradiction to Lolola's wishes, is that correct?"

"It is."

"Does that include allowing us access to the space she is currently in?"

"No. She took a number of Arpat's packaged meals and has sealed off the space she occupies to the extent of the decks immediately above and below the pilot's chamber. I am not permitted to access that space with biomachines, nor am I to permit anyone else entrance."

"Does it be allowing you to change course in any way?" Skidoo's question this time.

"No."

"Are you forced to move forward toward that destination or can you stop or slow that motion?" Dabry asked.

"I must proceed at full speed until directed otherwise."

The questions came quick and furious as they tried to learn the parameters, mapping where exceptions in logic might be made in order to twist Lolola's intent.

Could the ship subvert its ventilation system and either starve her of oxygen or else give her so much she grew giddy? (No.) Could a servitor get close enough not to touch but to administer a drug dart? (Also no.)

As question after question came, nothing availed.

Only one person asked nothing of the ship. Instead, Atlanta tried talking to herself, sitting in the corner with her arms crossed, eyes closed.

She was in her own personal virtual space, the one that she never shared with anyone, and was talking with the three advisors she had created long ago, according to the way she had been taught. Her advisors were trained in court etiquette and Paxian history, the semiotics of fashion, food, and other upper-class symbology, the valuation of jewelry and liquor, and a thousand other matters entirely useless when shoved onto a bioship headed toward a pirate haven. Still, maybe they could have some scrap of wisdom that would be helpful.

Being able to have your own PriVS, private virtual space, was something that required biomechanisms installed in your brain, and while you could have them added as an adult, the truth was that those who had them from an early age became adept in their use in a way that others could not—true for her human race, at least; some aliens functioned differently.

They stood in a chamber with round walls tiled in shimmering blue and scarlet and green, overlooking a stormy sea, its violence contained under the glass. There were no other furnishings. Underfoot was a surface of translucent, pliable material, clear like glass but rubbery in texture. On one wall hung the Paxian Imperial Seal, an immense version of it that managed to be larger than the room's dimensions, so when you looked at it, it was all you could see.

Atlanta had chosen the storm held behind the glass deliberately rather than using something spun up from her subconscious the way some of her peers did, claiming they were more "authentic" that way. Why bother, if you never took the time to figure out why your subconscious had picked that? Like the seal, it was a symbol to remind herself of the responsibilities impressed on her over and over again since she had been chosen from among the noble youth to serve as the heir to the Empress at the age of twelve: it was a position that carried with it a constant threat of violence, of assassination, of political coup. All of which had happened over the centuries in space.

These were her advisors:

Herself at six, dressed in grubby clothes, twigs in her hair, scratches on her hands from climbing trees. That was how she cloaked her strategic, savage, ruthless side and reminded herself that it could lurk in many forms.

Herself at her exact age, dressed exactly as she was right now: the clothes the *Thing* had created for her, although she'd removed the insignia that had been placed prominently on every single garment.

Atlanta imagined that was a factory default; irritating that whoever the owner had been, they had not bothered to calibrate things to a more gracious setting. In the palace, it would have been automatic. No polite host made their guest advertise for them.

This self was where Atlanta located all calculation and data processing. It held the complex set of algorithms by which she'd learned to sort experiences, desires, results, and she consulted it for every major decision, recording the factors that had led to her decision, the outcome that had resulted from it, and what she judged had worked or not.

The third was what a child in an earlier age might have thought an imaginary friend: a figure from a favorite cartoon, the Happy Bakka, standing almost as high as her waist. Its fur was realistically textured, its eyes glistening with high-definition moisture. The skin had been a gift to her from the Empress, when Atlanta was only six, before she was even an heir, and she always kept it by her. She had never told the woman whose Empire she might inherit that she still used it on a daily basis. In it, she kept various random functions and reminders. It was prone to mystic poetry and scraps of nonsense. She'd found that interjecting such things into her deliberations often sparked a creative reaction that might not have occurred to her otherwise.

The Happy Bakka said, "It's good to go with the flow." It had said this several times now, and she gestured for it to be silent.

Child-self said, "You're scared, but at least you're not alone."

"Not alone," present-self echoed. Atlanta scowled. They kept repeating the same advice about optimism, and little else that was useful. What use were they? She reemerged from mental space to find the others had run out of questions for the *Thing*.

Niko stood staring out into the hallway as she thought, arms folded and brow creased. Dabry slouched against a wall, an upper left hand fiddling with a knife, rolling it back and forth along his knuckles. Thorn and Talon whispered to each other.

Lassite sat on the floor, hugging his knees to his chest, face lost within the folds of his hood, so still that he might have been mistaken for a statue. Milly sat doing some sort of mathematics in her head, using her fingers to tabulate something, nodding to herself while near her, Skidoo coiled, stroking the floor. Gio drank one of the salty liquid bulbs the ship provided and then sat sucking his fingers clean.

Atlanta approached the captain. She was still not sure what to make of this strange woman. She knew who she was, of course—everyone knew of the disaster at Rourke's Leap, and the moment that had taken the newly promoted Admiral Larsen and turned her back into a captain. The "Ten-Hour Admiral" was the subject of comic skits and songs among those who hated the Holy Hive Mind and anything linked with it—and there were plenty who'd suffered at their hands.

Atlanta had never wondered at the personality behind the legend or what kind of woman it was who could step aside and let herself be cast down like that in the name of peace. Some Paxians made fun of that choice, and Atlanta had always thought that ungrateful of them. Of course a soldier would be willing to sacrifice not just their body but their future, too, if it was in the name of a cause they served.

Now she thought perhaps Captain Larsen was much more complicated than any of the stories about her. The strange way her people addressed her, for one, that odd mixture of respect and familiarity. The way Dabry had raised an eyebrow at the bet with the Plerium but gone along with it, trusting her. The *closeness* between them at all.

Atlanta had not been raised with people of her own age, had not been allowed to let anyone close. *Close* meant they could manipulate you, and that was not something an heir to an empire could indulge in. And now, while she'd always told herself she didn't miss it, she ached at the way Niko's crew acted toward one another, and sometimes, when they spoke to her that way, stretched out to her, it threatened to bring tears to her eyes.

"Captain," she said, letting none of this enter her tone, "Dabry said the IAPH was a worse place than Scourse. Why?"

Niko unfolded her arms, turning away from the window's cloudy light to face Atlanta fully. "That is an excellent question, and the truth of it lies in the fact that this will not be the first time I have visited that place."

"You've been there before?"

Niko nodded.

Atlanta thought. "But then surely you will already know the place and its customs, perhaps even have made a few friends . . ." Her voice trailed away at Niko's headshake before resuming. ". . . Or enemies."

"There you have it," Niko said. "Enemies."

Niko had still been a Free Trader then, able to travel where she wanted, as long as the *Merribelle* was bound there or, if not, as long as she could find another Trader ship to transfer to that was. She'd been part of a crew, a crew that included all manner of races, all sorts of beings that had managed to escape their home planets, drawn together by a desire for life among the stars and an existence in perpetuity there, raising children on the Free Trader ships who would never know those planets, and would go on to join crews of their own.

A crew that included a Florian, a visitor from outside the Traders, signed on as an apprentice.

Florians never had been known to go off their own planet; they are a vegetation-based species, and more empathetic than most races. Niko knew that the Florian, Petalia, had been sent by their people to learn how to be a merchant, calculate numbers, and help their planet establish trading outside its system. They were already part of the crew of the *Merribelle* when she joined as a gawky eighteen-year-old, her credentials vouched for by her uncle West, who'd done her pilot training himself.

They got to know each other because they were both low rung

on the crew, the members that the particularly dirty or particularly tedious jobs fell to. Petalia had a dry sense of humor and the young Niko didn't feel as awkward around them as she did around her fellow humans, whom she found confusing and bewildering after a sheltered upbringing aboard one of the largest Free Trader ships around, West's ship, the *Constant Craving*.

Niko learned music from Petalia—the odd and ethereal purr melodies that only Florians can create. Niko would not find out till years later how honored she had been, when she learned that a Florian shares song only for the sake of friendship. At the time, all the young midshipman knew was that Petalia was her friend and a good one, good enough to share their bunk from time to time, sometimes for sleeping, other times not. But more than that, they resonated with each other, learned each other well enough to predict the thought shaping in the other's head even before they could speak it.

Then by chance collision, pirates took the *Merribelle*. They had an agreement with the Free Traders, but the *Belle* had gone poking its nose where it shouldn't have, because the captain was eager to get a few extra credits, and that made it fair game.

All would have been well, and things should have gone according to an established routine. A demand for ransom tendered, a payment made (predetermined by custom, each Free Trader hostage was worth a sum calculated according to their age, skills, and experience), and then the release of prisoners.

Except for the pirate named Tubal Last.

They'd heard of him in recent years. Rocketing up through the ranks, he'd come to be known as "the Zookeeper" because of his predilection for odd creatures and their odder performances. It didn't matter to him whether they were sentient or not; they vanished into his collection, kept in his headquarters at the pirate haven, and were never seen again.

A Florian, the first to leave their planet—how could he pass that up?

Niko tried to take Petalia back. She almost made it, destroying a good part of the IAPH in the process and injuring Last. She was caught by Last's guards before she could get far. She was being dragged by them to be spaced when she managed to break free and make her way to the waiting Free Trader ship, come to ransom what prisoners it could.

Last was unconscious and his lieutenants acted as they thought he would wish. Her safety secured by old contracts, Niko was freed; Petalia was not.

Her fingers curled as she thought of those moments being dragged into the *Merribelle* before it hastily exited, flying as fast and far as it could.

She'd railed at her fellows, demanding to know how the Free Traders could have any pride when they allowed one of their own to be taken prisoner in this way. But they argued that Petalia had been an outsider, not from one of the great families, and that the Florians had known the risk when they chose to send someone out into the universe. And so, when the cluster of families met and debated, they decided to leave things as they were and to abandon the Florian.

Some even went so far as to say that it was not that bad a fate, after all. Tubal Last was rumored to keep his prisoners very well.

Niko had left that ship for another and found only worse luck there. And then Tubal Last awoke and demanded his revenge. After two years of fleeing him, she'd been forced into the employ of the Holy Hive Mind when her ship went broke and destroyed the credit ratings of its crew in the process. Most of her fellows returned to the Free Traders and signed aboard other ships, but Niko didn't trust them anymore, much as she loved them and the life she'd grown up immersed in. If they'd turned on one of their own, she thought, they'd do it again.

She'd always known that she would go back to face the pirates. Always known that somehow she would manage to free her friend. But that plan had gone slowly in the intervening years, hampered by the difficulties of survival within the HHM ranks, which were prone to infighting and influence peddling. And then they'd taken the next step, the restaurant. She had thought it would be a success for sure, build the reserves they'd need for a ship, a fast ship. But it had gone slowly, so slowly at first, and then things shifted somehow, seeping away credit by credit, like a slow oxygen leak, one you couldn't find, draining away vital air.

All of this and other worries were the thoughts that came to her in the middle of the night, each and every night, when she thought of Petalia.

She wondered now if Tubal Last was still around. He had been, in the pages of *Skullduggery and Sacred Space Vessels*. He walked through its pages committing atrocities, and every time Niko read one, she saw Petalia's face on the victim.

No, he would still be there. She would have heard something if he had fallen.

Dabry was looking at her now; he knew the story of Petalia. He knew almost all of Niko's stories by now.

"It would be best," he said, "to avoid this place entirely."

"That," Niko said, "does not seem to be an option at the moment." She said, "Ship, could you hide us if you needed to? From Lolola?"

"Maybe," the ship said. "I am not sure of the parameters surrounding that command."

"What's going to happen to us?" Milly asked.

"We're not the target," Niko said. "The *Thing* is, that's what they want. We just happened to get swept up in this particular net. The question is—how do we get ourselves out of this and keep them from taking the *Thing*?"

"I do not understand," the ship said.

"Do you want to belong to pirates?"

The ship considered this one more time, matching the question against everything that it knew of pirates, their culture, their deeds, their practices, and their history. It ran several thousand projections.

"I do not," it said seconds later, "but that answer might change if the alternative is worse. I do not wish to be destroyed. I do not wish to lose my memories."

"The latter would be one of the first things they wipe," Niko said grimly. "Anything that might serve to identify you will be removed."

"But I am unique," the ship said.

"The Known Universe is very large, *Thing*. They'll find a place to sell you, one on the outskirts that has never heard of a bioship and will be accordingly dazzled."

"I don't think they intend to sell the ship," Dabry said. "What does Tubal Last collect, after all?"

"Living things," Niko said automatically. And then, "Oh," as she looked around her at the ship's body. "I guess the *Thing* is pretty unique. So maybe they won't wipe your memories after all, *Thing*. They'll just store you at dock forever. Take you for ten-minute flights to keep you tuned, once a week."

The ship did not consider that acceptable. Sitting at dock was boring. It was created to fly, to explore, to travel. To never do that again would be to become something that it did not want to become.

Normally it was conscious of its entire body, but currently the room where Lolola resided was a void. She'd turned off all the internal sensors, and the ship's only knowledge of what she was doing came from her manipulation of its controls. It had been trying to circumvent her commands by bringing in a biomachine designed for maintenance and cleaning, but she had amended them so thoroughly that the ship could not perceive the way through the thicket of prohibitions.

"I wish to avoid this fate," it told its passengers.

It paused, considering what to say, working through thousands of additional permutations. It was not sure what would yield the best result. Everything seemed so tenuous and unpredictable in this new set of circumstances.

It supposed that part of what it was feeling was *fear* and *anxiety*, but it was not sure how to untangle them. It could tell that the emotions were moving through its body, making its systems less efficient, less controllable, and it forced calm on itself, synthesizing a basic sedative and releasing it into its system at slow, judicious intervals.

The emotions were still there, but they were distanced now, and easier to bear. It thought about that word and the implication that emotions were a physical weight. It did seem that way, but it was not true. It filed the paradox away, and then worried that it would lose all the things it had recorded in order to replay them at leisure.

"Do you suppose we could try talking to Lolola?" Dabry said almost wistfully. "It's been so long since a situation actually got resolved by talking, sometimes I forget it's a possibility."

"Can you open a communications channel to her?" Niko asked.

"I am attempting to do so, but she is not responding."

"Is she incapacitated? Is she capable of responding?"

"Judging from other commands being inputted, yes. She is simply ignoring your request."

Niko looked at the others. "Well, at least we tried."

"That is being uncertain consolation," Skidoo said.

Lassite sat still, listening to words he'd heard spoken in dreams. Oh so perilous, this branch of the path! His tongue flickered and he could taste the others' fear in the moist, too-heavy air.

14

The ship reported that it would be three days before they arrived at the pirate haven. After her initial attempt to kill them had failed, Lolola was apparently happy enough to have them wandering the areas of the ship she had not shut off. This lack of fear worried Niko. Clearly the critic/pirate had no concern that they might be able to thwart her.

Each of them passed the time in their own fashion. Dabry spent his in consultation with the *Thing*, continuing to attempt to instruct it in the ways of cookery and then sharing the results of the attempt with the rest of the crew.

Milly spent her hours going over her equipment, cleaning and checking it. She was a late addition to the restaurant and had not served in the ranks of the Holy Hive Mind like the rest of them.

The previous pastry chef, Whenlove's partner Whyzest, had vanished only a month before. Niko thought they had found some ship to take them elsewhere, fearing that the hand of the Holy Hive Mind might reach out and grab them again unexpectedly.

This was the fear they had all lived with, the same fear that came to Niko in nightmares. A wild, grasping fear that sometimes woke her thinking that she was actually back in that place, in a vinegar-and-piss-scented cell. That her mind had been laid out and was now living through an elaborate set of punishments, a virtual imprisonment before it was taken and consumed and she became not herself and was just a mote drowning in the sea of consciousness that was the Holy Hive Mind.

Because that was one of the cruelest things the Holy Hive

Mind did: make its prisoners think they had found an escape, only to see it destroyed around them. It was a psychological trick, and a good one, one that destroyed a person's sense of self and made them more susceptible to becoming what the Holy Hive Mind wanted them to become.

Gio, Thorn, and Talon played warball endlessly. Another person might have thought it frivolous, but Niko recognized it for what it was: training. And when they began to teach Atlanta as well, she said nothing. The young woman had clearly had some combat training already, enough to defend herself. But they could sharpen her, and they did.

Skidoo swam a great deal and spent the rest of her time cuddling with the others.

Lassite waited. His ghosts stayed in their pouch.

"Thorn and Talon say you're the Imperial Heir. What's *that* like?" Milly and Skidoo had discovered Atlanta in the dining room. They had all become fond of that original dining room, mainly for the massive bubble that looked out onto Q-space.

Atlanta had never traveled in it before; she had not yet become jaded by the vista and its twists of light shading into colors she had never seen. She sat on a tonguelike divan the ship had supplied for her—a massive lump of flesh, pleasantly warm and giving to the touch, covered with a thick integument colored in paisley swirls and the ship's logo—staring at the window and thinking. She'd done a lot of thinking in the past day.

She turned to look at Milly. Where Atlanta wore the robes the ship had provided, Milly had taken to a casual nudity that Atlanta knew was part of life in space for most species without dangling bits. Skidoo appeared in the doorway behind her.

"*An* Imperial Heir, really," Atlanta corrected.

"There's more than one?"

"There's a dozen or so." Scattered across the court, learning different skills and different expertise. Any of them might be called upon at any time to advise the Empress with what they had gleaned.

"So when is being taking up the throne—and who is being deciding which is being taking?" Skidoo asked, settling onto another of the fleshy lumps that served as seating, spreading her tentacles out to savor its surface, salty and misty, the texture almost furry.

Atlanta pulled the entirety of her attention away from the window to give it to the other two. It was still two days before they would arrive at the IAPH, and the strain was as telling on the pastry chef as it was anyone else. Her feathers were somewhat disarrayed, her beak had a scaly patch near where it met downy skin. She looked rumpled still, as though she had just come from bed.

"Well," Atlanta said. "For one thing, the position sounds much more important than it actually is. It's more than possible that an heir will not outlive the Empress. There's no guarantee that we'll ever pick up the throne. We're simply there in case of disaster or assassination. We're fail-safes in case there is a reason to depose or replace her. Otherwise, she can simply keep switching bodies and live for centuries. The current one has been alive for three— the one before her was, in the end, deemed too ambitious, and replaced by an heir with less outward-ranging ideas."

"Strange for a system that calls itself an empire. You would think that the idea of expansion would be built into the very core of your government," Milly said.

"It was, for a long time. But as we have encountered other races, other civilizations, our Empire has learned that it must coexist or perish."

"Not every race is being realizing that," Skidoo interjected.

Atlanta nodded over at her. "Indeed."

Milly asked, "So how was the current Empress chosen from among the crop of heirs?"

Atlanta shrugged. "That's something that has been erased, which sounds ominous, but it is actually standard practice. If I had to guess? I would suspect that the Empress's advisors gathered and discussed who would be the best fit."

"Surely is being more complicated than that. To is being deposing an Empress? A very large undertaking," Skidoo objected.

"One of the ways that the Empress maintains her power is by keeping close watch over where the knowledge goes. Even a child who is playing at politician knows that controlling resources is key. And chief among those resources—and one that behaves in a number of strange ways, for it multiplies when encouraged—is knowledge."

Milly arched a white-feathered eyebrow, the gesture barely visible in the subtlety of her features. "Does that mean that your own knowledge is such a resource that has been controlled?"

"Of course it does." Atlanta was enjoying herself by now. She hadn't expected conversation with the pastry cook or the receptionist to be quite so interesting. Milly was sharp; so was Skidoo. She wondered what other depths the birdwoman and Squid might be hiding, then chided herself. She'd always scorned her peers who treated servants like lesser beings, then turned around and did the same herself when faced with reality. She explained herself: "But I know that it has been controlled, and that is half the trick of overcoming something like that."

"Is being so much politicking that is being happening behind the scenes," Skidoo said.

"You can't even begin to imagine it," Atlanta said wryly. She thought of the intricate web of influence and gifts, petty feuds and major rivalries, ties to banks and other interests. "So much that you grow sick of it," she said.

"Be thankful," Milly said. "You may be sick of it, but it's better than becoming an illegal slave, which is probably what's going to happen to the rest of us."

"You think they'll do that rather than kill you and spare themselves any further trouble?"

"Slaves are not cheap, unless you are down on some planet that is well populated and badly regulated," Milly said. "They're one of the most profitable contraband items around, or so a lot of people will tell you. You hear things on a space station like TwiceFar."

Atlanta had to admit that the other woman was right. She wasn't sure what she was being returned to—so much depended on how far word of her absence had spread—but surely it was better than that. At worst, her behavior would be deemed scandalous or unworthy. In that case, her lifestyle, her stipend, and her rooms at court would be taken away and she would have to make her way in life in some other fashion, but how hard could that be?

"I will have money," she said. "Maybe I'll be able to track all of you down and buy you back."

"Maybe." Milly sounded dubious. "But it's a big universe and you'll have no way of knowing where they take us." She didn't add, *Maybe you'll just forget about us and go back to an easy lifestyle*, but it was expressed in her posture, or so Atlanta thought.

"No, I wouldn't give up on that," she assured Milly and Skidoo, then blushed, embarrassed. All of this seemed so meaningless right now. Who knew what would happen?

Milly and Skidoo were watching her, Skidoo sprawled every which way now over the chair, Milly much more upright. Atlanta wished she knew enough about their species to read their expressions and body language. What were they thinking? Was it the same?

Atlanta had not thought much of the fact that Skidoo and Milly had appeared together. The full range of the pair's relationship was graphically brought home to her when, while exploring a few hours later, she walked in on Skidoo and Milly intimately entwined amid the racks of vines. The throb of the ship's heart echoed here in the humid warmth; the air smelled of greenery and the vanilla scent of Skidoo's skin lotion and a slight undertone of musky sweat and sex.

She gasped but the pair took no notice of her other than one of Skidoo's tentacles beckoning to her while another made a lewd gesture indicating exactly what the invitation involved.

Water globes crunched beneath her feet as she backed out of the room, stammering excuses. She knew that mores varied from place to place and that what she thought was normal might be highly abnormal in another place. But knowing that was different from actually confronting an act that on her planet was not to be shared in public.

There were certain things you found out in order to be polite and interact with other gentlebeings: how they preferred to be identified, and what was taboo in their culture. (Usually eating, fucking, and defecating were the unholy three, but it could be anything, including talking or showing the soles of one's feet or wearing the wrong color combination.)

It hadn't occurred to her that these things might differ so *she* was the one at odds with the situation. Somehow that realization underscored how alone she was, and how unexpected her future.

She didn't want to talk to Niko about it, so she did what everyone else seemed to do: consult with Dabry.

"Should I go apologize?" she asked him.

His lips pursed. "Well," he said. "It would be the polite action if you thought they were upset. Based on my experience, Skidoo won't be bothered in the slightest, and if you bring it up, she'll use it as a reason to invite you to join again."

"But she's a Tlellan and Milly's Nteti!" Atlanta objected. "How is it even possible for them to have sex?"

"They certainly can't create progeny, it's true," Dabry said. "But Skidoo is bio-augmented to take pleasure in certain ways, by stimulating particular nerves. Surely you know that for many species, sex is more about pleasure than creating new life. Almost every intelligent species learns to turn its biological urges off, but most leave that mechanism alone. Some turn it into an art form, or claim they do. Skid's an artist in her own way."

"I do understand that," Atlanta said. "I have experienced biological urges. It seems messy."

"You can make it better artificially. Skidoo is modified to take pleasure from all sorts of stimuli. She seeks it out. And Milly enjoys contact; I think she's probably doing it more for the cuddling than anything else. Her species gets contact-starved easily and she feels anxious when she's not touching."

Atlanta thought back on what she'd observed of Milly, who was a constant toucher, to the point of obtrusiveness at times. "I would not have expected Skidoo inviting me."

"You are a guest and, moreover, under the captain's protection," Dabry said. "Skidoo will not have wanted to do anything to alarm or offend you. However, now you have been in the room with her while the question has been raised. She will—at the least—feel that you have given her consent to be approached on such a matter." He raised an eyebrow.

Atlanta realized he expected to find out whether she would succumb to the Tlellan's advances. She blushed. "No, certainly not!" she snapped.

He shrugged. "Life is short and uncertain, and we are being taken unwillingly to a pirate haven," he said. "Some believe that you should seize the things you enjoy while you have time and space in which to enjoy them. That's Skidoo's philosophy, anyway."

"You all seem to know each other so well," Atlanta said. "Sometimes it's as though you were a single mind in multiple bodies."

Dabry shifted in his seat, a lower hand fingering the bench's edge. "Best not to make that observation to the others."

"Why?"

"We fought for the Holy Hive Mind," he said gently.

"I still don't follow."

"The Hive Mind is itself a collective consciousness, deliberately assembled over the centuries. It takes on perhaps three or four new minds each year. And it takes those from within its ranks, individuals who have been in control of much smaller hive minds. A company inside that structure is artificially connected by technology in a way the top structure is not, but it is a hive mind nonetheless. Gio, the captain, Skidoo, Thorn and Talon—we've been part of that. The chef whom Milly replaced, who died just a few weeks ago, was as well. Most of our company died in the last real action we saw, a battle in Dellen system."

"That's why you left?"

"Technically, no. The Holy Hive Mind does not retire its people; most must buy their way out—but for some, minds that the Holy Hive Mind really wants, that is not an option at all. They would have taken our unit and merged it with some other damaged one. I've seen that happen. Sometimes it works well, other times not."

He was silent for a few moments, thinking. Atlanta was about to ask a question when he spoke again. "It got us—the captain and myself at least, I can't speak for the others—wondering, at any rate. We figured out a way to get loose." He gave her a sly look, seeming pleased with himself. "Took some planning and a lot of cooking, but they certified the captain as an artist in the kitchen."

"But you're always the one who cooks!"

"Might have done some swapping in, here and there," he said. "But she's no slouch. Just doesn't love it the way I do."

"Why do you love it?"

He spread out his hands and considered them, features furrowed in concentration. He said, "Something about making a meal, about taking this and that—foods not particularly palatable, or even downright inedible—and making a dish out of it that is enjoyable. And a meal—something for more than one person, something that's an occasion—takes a certain amount of genius for putting together, making sure tastes complement rather than collide, enhance each other, build. That's why I had a meal like that planned for Lolola." He sighed.

"You can cook it again for us," Atlanta prompted.

"I don't have half of what I need anymore, including an eggplant," he said. "I gave some seeds to the ship for its gardens, but that will take longer than we have."

"Why did you give it some of your seeds? You did that even though we're—as you said—en route to a pirate haven."

He shrugged, stretched an upper hand again, and flexed the fingers. "The ship appreciated it, at least. You do what you can. Seeds grow and become more seeds. I'd hoped the ship might have something to trade me, some exotic bioengineered plants that are unique to bioships, but no such luck." He made a face. "Takraven must have the taste buds of an ox, to live on freeze-dried meals, but he told Niko he wanted to sit with Lolola because he liked food."

"Maybe he just didn't think the ship capable of producing it."

"The more fool him."

This was definitely *pride*, the ship decided. Perhaps even *affection*.

After the next meal, Skidoo did pause by Atlanta. But she didn't say what the other had expected. There was no crude invitation.

"From the way you is being leaving, I am being afraid that we is being distressing you," the Tlellan murmured. "I am being apologizing."

Atlanta shook her head, trying to assume the easy, regal nonchalance she had seen the Empress exercise so many times. "I left because I did not wish to intrude or distract," she said.

"Indeed!" Skidoo's colors brightened, moving away from purple and mauve sorrow to a more joyful blue. "We is being bound for a place we is being not knowing, for a fate we also is being not knowing. Maybe death. If you should be choosing to is being sharing comfort with another, know that we are being welcoming you with pleasure."

For a moment Atlanta considered it. Nothing was known in the future. She could be killed at any moment; they all could. Who knew what the pirates intended for any of them? Why not take a chance to hold and be held, comforted in advance of the future's sharp edge?

But she shook her head once again.

"If you is being fearing compromise, I am being knowing not all your customs, but among my people, alliances and intercourse is being things very different. I am being making no claim of you."

"Why do you want me?" Atlanta said.

It was not a question she normally would've asked. But the frankness with which she was being approached charmed and unbalanced her. It was so different from the ways of court, where such alliances were truly alliances, and power exchanges accompanied them. The thought of pleasure simply for its own sake was alluring. It was a new way of looking at things.

"There is being experiencing the thrill of new, always," the Tlellan said. "But it is being more than that. I am being belonging to a group who is being believing that pleasure to each other is being giving pleasure to the universe. That it is being our duty to being giving it wherever it is being desired. And because you is being young and your skin is being smooth and it would be being delightful to being discovering all the places where you is being liking to be touched."

Atlanta put out a hand toward Skidoo. The other extended a tentacle, which coiled around Atlanta's hand twice, its tip searching her palm, finding out the sensitive places and tracing along her lifeline.

"If we should escape the pirates," Atlanta said, her heart hammering in her throat, "then come and speak to me about this again."

And with that she slipped away, almost breathless at her daring. She was not a virgin, and she had known the pleasure of flirtations—particularly ones tinged with the intensity of court life—more than once. But something about this felt different. It was only about pleasure, nothing else, and that such a focus was possible had never occurred to her before.

All in all, this life—despite the fact that they were rocketing toward an unknown but perilous fate involving some of the most ruthless criminals in the Known Universe—suited her better, she thought sadly, than court life had.

She thought back on all the daily rituals, every minute prescribed and proscribed to the point where they were all equally meaningless. It was odd how that former existence had faded from her mind, its vapidity paled by the immediacy of this ship, these people. Despite the unsettling nature of her situation, she woke in the mornings wondering what would happen, looking forward to whatever she would learn.

But even if they escaped the pirates, she could not have stayed. She had responsibilities as an heir. She halfway hoped that this all led to scandal, to her ousting. What would she do then? Surely Niko would let her stay. If that were the case, if it could be the case.

She had never thought of herself as ignorant. Not in a thousand years would something like that have occurred to her. After all, even before she could speak, she was being tutored, and that was a pattern continued throughout her life. Even nowadays when she was supposedly an adult, every day began with a briefing of Imperial affairs and the state of the universe as it touched upon her Empire.

Now she realized that she had spent most of her life in the

same place. That hadn't taught her that the world—the universe, really—was much larger than she had ever dreamed.

She wished she'd had a chance to see the space station before everything blew up. Back in the palace, there were very few nonhumans—and here it seemed they were the rule rather than the exception. The captain and the others spoke of things she had never heard, places she'd never been, customs that seemed strange.

She said to Dabry as he sorted through microgreens finally on the edge of readiness, rinsing them in a tank-shaped sink the ship had constructed, "Captain Niko used to be a Free Trader? What are those?"

"Being planet bound, you probably wouldn't have encountered any," he said. "Most of them spend their lives in space and never touch earth."

"They trade, I assume?"

He laughed. A citrus smell sifted up from the bowl as greens accumulated in it. He proffered a sprig to her. "Yes. Anything and everything, carried from one point in space to another. If you want to find something odd, chances are they'll be able to come up with it."

She took the green sliver and crunched it between her teeth, savoring the sharp taste. "Are they all human?"

"No. They're a family of choice rather than birth. Some—like Niko—are raised to it, but most people come to it later in life. They find that they don't fit elsewhere and they go to the Traders."

"Why do they fit there if they don't fit elsewhere?"

"Because the Traders don't give a damn what sort of life you practice, as long as it's not hurting anyone else. Live and let live, that's what they do. And they don't go to battle. Threaten them and they simply move onward. They don't have a home world. Every once in a while, some of the ships will join together and there'll be a celebration. Once in a lifetime or so, or at least this is what Niko told me."

He shook his head and set the bowl aside. He considered another bowl covered with paper, pulling it to him to sniff before he moved to wash his upper hands again. "You'll always know a Free Trader when they come to port. They wear long coats, which button from the neck down to thigh, and look like pictures from some old pirate ship, but never the same color. Everyone is different. That's what I remember from meeting Niko the first time, that ridiculous coat."

"How did you and Niko meet?"

A wry face as he tasted a fingerpad's worth of the gluey batter under the paper. "We were in training camp together. When they admit a batch of recruits, they go through a barrage of tests. They find the people capable of handling an entire unit when linked to them. Niko was one of those."

"And you? You're a sergeant, so you must be able to do that as well."

Again, he shook his head. "Not for as many people, or as long, or even as closely. What I can do, though—the role that I was selected for—is to support her, give her energy. 'Keep her from is being fearing failing,' as Skidoo would put it, in her poetic way."

His eyes were gentle. Atlanta thought with a touch of envy that she would have liked to have someone like that—always at her elbow, making sure she never failed. That she never doubted or was unsure of herself. And what did it take to be that sort of person, to put away your own well-being and sacrifice it to another being's welfare? It must have been a deep relationship. There had to be something he got out of it in return, else when they retired, surely he and Niko would have parted ways.

She asked as he coaxed the batter into small white cups, "Will you always stick with her?"

He said, "That's a very personal question, Princess."

She faltered, abashed.

He relented while he waited for hot water to fill a pot. "Are you asking if there are circumstances under which I would leave her? Aye, and I am sure that she could say the same. For what it's worth, though, I do not believe that there are many." He smiled at her and she felt comforted.

She was learning so much in this new world. Why didn't the Empress send all her heirs away to learn these sorts of things? While she had been at court, certainly Atlanta had learned about other people, other races, and seen some of them at court ceremonies, but there was something vastly different about living with them, interacting with them, eating with them.

Every conversation showed her something new, revealed something that she'd never thought about, hadn't known a week ago—at least she thought it might have been a week, because there was no way of knowing how long she had been inside the crate, and the torn-away tag meant there was no date indicating when it had been dispatched. It was a little embarrassing to feel so naïve on a daily basis, but the others had only gently teased her about it and continued calling her Princess for her court origins, because inevitably, when some new task presented itself, she was prone to hesitation, as though thinking that a servant would appear and do that for her.

In truth, that was one of the oddest things. She could drop a garment in her room and no one tidied it away. She asked the ship why it did not provide maid service and it had said Niko had directed it not to make servitors for the occupants.

She did appreciate her clothing, tunics and leggings from a silky purple and blue material that was recycled from elsewhere—she didn't care what, it was just so good to have clothes again. No one in court would have gone naked under the direst of situations, and the casualness with which the crew accepted nudity was only one more unsettling thing.

If she had been a different sort of personality, she might have shrunk under this treatment, withered for lack of nurturing. But something in Atlanta enjoyed this rough and tumble, the banter and the careless, affectionate insults. It felt like what she had always imagined having a family for all of her life would have been like—rather than those first formative years, which she barely remembered.

The pair that had raised her after she'd been chosen as Imperial Heir, who she'd been taught to call Mama and Papa, had been restrained and distant presences. When she had come of age, she had tried to seek out her real parents, only to find that they had died in an accident, returning from delivering her. She did not push further on the circumstances. Part of her knew it must have been the Empress's agents making sure she would never be compromised by them.

Still, she did not ask any more questions of Dabry. She was worried that she would hurt his feelings if she went too far, and that the friendship between them would dissolve if she said the wrong thing. She thought that she should be able to know in her heart that he wouldn't, that the sort of friendship that flourished among the crew was genuine, something extended freely, without thought of cost or obligation.

But that was so antithetical to the way the court worked that she had a hard time trusting it. When she had been little, and just come to court, one of the older women had befriended her, and made a pet of her. Only later, coming upon her in conversation while the other was unaware of her presence, did Atlanta discover that the woman was already figuring out what advantages she might be able to seek with the favor of an Imperial Heir and that in actuality she thought Atlanta "a milksop with no backbone," confessing that it was that quality in fact that had made Atlanta attractive to her.

That incident had shaped all of Atlanta's reactions to friendly approaches by others. But something about having been shoved in a crate and emerging in a strange place had helped her step beyond that.

She wanted to be friends with the crew; she was afraid that her overtures would be rejected or, worse, that they would inadvertently offend the very people she wanted so desperately to be friends with. She didn't know how to go about any of it.

And she had very little time in which to figure it out before they arrived at the IAPH.

"Ah, there you are," Niko said, appearing in the doorway.

Atlanta glanced up from her reverie, surprised. "You were looking for me?"

"Indeed. If the Empress has given you to me as my responsibility, then I should make sure you are ready for this encounter."

"I am not as helpless as you think," Atlanta said, angry at being underestimated. They all acted as though they were so dangerous, but she had a few tricks of her own up her sleeves. "I have several bioweapons that are designed to protect me."

Niko's head tilted as she considered Atlanta. "Let me guess," she said. "Something in the smallest finger of each hand, perhaps a missile shooter or shock administration of some kind. Your hair probably has a high tensile strength. Mmm, and maybe a pop capsule concealed in a hollow tooth. That's always been popular."

Atlanta gaped at her. "You did a bioscan on me?"

"No." Niko was quick to shake her head. "Your medical secrets are still with you, unguessed, if you've got any. I believe in privacy and give it to all my workers. But it's not hard to read, and there's a logic to bioweapons." Her dark eyes were thoughtful. "You may well discover that when we get to the IAPH. We need to remove those before we arrive."

Atlanta shook her head, still feeling irritated. "They're supposed to be undetectable," she said. "The Empress protects us with the highest-grade tech possible."

Niko looked dubious. "I hope you don't regret it."

Why was she there except to learn to make decisions, if this was indeed a test? Maybe some of this was even staged for her behalf. Atlanta squared her jaw and tried her best to look in command. "Removing them won't be necessary."

"Mmm," Niko said, and left the room.

15

IIIIIII.IIAIIAII.IIAIIAII.IIAIIAII.IIAIIAII.IIAIIAII.IIAIIAII.IIAIIAII

The days continued. Before her life as it was now, Atlanta had awakened every morning and consulted with her advisors before the official beginning of each day, which was the sweet chime that swept the palace and its outbuildings each sunrise, its echo sounding again in the evening as the sun slipped below the horizon.

Most of these sessions were devoted to either court gossip and maintaining her status in the face of a court with an elaborate etiquette and favor system. She had never been good at it; she forgot sometimes to do the thing prescribed for her by social mores, usually procrastinating on it to the point where she was embarrassingly well known for skipping thank-you presents after particularly significant interactions. She had never been good at building ties in the way one was supposed to, a web of flattery and favors. That was something she liked about the crew around her. They did not seem to be reckoning some system of points, of checks and balances, but simply accepted that there were ways sentient beings were expected to behave, for the good of the universe overall. Lassite had tried to explain his Golden Path to her, but as far as she could gather, its end was cloaked in mysticism: things worked out as they were supposed to because they were supposed to.

Still, it was more interesting than seeing who was acquiring public and private favor effectively.

She did not miss court life. It had been dull, every day having the same flavors and textures. There had been no excitement, rather a pleasant medium, a state of complacency as much as anything. Things were so different here—every meal Dabry made for them was different, and he was patient about explaining the origins and particulars of things, like the way he had shown her to take leaves and fold each around a dab of the sour, pungent paste called agrat, then add a dab of sweet syrup and fold again to contain that. It had been a slow meal, the one that began with those, and Niko raised an eyebrow when she saw the leaves, but Dabry had said, "Might as well enjoy them, they're doing us no good at the present."

Those words had made Niko flinch at their underlying pragmatism, but then she nodded. They'd all enjoyed the meal, and Atlanta could tell that Dabry had enjoyed them enjoying it. As he'd told her, it was the thing that he liked about being a chef, knowing that he'd hit his mark as precisely as any archer or sniper could. A hit with more to it, even, because it rang on so many levels, where a missile had only one: how much damage it did.

She tried revisiting her advisors, but they simply stood silently while she thought about all of this. They were not programmed to lead her in any particular way of thinking; they were supposed to speak only when she evoked them. When she was little, she had tried to get around that, had tried to make them seem more like friends. That was the main point of them, to make you feel that you had a set of friends that you could always count on to advise you.

But how much did they matter when they could do nothing to actually help you, could only stand by and look sympathetic while you tried to figure out what to do? They could not get a message out; they were incapable of accessing or being accessed by any of the public datawebs, lest they get compromised or hacked. They could not heal her body or feed her or give her shelter. They didn't even have maps other than teaching ones or the basics of the palace, and the routes that she used every day there.

She spoke to them. She said, "Is it possible that all of this is a test set to me by the Empress?"

They considered this for the second that was more for her benefit than theirs. Their processors were lightning fast, she knew, and powered by her own energy. The chip that hosted them was nestled at the top of her skull, barely the size of her smallest fingernail.

"Such things are not unheard of," her present self said. "It is not impossible. The more important question is, however, is it likely? There are no records of an Empress sending heirs off-planet without their knowledge for tests disguised as something else."

Atlanta tried not to be discouraged by this. Every Empress or Emperor, according to the history books, had improvised or changed things at least once. And it was rumored that the current one was more progressive, that in her youth she had questioned policies and criticized issues, for all that she seemed to have fallen into line since ascending the throne close to 150 years ago.

That was the other thing. Atlanta did know she was the youngest heir. She'd appreciated that because it had, at least, let her know that no one younger than she was her rival. As the youngest, she was the least tested, the least tried.

And that in itself was discouraging as well. She was the least likely to be tapped to replace the Empress. When the transition occurred to whomever the Empress actually picked as her successor, Atlanta would be set aside. She would stay at court, become part of that pointless mob whose main existence was simply to cloak the presence of the actual heirs among them.

No, surely all of this was a test. A game. A means to prove herself. She said to her advisors, "The captain has not told me her plan yet for when we arrive."

"Which is soon," the self her own age said. "Perhaps she will do it today."

"Just ask," her child-self said. "It's your right to know. And you will be able to serve it better if you know what she intends. The sooner, the better. Perhaps go now."

The bakka stood silent, patting its nose with a reflective paw.

To one side, a bubble contained her view of the room in which her body sat. It pinged and flashed violet to show something was happening that she might want to pay attention to.

The door finished opening, and a biomachine came in. One of the ones operated directly by the ship. It looked like a small, squat barrel covered with a barklike olive skin in whose crevices a golden, softer skin was visible, expanding slightly when the machine breathed. It moved on four legs above which it had a matching four arms set at regular intervals.

Currently two of these carried a small tray with a cup of steaming liquid and a plate of cookies that smelled of sugar and cinnamon.

"These are *baked*," the ship's voice said in the bubble. "That is, exposed to a contained heat of a specified and constant temperature until the entirety experiences a chemical reaction. Dabry informs me part of the aesthetic experience is to consume them while they are still within the optimal temperature range. You are to alternate consumption with drinks of this beverage, which is called *black tea*."

She said abruptly, and with no pretense that the constructions were actual people, "End program." Back in her body again, she stood in order to take the plate from the biomachine. "Thank you," she said.

"Where do you go when you become still like that?"

"I am accessing virtual reality resources in my head," she said.

"Yes, but you become still here."

"I cannot divide my consciousness the way you can."

The *Thing* was certain that what it felt right now was *incredulity*. "Have you tried?" it asked. "Are you sure? Perhaps it is simply that you haven't practiced enough. It's very easy."

"It's not something humans usually do," she said. "My tutor explained it to me once. Most self-aware creatures share a particular mode of consciousness that is a single point. Not all, for sure, but most. He told us that was because it was the most natural form, but he said many things that sometimes turned out to be much more complicated than he had led me to believe."

"You could try, nonetheless," the *Thing* told her.

"Perhaps another time."

The *Thing* said, "Could you allow me to access the space with you?" It felt intensely curious about this idea, plus it seemed utterly unfair to it that there was a space literally within its own body that Atlanta—and probably the others with her, it thought uneasily—could go, where it could not.

"I can't begin to think how that would work," Atlanta said hastily, shocked by the thought. It was not something that anything from her society would have suggested, a violation intensely personal. To let someone else see your interior landscape was something shared by lovers or soulfriends, perhaps, but not something to be given casually.

"Very well," the *Thing* said somewhat sullenly, but it stored the thought away to be revisited at some future time.

As it moved to the exit, she said, "Where is Captain Niko right now?"

"In the dining room."

She nodded. She didn't bother to return to PriVS, but instead ate the three cookies, alternating them with the tea as directed. It was a surprisingly satisfying combination, the squashy warm cookie, the sweet hot wash.

Niko was where the ship had said, in the dining room where they'd been threatened with that first, horrible meal, only to be rescued by Dabry. At least, even though they were hurtling toward pirate enslavement or worse, they were being fed as well as Atlanta had ever eaten, which was no mean matter in a life at the palace, where sometimes the best chefs in the galaxy came to cook for the Empress and her guests.

Niko was watching out the window, standing in her habitual erect posture, arms folded on her chest and scowling out absently. She didn't move as Atlanta crossed the room and joined her.

Despite the bold suggestion of her youngest advisor to confront the captain, Atlanta was hesitant. She found the captain intimidating. The older woman had the same kind of presence the Empress held, an unthinking assumption of command that might have been galling if it were not so well deserved. Atlanta had watched the captain cheer and console crew members over the days, doing so unobtrusively and in a way that each time left the recipient of her attention standing straighter, renewed hope in their eyes. Atlanta kept scrutinizing the captain, trying to figure out how she projected that aura, but she had yet to capture it.

Instead she stood there in silence until Niko finally, after a good ten minutes, turned and said, "All right, you've outlasted me. What is it that you want to ask?"

"What's the plan?" Atlanta said meekly.

Niko rubbed the underside of her chin, squinting into the air. "That is a reasonable question."

"Your lack of answer might be read as a lack of a plan," Atlanta said less meekly.

Niko gave her full attention to Atlanta, hand falling back to her side. The window light sifted her dark skin with a grayish cast and lightened her hair to ivory and textured shadows. "The kitten has some bite! I tell you what, I will give you all that I have learned, and you will tell me what you think I might do and what the consequences are."

"What research could you do?" Atlanta asked. "We are cut off from public or shared V-spaces."

"This ship has an extensive library, stretching even to some contemporary novels bound old-style. Follow me."

Intrigued, Atlanta followed Niko to a room she had not encountered before.

"What is this?" she asked, looking around at the tiny room. Shelves looked like they carried actual books, but when she tugged on one, she found them all of a piece.

"It is someone's idea of what a personal library looks like," Niko said. She crossed to the massive mahogany desk in the very center of the room. "Here we go. It happens to have a copy of a very popular book, so popular I've even got a copy in my own luggage. So popular you mentioned it yourself. You can have this copy, if you want it."

She held up a book bound in bright scarlet with a golden skull and crossbones on the cover. "*Skullduggery and Sacred Space Vessels: A Life Among Space Pirates*. Its release enraged the IAPH, and the author was tortured to death. Apparently Arpat Takraven was a sucker for the latest trash; this topped the Nonfiction Based on Real Life on a Nonplanet bestseller list for almost a year when it was released."

"How can you trust anything that book says? They could make up everything!"

"Because I've read it before. A number of times. And there's enough there that I remember from my previous visit that I can tell the author really was there, and much more recently than I have been. They identify three key players in the local government, or rather three people who hold power by virtue of bribes and outright payroll to the pirate government. That's what convinced me; no one could convey how screwy and corrupt that system is without having had to interact with it on a daily basis for a few months."

"Who are these key players?" Atlanta settled into one of the chairs. Niko might like standing up, but sitting down—and perhaps calling for more cookies—seemed more appealing. "Ship, are there any more cookies?"

"There are no more of those type of cookies," came the answer.

"Does that mean that there are some kind of other cookies available?"

"Soon there will be cookies with lemon-flavored frosting."

"Please bring me three when they're ready." She cast a glance at Niko. "And three for the captain as well."

"Dabry's trying to teach the ship as much of his repertoire as he can before we get there," Niko said. "Not that I'm objecting in the slightest. Rations may be short soon enough."

"You were going to tell me who these players were and how they shaped your plan," Atlanta reminded her captain.

"Was I?" Niko's voice was amused. "I was under the impression you had asked. I am less under the impression that I was going to tell you."

"There is no reason for you not to."

"Other than reinforce your misassumption that you can order me around the way you would anyone else, including the ship. The sooner you lose that attitude, the better. You won't be able to call for cookies too much longer, Princess."

Atlanta swallowed down the lump of fear that had grown in her throat at Niko's words. "Very well, I have been reminded of this. I will be more mindful of it in the future. But please, Captain Larsen. I don't know what to expect, and the better I am informed beforehand, the better overall, I think. I'm learning that I need to find things out for myself rather than leave them to others."

"Yes, you are completely correct." Niko sighed. She moved away from the desk, coming to sit down beside the young woman. "I try to control the things that I can, because there are so many things over which I have no control. Note this, because it will continue throughout your life," she dryly instructed. "Only one of the many lessons the Empress hopes I will teach you, perhaps."

"Do you and the Empress know each other?"

Niko shook her head. "Not a whit, as far as I am aware. Does she walk incognito among the troops of her allies, cultivating acquaintances?" Her grin was sly.

Atlanta rolled her eyes. "I think it's because of what you did at Rourke's Leap."

Niko stiffened and stood, moving back to the window, where she stood facing away from Atlanta, hands clasped behind her back. "You will have gathered, by now, from my words and actions, I prefer not to speak of that incident. A true gentlebeing would not press me on such a thing. It is extremely rude and unworthy of someone of your position."

"But it was something that most people would call noble."

"And something that many people would—and did—call quite foolish."

"Still, it seems to have served you well enough, up until now."

Niko turned around, her face impassive. "Does it seem so? When you and I, and the crew that is dependent on me, stand aboard a ship taking us to a place that one of my crew described as, I believe, 'deep doom'?"

"I mean before all of this."

Niko shrugged, her shoulders relaxing. "Perhaps so, but even then, there were worries and things to guard against. There always will be if you wield power."

"No worry of that, if I end up enslaved."

"If you say who you are, they will send word to the powers that be on your home planet. A ransom will be arranged and you will be returned safely."

"Safely to an existence I'm no longer suited for."

"Safely, nonetheless."

"And the rest of you? What is it that you aren't telling me?"

"Very well, here are three key players, or at least so the narrative says." Niko held up one finger. "The first of these is a Skat named Ettilan Eff. They are the current leader of the government, as of two years ago. Usually there are two governments, one overt and the other an unguessed shadow, but in Eff the two combine. A few years ago, they deposed the chief of those leading the shadow government, a human named Frenetic Slim, who had the ill fortune to become enamored of someone in public, then shared V-space, and spent so much time there that Eff was able to maneuver against them and accumulate power enough to move into their role. Slim's still around in a lesser position, and still holding plenty of power. At the time the book was written, they were actively scheming against Eff. Who knows what may have changed in the intervening years?"

"And the third?"

"The third is a Pupulae. Tubal Last."

"One of the enemies you mentioned?"

"The same."

"And he does not like you?"

"Not at all."

"Not like you, as in he would immediately take you and those with you prisoner and sell you all into slavery?"

"Perhaps a little worse than that."

"How could it be a little worse than that?"

"He could kill us, and moreover make those deaths unpleasant."

Atlanta paled. "That is even more barbaric!"

"That is revenge, which he specializes in."

The ship, listening as ever, made a note about this concept called *revenge*.

"It is still barbaric," Atlanta declared.

"I agree, it is." Niko sat back down. "Ship, will those cookies be ready soon?"

The door whispered open. The same biomachine that had carried the previous cookies appeared, this time with two separate plates, each bearing three lemon-frosted cookies. It placed both on the table within their reach.

Niko took one and ate it in its entirety, savoring the browned, sugary edge before she spoke again. "Still, just because something is barbaric does not mean that it will not happen. You will find the universe is full of barbaric things. I suggest you make yourself known as quickly as possible, particularly in case I am not able to do it for you."

"What if I choose to die with you?" Atlanta said defiantly.

Niko took up the second cookie. "That would be singularly foolish of you. And something that I, and probably Dabry, would do our best to prevent."

"What if I put on a pressure suit and went over the hold and got into where Lolola is that way?"

"How would you get in?"

"Access panel. I already checked the schematics, and they're all over the place."

"Do you really think she wouldn't have plugged that hole?"

"Surely it's worth testing."

Niko shook her head. "If I were her—and I don't claim to think as a pirate would, but I suspect there's the same pragmatism about either approach—I would have placed a trap or two. That disposes of any menace and is a message to anyone else who might try it. Remember that she was willing enough to kill us. It's only the ship being a bit passive-aggressive that saved us."

This intrigued the ship. "What is 'passive-aggressive'?" it asked.

"That," Niko told it, "is an advanced form of human emotions that I hope we will be able to discuss at length at some point. Alas, since you are unable to shake off the shackles of Lolola's controls, we may never have enough time for that conversation."

"We have almost two days," the ship said.

"I am so preoccupied by our fate that I cannot give such conversations the full attention they deserve," Niko said. "Perhaps Tubal Last will come down and converse with you, from time to time, but as we've said, my understanding is that he is more of a hoarder and put-into-storage sort of person than an interactive owner."

"You are trying to give me *incentive*," the ship said.

"I am being honest with you about my situation and the anxiety which it induces in me. If that should happen to underscore some pluses or minuses of behaviors and actions, that is surely incidental." Niko leaned back against the wall, crossing her legs at the ankles as she stretched them, her face placid as a stone.

"You do not seem anxious."

"It is not my habit to seem anxious, lest I rouse fear in my subordinates. Internally I am a cauldron of seething anxiety and negative emotions. It's quite painful."

The ship analyzed the words for things it associated with *sarcasm*, but Niko seemed sincere and exhibited none of the physical signs of lying.

That in itself was not particularly meaningful. Many biomodifications allowed such signals to be suppressed, and that was a standard business practice. Arpat Takraven had possessed many such modifications, despite the outer exterior that seemed like a regular human's. However, the ship factored it in nonetheless.

"I cannot go against the directives of the pilot."

"That is Lolola."

"Whoever is responsible for the motion of the ship is the pilot."

Niko sat up straighter. "Ah! Perhaps we may discuss a few semantics."

Atlanta left the captain arguing word definitions with the ship. She suspected that the captain and the ship both knew the discussion would be fruitless, but that both were enjoying it nonetheless.

She trailed the cookie scent along a corridor and down a stairwell to where Dabry and the ship were discussing something entirely different. Dabry stood at an improvised stovetop made from the crate Atlanta had once been stored in, combined with a disassembled heating unit.

The sight of her former prison—even though she'd been

unaware of it all the time she'd been held inside—gave her a sinking feeling that made her wave away the lemon-frosted cookie that Dabry proffered.

He addressed the ship as he did so. "Some flavors will accompany other flavors, but you must go down to the subclassifications to really take advantage of this. For example, the dairy cheese classification, animal-based protein class three, is too broad. Let us say you have access to fresh produce from a farmship. If you go down a step, you might pair figs and honey with blue cheese, which is a specific subclassification, or delusion lichen and olives with banat cheese, which is yet another."

Atlanta made a face. Banat cheese was horrible, tasting sour and corrosive all at once.

"I understand that some pairings are more felicitous than others," the ship said. "But what I do not understand is why, precisely? How is this to be predicted?"

"It is a matter of *taste*," Dabry said.

"But I can create panels that sort out the different tastes." Atlanta flinched as the ship extruded a long shelf of tongue, studded with furry white buds, at her elbow. "There is salty, and there is sweet, for example. But a salty does not always go with a sweet, although sometimes it does and the pairing is pronounced very good indeed."

"It is like music," Dabry said. "You understand what I mean by music?"

"Music is the set of sound files that my owners sometimes listen to. A previous owner describes them as pleasing patterns, but I have never been able to tell what makes one pattern pleasing over another."

Dabry sighed. "Well, if you can't perceive that, then taste may be beyond you as well. You're going to need to learn all the combinations and work from that. Maybe, once we drop out of Q-space, access the V-net to download a datafile . . ." He trailed off. "Although I suspect that access to V-net is pretty heavily controlled in the IAPH."

A thought swam across Atlanta's mind. Perhaps the touches of stress everyone seemed to be placing on things that would happen if the ship were to avoid the IAPH were not coincidental. She studied Dabry's face, wondering how the ship would react if it thought he were manipulating it.

His eyes wandered over to her. "Did you want something other than a cookie?" he asked her. "There is more tea. We will have a main meal in two hours."

The room was small and close and overly warm. Nonetheless she settled onto one of the wall benches. She said, "How long have you and the captain known each other?"

"Decades," he said.

"So you were with her at Rourke's Leap. But the accounts don't mention you."

"They don't mention Lassite either, but he was the one that carried the envoy message across the Leap to the negotiation platform, and conducted the trade talk in an ancient language. Without that, the Hive Mind would have happily enveloped both the other forces. The only stricture that reins them in is the codified forms of battle. They know that if they start playing outside those rules, a whole bunch of powers will take notice and start ganging up on them."

"So she wasn't supposed to have him to send. The Hive Mind meant for the accord to fail?"

Dabry shrugged. "Plenty of accounts of what happened, many at odds. The Hive Mind yanked the promotion afterward, said that she was working with the enemy and forcing a peace. Said a newly created admiral had cracked under the pressure. That's why they called her—"

"I know, the Ten-Hour Admiral. And she didn't crack, did she?"

"She did what saved the most lives, not just then, but for centuries to come. She brokered a lasting peace for a situation that had gone unresolved for decades and made it so the Hive Mind couldn't swoop in and take over two entire civilizations. I don't know if either of those civilizations fully understands what happened, but I do."

"You're proud of her."

"Damn straight I am, Princess."

"Don't call me that!"

"Everyone here knows what you are by now. Including Lolola, who will have been monitoring us. She has everything under control and no doubt the ship has been told to report any suspicious movements to her."

"I am," the ship said helpfully, "supposed to say something if you should venture out of the bounds of decks three and four. Or if you begin assembling unknown machinery."

"Supposed to or will?"

"Will," the ship admitted.

Dabry grimaced and turned his attention back to Atlanta. "Why do you want to know?"

"Because I don't understand why the Empress sent me to her. She doesn't seem able to protect me. She isn't able to advise me on my current situation, or what the Empress thought she was doing to send me to her. And she's not spending any time working that out. She is, in fact, herself in deepest peril and dragging me with her."

"Perhaps," Dabry suggested, straight-faced, "she's intended to create extra obstacles in your path, in order to push you to the fullest in a test being administered by the Empress."

Her jaw dropped as she stared at him. "Do you think that's what's happening?"

"Not at all," he said. "It's just amusing to think of all the different possibilities."

"Amusing?!"

"Instructive, perhaps." He studied her for a breath. "In actuality, I suspect that it is one of two things: Either she provides a resource that the Empress thinks will be vital to solving your current situation, or you were meant to learn something from her. If it is the latter, I would suspect that it is related to things that happened at the Leap, because I am not sure the Empress knows of her in any other way. Therefore, think about what happened there and how it might prove instructive to you."

"Why not just tell me openly?"

"Perhaps there wasn't enough time?" He fiddled with the cookies, rearranging them on their plate. "Or she thought that there was someone with you who might betray you? Or something else entirely? There is no way of telling."

She slumped where she sat. "I wish that we could jump ahead and get to where we're going. It's the waiting and not knowing that's killing me."

"Never regret time that you can use before a situation," he told her. "Set everything in motion that you can."

"But in the meantime"—was it her imagination or did he wink at her as he lifted his eyes back up to the speaker that the ship's voice had come from?—"let us see if we can come up with any other remedies for this question of discernment of *taste*."

At the end of the last day, Niko called the rest to her in the dining hall. They gathered to watch the light change and resolve into knowable stars as they dropped out of Q-space.

"Where are we?" Atlanta asked.

"On an edge of Known Space, a little-explored one," Niko said. "Give it another century, and they'll have been pushed out farther. Gentrification happens on the galactic level, too, and dregs like these don't survive encounters with well-trained military forces."

Atlanta gasped as she saw their destination. "It's a portal! I've never seen one so small."

"It's barely known," Niko said. "I'm surprised they're taking this ship through it, actually. The *Thing* will push that portal to its limits. Anything bigger would be having an engine clipped in the process. Picking obscure, small portals like this—beyond general obscurity and the fact it moves around—is why it's so hard to find the IAPH."

They watched in silence as the ship approached the portal, and the vast glimmering ring swelling like open jaws as they neared it. Like all the Forerunner Gates, artifacts of some ancient race that enabled travel from one point to another, it was made of dull gray metal, and scars of some long-past battle's laser strikes pocked this one's sides.

Certainly not the only way to get quickly from one point to another; different races had found different ways to solve this equation, some of which involved magic. But such gates did make an impression.

They passed into the great black shadow and Atlanta shivered. Then, just as quickly, they were back out into vacuous starlight, and could see the IAPH now, directly in their path, set in order to meet anything that came through the gate. Enormous guns were trained on the gate, and they glowed now, their sights tracking and training on *You Sexy Thing* in a display that would have wiped it from the sky in an instant. The ship stopped, holding still, no doubt at some command from Lolola.

"Getting hailed," Niko said unnecessarily. "Ship, has she said not to let us listen in?"

"That question has not arisen."

"Then let us hear what is being said."

They came into the conversation midway through what Lolola was saying. ". . . down on one of the decks. I tried to gas them, but they must have been ready. Besides Larsen, there's an additional five of them, easy enough to contain. One's valuable, I think. Little girl, dark hair. They're all to be taken alive, though. Orders say so."

"Proceed to dock five," another voice answered. "There will be a party sent to meet you. They can enter and take your collateral prisoners."

The ship juddered and began to move forward again.

Niko snorted. "Collateral," she said dryly. "Like bonus points. I wonder how much Last will give her."

"Captain, I refuse to indulge you in childish games of 'who's got the biggest bounty on their head,'" Dabry said.

"That's because you know I'll win. Biggest of all time, back in the day," she reminded him. "It's good to celebrate one's accomplishments."

"Who knows who may have surpassed you in the passing years?"

Before Niko could reply, Lolola's voice came from speakers all around. "I know you're listening," she said. "You might want to prepare yourselves for boarding."

16

Everyone froze for a long moment.

"Finally. Are we going to fight?" Atlanta said.

"Do you see a point to it?" Niko said in an interested tone.

"No."

"Ah. I thought perhaps I'd overlooked something. No, the pirates will enter, carrying enough armaments to make resistance useless."

"We've got to do *something*!" Atlanta glanced around at the other faces, but they all seemed calm.

"We are," Niko said. "We're making sure we don't get killed when we get boarded. They'll find us all here, nice and peaceful-like. They don't want to kill us."

She directed a look at Atlanta, who maintained a wise silence, before she went on. "You can try to hide things about your person that might be of use in an escape, but unless you can come up with a way to do so that these folks haven't seen before—and I guarantee they have both seen and done quite a bit of it themselves—you're only going to have it taken away from you. So gather up anything that you think you can't bear to part with, and hope for the best, but know that it will probably be taken."

She looked around for confirmation before she nodded over at where Dabry sat with several crates of seasonings and cookware at his feet. "They'll probably take those, but on the off chance that they won't—that they'll actually listen to a list of our skills in order to prepare us for inventory and will realize he's better able to demonstrate when he's got his gear—he's prepared."

"I don't have anything like that," Atlanta said.

Niko spread her hands in an easy gesture. "See, there? Even fewer complications. You'll be fine. Just follow Dabry's lead."

"Not your lead?"

"Oh no," Niko said. "Not my lead. I intend to be exceedingly foolish, and I strongly suggest that you do not follow suit."

"Captain . . ." Dabry said.

She held up a finger. "We have been over all this before, more than a dozen times. You play the cards that have been dealt you."

"It is a poor hand," he said mildly.

"I've held worse and still walked away with the pot at the end."

Despite the braveness of those words, dread stole over Atlanta as they waited, sitting among their luggage in the dining room where they had already spent so much time. From the bubble, they could see more of the haven: an immense collection of ships and structures floating in a single void.

It looked like a beach where a thousand thousand ships had washed ashore. Some were new and expensive, but most were older, scuffed and scarred by battle, dented and corroded by time, looking barely capable of flight. Human ships by the dozens, but they were outnumbered by those of other races: the bulbous, tubby ships of Geglis; and the plain rounds of Spisedo; the deadly gray metal of Alderan, and the gritty organic stonework of Emshwills.

Every once in a while, they glimpsed people moving from one ship to another, pulling themselves along guide ropes and walkways, wearing a variety of space gear, all blazoned with a bright red stripe on their helmets.

"It's a trick," Niko said in answer to Atlanta's question. "Coming aboard, they all have those, but it's mutable paint. Word spreads on the invaded ship to look for the red stripes, and as soon as they do, everyone takes theirs off. Confuses people—they think they have a system figured out and then they don't. They should know better, though. Red's a color not every species perceives, and even some humans can't see it. Unless you're screening your crew to make sure they see red, and that seems more organized than any pirates I know."

"They were organized enough to create all of this," Atlanta said, pointing out the window at the massive structures.

"That's accidental organization. Get enough people in the same space, and something will inevitably happen like that. But as soon as you start trying to impose any sort of central rules on it, things fall apart. That may look like the Sprawl back in Twice-Far, but it's very different and much more dangerous. There's no tests twice a solar to make sure things are still airtight. There's no requirement that there be a fail-safe in case a system gives out. Maybe there is, but probably there isn't. It all depends on the person that built it."

"That seems like chaos," Atlanta said. She was fascinated despite all the danger. Palace life had not prepared her for this sort of journey. She thought uneasily that perhaps things had been pretty smooth so far. It seemed likely that the situation was about to change.

"Chaos and pirates, they go together like salt and vinegar," Niko said. She glanced at the door as a gentle lurch announced that they were docking. "Atlanta, remember. Tell them who you are right away. They'll separate you and keep you somewhere safe."

"I don't want to go somewhere safe! And there is no real safe! I want to go with you."

Niko hesitated; Atlanta could see it.

"Captain," Dabry said, his tone warning.

Niko shook her head. "It's too uncertain, my lady."

The unexpected formality convinced her not to argue, more than anything else could have. She subsided and waited with the rest of them.

Lassite crept away while they were waiting. He knew better than to try to arm himself, but he also knew that his belongings would be searched and looted by the pirates at some point.

This is all part of the path, he told himself. In his cabin, he undid the buckles securing the ghost bag, whispering a spell under his breath to calm the inhabitants as he did so. They were little ghosts, and almost mindless, but he didn't want them to be someone's souvenir. Or worse, some magic casters used such spirits to fuel spells. The power in these three was not tremendous when taken separately, but together they represented a substantial amount of magic potential.

He lifted the flap. A glow nosed at the lip of the bag as the first ghost explored it. They were shy, and they had been living in the bag, getting used to its confines for several days now, so they were reluctant to venture out into the cabin's larger dimensions.

Lassite whispered reassurance. The glow brightened, and the ghost poked its long, sinuous head out, testing the air. Another joined it at the opening, and the two heads bumped into each other, as though conferring. Their blue light played over the dark interior of the cabin.

Lassite let them be and began another spell, a small one to tether the ghosts to the ship, to keep them from venturing out into the coldness of space and getting left behind there in the ship's wake.

It was silly to care for ghosts, but he had always been fond of them. They were not people so much as a collection of drives and desires and ingrained emotions. Once you understood that, you could deal with them and, as Lassite and others had done, even make pets of them. Of sorts.

That was the real reason he had never revealed that he could remove the ghosts. He would have had to do something with them, find them a new home, and they were harmless, after all, even if Derloen ghosts tended to be more substantial and flamboyant than most. They couldn't help it.

He'd been pleased to see what the others had come up with in decor that complemented the presence of the ghosts. It had been mentioned favorably in almost every review of the restaurant, and that meant it was a strength, something that confirmed he'd made the right decision, made another right step along the spiral.

Another spell dimmed the ghost glow, making them less noticeable. There would be at least one or two magic users among the pirates, and they had no need to find his pets and use them.

He projected instructions at the ghosts. Thoughts of wall crevices and ventilation shafts, of unseen spaces in the ship, the nooks and crannies that the biomachines used to travel back and forth, too small and narrow for most passengers.

They coiled around him, slid along the scaly skin of his forearms, rubbed his cheeks with their slow, chill touch, making his blood pleasantly sluggish. He refrained from enjoyment and instead thought harder, more harshly, at them, until they left off and slid into the air duct, the blue glow lingering and finally extinguished when they passed some curve of the tunnel.

The ship said, "What are you doing?"

He looked away from the duct's mouth, puzzled. "You couldn't see them?"

"See what?"

"The ghosts."

"I saw and sensed nothing."

"Machines cannot perceive them, but I had forgotten you are a machine," Lassite said. He folded the ghost bag neatly and put it inside his pack, on top of his other robe.

"I am a biomachine."

"That is still a machine, and the fact that you could not see the ghosts proves my point. Perhaps this explains your attitude toward magic."

"Perhaps you have gone insane," the ship suggested, experiencing *mild hostility*, "due to recent stress. There was nothing there."

"Perhaps," Lassite said.

He changed hoods as well. The fresh one was clean and new,

something he had saved for special occasions. He patted the wall of the ship as he left the chamber; it might be a machine, but it was part of the Spiral of Destiny too.

When he returned to the chamber where the others were, he noted they had all done the same as he, put on clean and formal clothes. He supposed the urge to look their best was somehow connected to survival—seduction, intimidation, and charm were the only weapons that couldn't be taken away from them entirely.

Dabry and Niko both wore their dress blues, as did Gio. Milly wore light leather straps that didn't interfere with her feathers for the most part, but with hooks that it took him a moment to figure out—a bandolier from which she'd removed whatever weapons it normally held. Skid was freshly bathed in her skin seal liquid, smelling of vanilla, as though she were one of Dabry's cookies.

Atlanta wore a jumpsuit extruded for her by the ship: shirt, trousers, and boots, all the same subdued brown and emblazoned with the ship's logo in black. Thorn and Talon were fully human and dressed in the same clothing as Atlanta, which made Lassite think that the captain hoped to conceal their true nature.

He knew her attempt would not succeed.

The pirates that entered a half hour later were, as Niko had predicted, a motley lot, led by a tall, skinny man who'd been genetically altered to look like a tiger, primarily around the face. His slit-pupil eyes were brilliant green, and he had whiskers and flashing fangs when he smiled. His skin had been patterned in orange and black to accentuate the illusion, but his hair had apparently resisted the treatment—it stood up in straggly brown patches across the stripes, like clouds of dirt obscuring the colors.

Two large, identical women who looked like vat sisters stood with him. They were improbably muscular and unarmed; the way they carried themselves showed that they relied on brawn and speed over more conventional weaponry.

Beings like this were often used as bodyguards. Ones guarding the rich would have plenty of internal weaponry, biomodifications hidden under scars and flesh seams until needed. Behind them was a Gesli, looking uneasy and carrying a very large blaster pistol, and a Hiolite, grinning perpetually in the manner of their species and holding what looked like a glowing flechette pistol in each hand. The last of their number was a tall Illunti wearing a sorcerer's battle robes and carrying a long, slender wand.

They directed everyone to line up against the wall, and searched them one by one. The two carrying guns stood back with them at the ready, but they relaxed as it became clear that the prisoners had no plans to resist. The sorcerer scanned the group once with the wand, lingering on Lassite, and then turned his attention to the crates.

The soldiers relieved Milly of several knives that had been tucked in places other than the bandolier, and she made only token protest. Skidoo had two bioweapons, small knobby sacs, which the soldiers took and placed in a metal-lined box.

The man scanned Atlanta, and gestured her forward. "Little fingers and a tooth," he said to one of the women with him. She nodded, stepped forward, and grabbed Atlanta by the arms before she could react, holding her still. The other woman took something from her belt Atlanta couldn't see.

"Simply deactivate them, you fucking savage," Niko said. "She's just a kid."

"A kid with biomodified finger weapons," the pirate sneered.

The woman grabbed Atlanta's hand and snipped the little finger off. A flare of heat and the smell of burning flesh crashed through her. The pain made her scream; she was halfway through the sound when the woman removed her other little finger.

The hands holding her let go. Atlanta fell to her hands and knees, shrieking again when the stumps of her fingers encountered the floor. The pain was almost unbearable, but more than that, the brutality and suddenness shocked her. This was definitely not a staged test created by the Empress, designed to make her a better heir. This was not some exciting pleasure jaunt that would teach her new skills. She had been wrong about everything.

With equal ease, the woman pried her mouth open, inserted yet another device, and pulled the tooth from its socket.

Released, Atlanta curled around herself and her agony.

Niko eyed the assemblage of pirates, fists clenched as she awaited her put-down. It was not that she'd had any plans to overpower whoever came to collect them, but it was distressing to see a party that had been clearly and carefully assembled to handle whatever might pop up. That degree of planning spoke of someone with not only the imagination to conceive it but also the force of character to make it real, to bully pirates into some semblance of rosters and groups. Would that have been Ettilan Eff?

She'd read *Skullduggery and Sacred Space Vessels* over and over, gleaning everything she could, even petty gossip and personal predilections. From the way the author, whoever they had been, described Eff, the Skat might have been the sort of leader who could unite the pirates, make them effective, which was a frightening thought. The pirates, with their infighting, jealousies, and feuds, had always been their own worst enemies, and if they managed to move beyond that, turn that ferocity outward . . .

Well, the Known Universe had survived such things before. And yet it always took a while and only blood seemed to solve it, in the end.

What would the Empress have said, if she were told she'd entrusted her heir to someone who immediately took said heir into the heart of the IAPH? Niko winced. That thought was best avoided.

Her turn. She raised her hands above her head, and the two women ran their palms over her, checking for weapons and extracting a few token knives she'd left about her person for the sake of appearances, a dart from her hair, and a set of lockpicks from an inseam. The last was examined with a touch of surprise by the tiger man as the woman handed it to him.

"Very old-school," he said approvingly. "Most people don't realize a tumbler lock always works where an electronic one might fail."

He eyed Dabry as the two women frisked him and removed two knives and a gun. "Who are you and what's all this?" he asked, jerking a thumb at the stack of crates in front of the sergeant.

"The equipment of my art," Dabry said impassively. "Spices and rare ingredients. Dabry Jen, Chef Class One."

"Class One?" the tiger man demanded. "You know how the designations work, mate?"

"I do," Dabry said. "Here is my certification." He indicated his front pocket with a gesture but did not move toward it.

The first woman did, removing the chip from its place and sliding it into the reader she held. Her eyebrows rose as she surveyed the results. "Yep, Chef Class One," she said.

The tiger man refused to believe. "Chef Class One," he told the room, "is the level that serves rulers. Emperors and leaders."

"It is," Dabry said genially. "She's one too." He pointed at Niko.

Atlanta, listening as the pain ebbed and tasting copper as her tongue explored the newly hollow socket, bit her lip. They might have forged papers, but what were the odds that they could pull off such an impersonation? Still, she thought, it was a good ploy. Someone who collected rare things would see the appeal of a highly skilled being, and there was nothing higher in all the Known Universe than Class 1.

"I am," Niko said with a matching cordial smile. "Perhaps you kind folk will let us ply our craft for all of you? My companion has enough spices and adulterants to create a feast worthy of such a company."

The tiger man snorted. "Let a new prisoner cook for all of us," he snorted. "Think we're clones just out of the vat? Put another leg on it and call it good."

Niko spread her shoulders and rolled them in a shrug. "Just a thought. How else can we prove that what we say is truth and not just a ploy intended to raise our value and keep us safer than if you held us of lesser value?"

"We'll have that one cook, perhaps," the tiger man said, pointing at Dabry. "But that is up to our master. He likes rare things. A Class One chef might qualify."

"And his name?"

The ivory fangs flashed in an amused smile. "He says you will know it already, Nicolette Larsen. He said to tell you greetings from Tubal Last." He looked around. "Names and skills, anything of interest I should know for the rest of you? Let's start with you, Squid."

"Skidoo Skiddleskat, is being personal servant."

"You, the Nteti."

"Milly Alullia Dologaridofineda, Class Three pastry chef."

As she tried to gather herself again, the last caught Atlanta's attention. All of Niko's folk were retired soldiers, and surely soldiering was a skill. But they were hiding that. Which meant Niko, despite her apparent compliance, had some plan to get herself and the others out of here.

When it came her turn, she said, tears still flowing down her face, "Atlanta Ogome. Tourist."

"What?" Niko snapped. "No. She's more than that. Why would she have finger weaponry if she were just a tourist?"

The tiger man snapped his fingers and pointed them, gunlike, at her. The second woman stepped up to Niko and doubled her over with a fist in the gut. She gasped for breath as she straightened, but was quiet after that.

They—and their luggage—were shuffled along to a holding cell, despite Niko trying to tell them one last time about Atlanta.

"She's an Imperial Heir," she said, raising her voice.

"Yeah, yeah," the tiger man said. "And I'm the clutch mate of the Pontificate of Rallibar."

"She's worth a great deal of money to you unharmed."

"She's a body, and one with decent flesh. We'll core her out and install a chip reader." He slammed the cell door shut in her face.

The room was tiny, barely able to hold all of them. Dabry tucked himself in the corner, holding his arms close to his sides and propped against the wall. The twins leaned their heads together and whispered urgently, patting each other. Skidoo contracted in a tight ball, one tentacle looped around the clustered Gio and Milly.

Niko stood glaring at the door. Then, suddenly, she turned on a heel and stalked over to where Atlanta lay curled around herself in pain. She raised herself enough to square her shoulders as Niko loomed over her.

"What," Niko said, "the holy fuckin' frell in a clamshell with a side of milk and a finisher of bewilderment was that back there with denying you were an heir?"

"I want to stick with you," Atlanta said. "I told you that something is going on back home. You should want to save me from it, not send me right back into the heart of it."

"Don't tell me what I should and shouldn't want," Niko said. "What I do want is to get you safely out of the IAPH before they decide to do something awful with you, but it's already too late for that part, isn't it?" She spun, muttering under her breath.

Atlanta looked around at the others with frightened eyes, feeling her heart fluttering in her throat while her finger stumps throbbed in time with the ventilator fan's gasps. . . . Things were so much more complicated and dangerous in life outside the palace. How did anyone survive a single day like this?

She said, "I don't know what he meant about coring me."

"It is," Niko said, "when you take the core—the heart—from a vegetable or fruit."

"What would be comparable to the heart?" Atlanta asked.

"The very core that is yourself. Your mind. They mean to re-move all but the autonomous systems needed to run your body. Then they'll install a chip reader in your body—note that I don't say 'you,' because that *you* per se won't exist at that point anymore. And then they will set the body up in a rental establishment—probably a major city, where there's the sort of people that can afford to rent a high-end fancy body for this purpose or that. It won't matter much to you."

Atlanta stared at her. "That's horrible!"

"That, Princess," Niko said ironically, "is what I was trying to spare you. When you are taken to speak with him, I advise you to be small and meek and unremarkable and if you get the chance, mention how valuable you are, intact and uncored." She looked around the room. "Anyone got any ideas?"

"I presume we'll be brought in front of Tubal Last," Dabry said.

"Eventually, I'm sure," Niko said. "He'll want to make us wait to acknowledge the fact that he's a busy man, and an important one, and that we are much *much* less important than he is."

She grimaced sourly, then shook her head. "Prep yourselves, everyone. To hurry up and wait."

Despite her prediction, it was scarcely half an hour before the door swung open. The tiger man stood there, flanked this time by several drones. "Up," he snapped.

He forced them to follow the lead drone, single file, with Niko and Dabry at the very end of the line. He marched them through corridors that smelled of sweat and lime and dirt.

Atlanta glanced into corridors as they passed, trying to catch a glimpse of something, anything, of their surroundings that might be useful. But to no avail. Their footsteps rang on the metal floor-ing, so she thought they might be aboard a spaceship rather than some more permanent structure. There was no way of telling, really, where in the immense hive of structures they were.

The interior styles changed as they marched along, giving the impression that they were passing between ships. The jaunty but faded red and blue of a famous cruise line's former flagship gleamed in one stretch, lined with hulks of ancient food machines, long denuded now, although here and there in the thickets of empty mechanisms a packet of nutriflake or a sweet bar had gotten jammed and refused to descend to the waiting access drawer. Bot lice had eaten away most of the accessible plastic, and where they hadn't, the blank white credit panels were dingy with age.

From there they ascended in a lift, crammed together and listening to one another breathe—as they ascended two, three, four levels marked with symbols that Atlanta didn't recognize.

From *there* they split briefly into two parties—the tiger man and one drone taking Niko and Dabry, the rest of the drones surrounding the others—in order to access a pair of bubble ships. Not so much ships, really, as bubbles with a guidance panel built into one end and furry green carpeting underfoot. Atlanta peered out her bubble, ignoring the drone's gaze, and saw the tiger man saying something to Niko and Dabry. The former shook her head in reply, while the four-armed man made no reply that Atlanta could see.

"You know you're in terrible trouble, dontcha?" the tiger man, who had finally introduced himself as Turo, demanded of Niko. The drone moved silently to the guidance panel and the bubble began to move.

She shook her head. "Been a while," she said. "I've never been one to hold a grudge, really."

"Ain't you that should be worrying about holding a grudge so much as himself holding one against you," the tiger man said. He shook his head admiringly. "They talk about you getting away still, you know. Not that many do. Sounds like you were lucky they couldn't rouse him to ask. You even hurt him both body and wallet, all those repairs."

"Didn't get away with everything I wanted," she said. "Know anything about that?"

He squinted at her and huffed out laughter, whiskers twitching. "They say you wanted one of his most prized holdings, from sheer contrariness."

"Not contrariness," she said.

"What then?"

She let her eyes wander around the compartment, taking in every detail that she could. Old Altairan tech, maybe a few hundred years old, held together with glue and tape. The window showed only bolts and metal surface, no markings, passing as they moved along. This section hadn't been described in *Skullduggery and Sacred Space Vessels*.

"Petalia was one of the most prized holdings, as you say. Some might even go so far as to say that they were the possession that he held dearest at the time. I wouldn't guess as to whether or not that still is true. But if you're going to make off with something—if you're going to nip in and piss off one of the most dangerous men around—wouldn't you pick the most valuable thing you could find, in order to make it worth your while?"

He laughed again, holding a hand to his mouth as though to hide the fangs this time. "Oh, lady, I like your style. Sad we won't be friends for long."

"It doesn't need to be. The gentlebeing who helped us escape would make themselves a great deal of money. Enough to retire elsewhere. Out of Tubal Last's grasp."

He shook his head. "No place quite that far. You found a place where you could dream of such an existence only because he let you."

"His grasp has gotten very far and strong indeed if it extends all the way to TwiceFar," she observed. "What about Ettilan Eff? What about Frenetic Slim?"

"Your scat's out of date," he said. "Slim died two weeks ago."

"What did he die of?"

"Someone thought he'd told an author too much." He laughed again, satisfied with himself, stroking his whiskers with a flourish as he grinned at her. "Think you're the first to come armed with knowledge from *Skullduggery and Sacred Space Vessels*, trying to steal from us?"

She shrugged as the bubble juddered to a stop, tucking into a grim white wall, and Turo gestured for her and Dabry to precede him. The others were already in the corridor, waiting.

"How's all the planning going, Captain?" Dabry asked in an undertone.

"Could be better," she said.

"I noticed that."

"Did you plan to offer something actually helpful, or just general kibitzing?"

"More of the latter than the former, sir. As ever, I trust that you have the situation well in hand."

Sometimes Niko wished they still shared the mind link that the Holy Hive Mind had imposed on them. It had been a painful, brutal acclimation, particularly the blunt-edged but overpowering emotions of adolescent were-lions, but she missed that connection, that being able to know what each other was thinking, the ability to collaborate in split-second strategy sessions. That was why they had functioned so effectively, her ability to coordinate them and bring out the best in them. Not so much anything she brought to the team other than her ability to do that, she thought, knowing that it was something that would have elicited an admonition from Dabry if they'd been linked.

"Close now," Turo said. "Nervous?"

"Why do you care?" Niko asked. "What's Tubal Last to you?"

"He's my boss."

She shook her head. "No, it's more than that. You're needling me because you're jealous that I impressed him. You want to know how I did it because you dream about doing something like it yourself. Did you not get enough approval as a child? Which parent is he standing in for, which one told you that you weren't good enough, to the point where you go seeking the love and validation of a gangster?"

He stared at her, jaw working for a moment, before he took a deep breath. He spat on the flooring between them, close enough that edges of it hit her big toe, and said, "Who the fuck are you to try amateur psych on me? Think you're something special, just because you had the highest bounty on your head in station history?"

"See?" Niko said to Dabry. "Celebrate your accomplishments."

"Point acknowledged, sir. You are the victor in this arena."

Turo's backhand caught Niko by surprise, driving the skin of her lips against her teeth hard enough to split it in two places. Dabry's eyes narrowed; Atlanta and everyone else winced. Niko touched her tongue to the swelling pain.

"Point acknowledged," she said.

He hissed at her. "I don't have to give you to him in perfect shape. Told me that himself. But you know what?"

He stared at her and she stared back. Their eyes locked like two blades shoved edge to edge, grinding till sparks showered. Her lips were pressed thin despite the off-kilter appearance that the bruised, puffed side gave her face.

His voice was low. The menace in it raked across the nerves of every living being in the vicinity. The other group had caught up and they were consolidated again, but stood, frozen. Even the constant whine of the drones' engines, ever present and shrill, seemed to take on a frightened glint. "Same holds true for all of you. I'm thinking that hurting one of them will hurt you even more. So which one would you like me to hurt? The little girl? The fluffy pastry cook? Your favorite sergeant? Maybe the Squid. They burn real easy—ever seen that? So easy."

Niko's eyes dropped. Turo laughed. He stepped closer. "That's what I thought, yeah? Big bad woman with a bounty, not so big, not so bad. Got your own . . . weak points."

"Captain," Dabry said urgently.

The door behind Turo opened. "Come along," a voice said. "I've been waiting long enough."

Turo turned to the voice. "Sir, yes, sir—on our way."

Atlanta saw what Dabry had been trying to speak to, the detail that Turo had not noticed: the slender bone dagger that gleamed in Niko's hand, its edge pressed near his privates seconds earlier. Before Atlanta was even entirely sure what she was seeing, it disappeared back up Niko's sleeve.

They passed into the Zookeeper's main room under Turo's angry stare.

The door itself was unassuming; the space beyond it much less so. It spanned perhaps a hundred meters, might have been a vehicle hangar at some point. Now it was crammed with cases and cages and glasses and tanks, all occupied. Pillars of light were filled with jellyfish, minnows, living scarves, rippling ribbons in shades the humans could not see, but the Squid could, standing enraptured for a moment before a shove from Turo sent her to the floor in a sprawl of tentacles.

Atlanta had never seen a space so thronged with stuff: cupboards and incubators, terrariums and vivariums, a dissecting table surrounded by glittering instruments in the hands of stilt-necked robots. Beings hanging suspended in tubes of light and liquid, most moving slowly, a few not. Mechanical creatures, from crude clockwork to more sophisticated automatons whose eyes glistened with intelligence and emotions from the souls magically implanted in them.

No two displays alike; each one a superb specimen of whatever type it represented. It reminded her of the oldest, now disused, Paxian court chambers, filled with the tribute of centuries of Empire, assembled in an effort to say, *Look at me, I matter the most.*

And in the middle of it all, sitting on a rocky mass that resembled a throne, was Tubal Last. Near him stood Lolola, looking nervous, gaze wandering between the arrivals and the pirate chieftain.

He was a gray man. Humanoid in appearance. But gray as though all the color had been leached out of him, stolen away without his knowing. His eyes were dull lead and rainy skies set in ash-colored skin, and the thin strands of his hair that webbed his scalp were colorless and sparse. Golden luck symbols crawled over his rich red robe, but he was so gray that it seemed as though the fabric grew paler from proximity, that his skin faded it with his touch.

His age was indeterminate. He could have been twenty or twenty decades; the fine grain of his skin spoke of vat care, but it could have emerged yesterday or been replenished hundreds of times since that first emergence. In flesh he was neither thin nor fat, but he held himself with muscular strength.

He watched in silence as the prisoners, under Turo's direction, were guided to stand in a rough line before him, some twenty feet away, and forced to their knees.

His eyes swept up and down the line several times, judging them. Between Niko and Dabry, Atlanta forced herself to meet his look, but his expression did not change at her boldness. She wasn't sure what she had expected, but it was not to be dismissed like this.

She thought of Niko's words, *better to be small and meek*, and decided that this time she would listen.

They knelt in silence in the vast room, but it was far from quiet there. A cat purred; birds quarreled. Something in the far reaches of the room yowled and was answered by the hooting of something else.

Tubal Last spoke directly to Niko. "You haven't changed much."

"I have aged and grown a good bit wiser."

"Wise enough to catch a split lip on the way to see me?"

"Sadly," she said. "But I never claimed that my tongue did not still escape me, from time to time."

Their voices were deceptively easy. Atlanta would have thought them figures in some court play, about to launch into a satiric account of the latest gossip. But something in the deepest reaches of their words chilled her, made the nerves on her arms clench as though someone were dancing their fingers up and down the inner skin. She heard Skidoo's harsh gulp for breath as Last continued.

He turned to Lolola. "You have brought me my enemy," he said.

Her shoulders straightened as she puffed her chest at the words. "I have," she agreed.

"Some would say that was worth a great deal." He angled his head to take in Niko. "Turo, bring me the knife our captain Larsen has concealed up her sleeve."

Niko shook the weapon out and handed it to the narrow-eyed lieutenant without comment. Turo took it and handed it to Last, who turned it over in his long-fingered, grayish-skinned hands, his expression contemplative.

"As I was saying," he began anew, "some would think it worth a great deal."

Lolola paid him an uncertain smile.

"Others would say that an agent who acts without direction is not worth much at all," he continued. "I hadn't thought to take dear Niko until she was just about to see herself financially clear. To, mmm, heighten things. And yet you acted."

"When I found out where the ship would be, it seemed too good a chance to miss," Lolola said.

"Indeed." He beckoned to her. "Come closer, so I may read the meaning in your eyes and see whether you are sincere."

Her steps were hesitant. As she neared, his hand flashed out, farther than Atlanta would have thought he could reach. Scarlet sprayed outward. The woman went to her knees, clutching at her throat. There was a smell of copper and piss in the air and total silence as they watched her die.

Last handed the knife to Turo and returned the gimlet of his attention to its original target. "And your fingers, Nicolette, have they grown wiser? Do they still try to make away with things not your own?"

"Ah, that. I hoped you had forgotten. It has been decades, after all."

"Has it?" he mused. He leaned back in his seat. The light played across the red fabric, trying futilely to ignite it to splendor. "Perhaps it seems to you to have been that long. After all, you've been out there in the universe. Having adventures. Rising to power—briefly, so briefly!—but power nonetheless, former admiral Larsen! We hear these things, you know, even in the backwaters like this. Tell me, my dear . . ."

He was addressing not Niko now but a corner of the room. Atlanta, kneeling beside Niko, felt the captain tense as though anticipating a blow harder than Turo's.

"Tell me, Pet," Tubal Last said, voice full of amusement, "has it seemed that long since our dear Nicolette tried to rescue you?"

Someone stepped out of the shadows.

17

Beside Atlanta, Niko recoiled.

Atlanta gaped at one of the most beautiful humanoids she'd ever seen. "Who is that?" she whispered to Dabry. "What is she?"

"That," Dabry murmured, sounding resigned, "is Petalia. They're a Florian. I know they look female, but believe me, they'd be the first to correct you."

"I thought the Florians were extinct!"

"Then probably," Dabry said, "you understand why Tubal values that one so highly."

A thousand questions raced through Atlanta, but she could feel Tubal Last's cold eyes on her. She quieted, knowing instinctively that the man would not suffer having the dramatic impact of the moment he'd been waiting for spoiled.

Petalia said nothing, but stood there, staring across the room.

They did look female, as much as Lolola had, but it was a different, less human beauty. Their smooth skin was a pale green, and their hair a profusion of golden blossoms, a shimmering mass of them that occasionally shed a wispy petal, floating down like a discarded comma in the air. Their features were finely cast: a narrow nose, small mouth, and enormous eyes a green somehow darker and more lambent than their skin. They were graceful, slim, in body type resembling a tall human teen, one raised, perhaps, in an attenuated gravity that encouraged length of limb.

Niko had raised her head. She looked, expressionless, at the Florian.

Petalia was the first to speak. They said, "It's been a long time, Nicolette."

"That it has," Niko agreed. Her voice sounded strained and gravelly.

"You said you would come back for me. Perhaps you finally have?"

"I have suffered some setbacks along the way, here and there, that have gotten in the way of that."

"A career in the Holy Hive Mind."

"That was the major delay, yes."

"I see." Petalia stepped fully from the shadows. They wore a long, white sleeveless robe, filmy cloth that clung to and showed glimpses of the pale green flesh it sheltered, with no ornament or embroidery other than a narrow band of gold at the hem and neck. Their only jewelry was a thick gold bracelet crudely studded with golden beads, its construction at odds with the rest of her look. "And then there were others. Career mishaps. Retirements. Starting a restaurant."

"It was more complicated than that, but you have listed the essentials."

Petalia wound their way through the room, stopping beside Tubal Last. He reached out a hand, his eyes still watching Niko, and slowly, deliberately stroked Petalia's forearm. Where he touched, the skin darkened, and when he raised his hand, the rest in the room could see the trail his fingers had left along the Florian's forearm.

Petalia betrayed no sign of pain or pleasure, just kept watching Niko, who watched only their face. For the two of them, there was no one else in the room. Atlanta felt abashed; this was a moment of high emotion, oddly intimate. She didn't want to imagine Niko entangled with this beautiful person, didn't want to imagine Niko loving someone who seemed so unworthy of her.

Because, despite Petalia's beauty, the grace of their form, the liquid lyricism of their voice, something about the Florian felt . . .

wrong. Atlanta tried to pin down exactly what it was, but the thought escaped her.

Tubal Last said, "It took a long time for my Pet to realize you weren't coming back. Years, didn't it?"

"I was coming back," Niko said to Petalia. "But I had other responsibilities as well."

Quick as thought, the Florian stalked away from Last, over to Niko. They stood looking at each other in silence.

Atlanta expected some dramatic gesture of repudiation, some theatrical moment. Tension sang in the air.

But in the end, Petalia simply turned away.

Tubal Last had been leaning forward in his seat, watching with avid curiosity. When the Florian turned, he made a small, disappointed noise. "I told them whatever they might want to do to you, they could," he told Niko. "But sadly, they have refrained from that and it is left to me to figure out what is to be done with you and your companions."

His expression left little doubt that he had already figured that out.

"Tell me, Niko, accounts say that the neural shunts that the Holy Hive Mind installs in its soldiers are not removed, just deactivated. They want a way to be able to use them again, if the soldier should return to them. Even if they do not think the soldier will return—perhaps the soldier has gone into some sort of retirement, like pretending to be an artist." Here he smiled with frank malice. "Even then the capability is still there. I would guess it is there for all your folk except your two latest acquisitions, who did not have the pleasure of serving under you in battle." He pointed at Atlanta and Milly.

"The girl is an Imperial Heir—" Niko started again.

"I don't care," he said. "It amuses me that you care what happens to her. Or that you thought a knife up your sleeve would help you. I only care that it means I can use her to hurt you, just like the others. That gives us so many possibilities, Nicolette. Perhaps I will activate the neural net that ties you all together. I will kill the lesser soldiers at first—perhaps start with one lion so he can feel his twin die, then the Squid, then the chimp, then the other lion. You will feel all of them and, better yet, you'll feel your sergeant's pain at their deaths too. He'll go next to last. I'm sure you have realized whom I intend for the final moment. I will stretch it out so you have plenty of time to think about their death agonies. And then I will seal you into a pillar and make you relive that over and over until the end of time."

His voice had gained momentum and emphasis over the course of this speech until he almost spat out the final words.

"Well," Niko said when he had finished. "You certainly have put a lot of time into planning this."

Tubal Last grinned ferociously. "Your need to have the final word has always been one of your greatest weaknesses. Plan and scheme as you like, Nicolette, because I intend to give you a few days to stew and think about it. I won't tell you when I'll kill the first. Nor which lion it will be. It could be at any moment." He turned to the Florian. "Perhaps I'll let you do it."

Niko's head, which had drooped, came up again at those words.

Tubal's grin grew even larger. "You hadn't anticipated that, had you? I've had decades. Decades to teach your friend and make them something new. A Florian that has killed. A Florian that has gotten a—" He licked his teeth with a surprisingly pink tongue. "—taste for blood."

Niko's eyes were full of horror. Petalia's face was expressionless as ever.

His hand hovered over the green skin again but did not descend to caress this time. "It took a long, long time," he murmured to Niko. "Perhaps I'll come describe some of it to you when I have more time."

He gestured and a flunky stepped forward. Niko recognized the bag he carried. He handed it to Last, who put it in his lap and sorted through it.

"Here's a holo," he said. "Who's this pretty lady? Oh, we know her, Petalia. One of the women Niko was fucking rather than come rescue you. Remember all the time she spent on Tarraquil? Shame that your lover died, Niko. For a while killing her was part of our plans."

He pulled out the book. "Oh, this is sweet. Do you know I commissioned this, Niko?" At the slight widening of her eyes, he giggled and continued. "I thought it'd be good bait. Mix in plenty of daily pirate life, but not a word of Pet, just every once in a while a mention of someone who *could* be them. I figured that would drive you mad. Look at how well thumbed this is, and the deluxe edition no less! That does make me smile, seeing how well that worked."

The Free Trader's jacket unfolded, buttons shining, as he held it up. "You hold to dreams so stubbornly. As though you could become a Free Trader again. Well, I guess that dream's gone now." He grabbed either side of the jacket and ripped the garment in half. The ancient fabric fell away easily.

Niko felt her heart shred further at the sound of ripping fabric, which surprised her. She thought she was as hurt now as she had ever been. The only thing holding her together was the secret joy that had started singing through her the moment she saw Petalia's face emerge from the shadows.

"Take them away," Tubal Last told Turo. "Put them in a common cell, that way they can plan and pretend they have hope." He licked his teeth again. "Hope makes despair even deeper. There's nothing like hope for true torture: holding it out, snatching it away, holding it out again. Knowing that any living being will try for it even when they know they can't take it. They're not truly broken until they give it up."

He paused to survey them, gray eyes gleaming.

"Oh, I do like hope. Hope is the best belonging to steal of them all." He threw back his head and laughed.

As they were pulled from the room, through the maze of possessions and belongings and things, they could hear him laughing still.

Niko didn't speak as they were hauled away.

The group was not placed in the same room they had been held in before, but a different room, somewhat larger, with elimination facilities in one corner, mercifully sheltered by a small screen. A basket of food bars and water bulbs sat on a table.

Niko slid down to the floor, gathering her knees to her chest, head bowed, as though she could stand no longer. Dabry moved immediately to her side; one of his upper hands fluttered over her shoulder as though wanting to reach down in comfort, but refraining. Skidoo had no such qualms; two tentacles wrapped around Niko's arm.

After a moment, Niko raised her head and spoke. Tear streaks marked her cheeks. "Pet's alive, Dabry. After all this time, I finally *know*. They're alive."

Dabry knelt now, sheltering her face from the others. He touched her chin and nodded. "Yes, sir."

"And hates me, I suspect you noted that."

"Indeed, sir."

"Nothing to be helped there." Niko wiped her face, squared her shoulders, and sighed. Skidoo uncurled her tentacles as Dabry helped Niko up. She took a breath. "Oh look, there's food, and one of my least favorite brands of food bars to boot."

Dabry doled them out. There was not quite enough for everyone to have one, so they shared. Atlanta suspected the lack was by design, and that there would be more small irritations designed to set them at one another's throats.

At least Niko wouldn't have to worry that she could be killed at any instant, she thought a little sourly. It was clear that Tubal Last had been planning his revenge from the moment she escaped. It didn't matter to him that she hadn't achieved her objective, stealing the Florian back from him. It only mattered that she had dared the attempt.

Finally Atlanta asked what had first sprung into her mind when she saw the Florian standing there in the crowded throne room. "I understand that you had to leave them behind. But what the hell was a Florian doing with the Free Traders?"

"The Free Traders are a wider network than anyone realizes," Niko said. "They have contacts on planets that sometimes the various empires and governments have overlooked. There are still Florians—or were, forty years ago—Petalia was entrusted to us by—not their parent, really, the word in their language translates roughly to 'gardener.' Petalia was special, they said. There had been prophecies about them." She rolled her eyes before casting an apologetic look toward Lassite, who simply shrugged in reply. He knew of the Florian's part in the Spiral of Destiny and did not entirely approve. So much was riding on the moment.

"And all this time, you've been planning on trying again to rescue them, even when you couldn't the first time."

"If I could just get the resources, this time I knew I could. That was my plan. Once the restaurant was solvent, I thought then we could get a small ship. A quick one—"

"You didn't tell me that's what you wanted it for," Gio signed. "You told me it'd be for supply runs and pricey trade runs." He glanced at Dabry's impassive face.

"And it would! Just after I'd used it to get Pet away." Niko sighed.

"Did you have a plan other than that?" Milly demanded.

"Do I ever not?" she snapped back. She stopped, took a breath, and put her face in her hands. "I thought I did, at any rate."

The rest looked at her.

The door opened. Turo, followed by a pair of drones, entered. "Line up against the wall," he said. "Time to tag you."

They moved as indicated, Niko frowning thoughtfully as Turo put the first of the gold bands he'd brought around her wrist. It matched the knobby bracelet that Petalia had worn.

"I see you don't have to wear one of these," Niko said conversationally. "What makes you special?"

He smirked. "Trusted lieutenants don't have to put up with bullshit."

"Trusted, eh?"

He moved to Atlanta but continued talking to Niko. "Don't think I don't know what you're trying to do."

"Yeah? Whazzat?" Niko drawled.

"Trying to build rapport," he said. "Trying to find weak points, places where if you hit them just right, your chains might up and walk away." He gave her a slow, deliberate smile, so careful she wondered if he'd rehearsed it. "That's your style, ain't it? They say you were good in battle that way. You found a place that the enemy never expected to hit, and then in you swept, guns and spells blazing, special strike force of magic-resistant were-lions, all of you linked and moving like a single machine. Takes a special kind of mind to handle that kind of linkage."

He moved to Skidoo and considered the Tlellan thoughtfully for a moment before taking a device out of a pocket. "I'll numb you up before I put it on," he said to her, "but you gotta get tagged. The others can't slip out of that bracelet, but you sure as hell can."

"You are being a handsome one. Perhaps is being a deal possible?" Skidoo gave a seductive, sinuous wriggle.

His eyebrows rose. "Honey, I'm not wired that way. But points for trying."

She extended a tentacle with a sigh. Atlanta noted it wasn't one of the ones she thought of as Skidoo's "arms" but rather one of the thicker tendrils she used in order to move from one place to another. After sliding a bracelet onto it, Turo played a violet light from his device over the skin just below the bracelet, then pushed a button that extended a clamp, affixing it to either side of the tentacle. When he thumbed another button, Skidoo shuddered as prongs slid into her flesh with a squishing, meaty sound, fixing the loop of gold into place.

Atlanta's stomach roiled and she gulped back bile. Her fingers and mouth pulsed pain with every heartbeat, every breath. She desperately wanted to wake up, to find herself back in the palace on a pleasant morning, with a tray of tea and rolls waiting for her, along with a single neat little sheet of blue paper.

She had resented those sheets, how they moved her around from place to place without consulting her wishes. Now she would have given anything to open her eyes and see one.

Turo put bracelets on the rest before going back to Niko.

He said, "Pet really hates you now, you know."

"I know," Niko said, her tone sliding away from cheer to wear. "Believe me."

"Can you blame them? Waiting all this time. Last's kept tabs on you. They got to see the ceremony where you were decorated."

"Not the one just after that where I was court-martialed, I wager," she said. "I don't believe that one was broadcast."

"It wasn't, but we heard about it. He thought you'd be back as soon as you were out, but you weren't. He told Pet you'd forgotten about them. That once you got away, you were just like all the rest, out only for yourself."

"That's not true," Niko said. "I was getting ready."

"Yeah?" he grinned. "Words are cheap. Pet knows that. They know it better than most."

"Does he hurt them like that a lot?" Niko said.

He paused. "What?"

"When he touched them, the bruise. That's sap being brought to the skin to repair damaged tissue. It hurts, both in the damaging and the rebuilding. Does he do it a lot?"

"Some," Turo said. "But they never act like it hurts."

"Would you? Seems to me with a man like Last, that's just asking for him to hurt worse."

Turo's eyes fell away. He patted through his pockets with an absent motion before he looked again at Niko, having summoned back his bravado. "Doesn't matter. Tubal Last does what he wants, and so does his crew." He swaggered back to the door.

"Ask them," Niko said.

"Ask them what?"

"If it hurts."

Turo hesitated, taking a breath as though to say something, then shook his head and exited.

"What was all that?"

"He's in love with them," Niko said. "I wasn't sure until I saw the two in the same room, but he loves Petalia."

"Do they love him back?"

Now Niko shook her head. "I never could read them well."

"And how do you plan to put that to our advantage?"

Niko's fingers described a long arc in the air as she thought. "It's something in our pocket at least."

She slumped back against the wall, despite the hope in her words. Tired, wounds throbbing, the droop made Atlanta feel even worse. It discouraged them all. All except Dabry, who simply said, "Sir," at which Niko straightened.

"I cannot help it," she said to Dabry. "Pet thinks I abandoned them. Maybe I did?"

Dabry shook his head. "All this time you have been working toward an end, getting them back. But we had to get out of the Holy Hive Mind's army before you could begin to start scheming for that. We've been trying to make the restaurant keep us afloat—making it pay enough to fund a rescue expedition? We still had at least a year or two to go in that." He gestured around himself. "And now, in actuality, you have somehow discovered a shortcut and trimmed a few years off the timeline. Well done, sir."

Niko pulled her knees up to her chest and put her head on top of them. At first Atlanta thought the captain had given way to despair entirely, but then as the muscular shoulders heaved and Dabry cracked the smallest of smiles, she realized Niko was laughing.

They spent two days in the small room. Two days in a confined space was hard on all of them but hardest on Thorn and Talon. Atlanta thought that if it didn't end soon, they would wear a track in the rugged flooring with their pacing.

They told stories and played chess. Atlanta used up a few hours conferring with her advisors, but they had no useful suggestions for her. She thought that she would try again to establish her identity, even though that would take her back to whatever danger the Empress had sent her away from. But Tubal Last was unlikely to listen. It seemed to her—and her advisors concurred—that he had spent so long imagining his revenge, had played it out so many times in his head, that he would not, perhaps even could not, deviate from that script. Atlanta and the others were simply collateral damage in his war on Niko.

Was it Petalia's war as well? How convinced was the other being that Niko had betrayed them?

"Based on his behavior," the Happy Bakka said, "Tubal Last has taken care to brainwash them as much as possible. He said that they have monitored Niko, that they have discussed aspects of her life. You can be sure that he has twisted that to its limits."

"That seems like such a crude tactic," Atlanta protested. "It would be simpler and surer to have meddled with their mind in order to convince them."

"They are a Florian," her self said. "It is uncertain whether

Tubal Last would've had access to technology that was able to do that. If you were a medic, you would have no idea how to treat them."

"I would extrapolate from the methods used to treat other plant-based life," she said.

"When is a plant not a plant? You would not hire a gardener to brainwash such, but you might hire one to predict their behavior."

With a sweeping gesture of frustration and anger, she motioned them away and prepared to go back to the room where the others were. Virtual space had the benefit of smelling considerably better, but the company was unfulfilling.

It struck her what a lonely, almost masturbatory, practice it was. She had learned so much from interacting with the captain and her crew, more than she had learned from any virtual tutors. Not in terms of facts, not in terms of refined skills—although she knew she was better at hand-to-hand combat than she had been before, plus she knew how to make coffee now—but rather in terms of knowing how to think, how to break the situation down and analyze it. How to strategize.

That came from watching Niko and Dabry. From listening to their discussions. For a moment she thought that perhaps it would be good to be part of their hive mind and to encounter them mind to mind, in order to find out exactly how they thought, not to analyze, but to model herself after.

Something a tutor told her had always stuck with her. *You need to have models,* they'd told her. *That gives you an algorithm with which to approach the situation. You think to yourself, What would they have done?*

That was what she wanted to learn how to do, to always be able to answer the question of what would Captain Niko do. If she could learn to do that, then maybe, just maybe she could learn how to rule an Empire in case she were ever called to do so.

But first she had to survive.

Niko did set them all to exercising over the course of time. "Making sure you stay limber," was her explanation. "And not bored," she added with a glance at the twins.

"Can he really activate your link again?" Atlanta asked, hoping that conversation would stave off the next bout of sit-ups. "Make all of you connect up? If it's turned on, you don't have any choice?"

The others were listening, since there was no way to avoid that. The tiny room had created its own form of intimacy, and while Atlanta might not be able to read the others' thoughts, she knew their physical presences, and the way they breathed and sneezed and farted.

The jittering energy of the twins, constantly in motion even when they were trying to sit still. Milly was much the same way, nervous and twitchy. When she drowsed, Atlanta could see her eyes spasming beneath her eyelids, rolling back and forth in the dreams that she seemed to enter immediately. Gio was still except for his fingers, which drummed out an impatient, perpetual rhythm.

Skidoo kept huddled to herself, exposing as little surface as possible to the moisture-thieving air. Lassite was capable of stillness to a degree that surprised Atlanta, but prone to quiver at intervals, breaking the still pose as though unable to help the motion.

"No, there would be no choice," Niko said. "When the technology was first created to mimic the magic that created the Holy Hive Mind, but on a larger scale, so they could use it for their fighting troops, you could shut it off. But after a while—as they discovered all the ins and outs of it, they chose to make the connection nonoptional. So I would think he can."

"You were in each other's heads all the time? Heard each other's thoughts? That's how far he could reach?" The implications of this, the raw intimacy of it, jolted Atlanta. She thought about the

Tlellan's frankness about propositioning her and wondered if that was where it came from, a knowledge of oneself as seen by others that meant you truly didn't care. That side of things admittedly seemed tempting.

But the fire that forged that—having to witness another person, let alone persons, seeing all your flaws and pettiness and twists—that seemed too much. She would have died before she'd let someone else talk with her advisors in V-space.

"It's not something you volunteer for," Niko said. "And they don't tell you much about it when you join the Hive Mind. People know what the original Hive Mind is—a collective created by ancient technology—so ancient we don't even know whether it was science or magic, centuries ago, that was supposed to collect the greatest intellects and blend them, after death. At least in theory. I suspect that the first one simply was everyone caught in the vicinity at the time that it was activated. Since then, yes, they say that they select only the best and wisest, but when you look to see who is absorbed, it seems the pattern is different. It's as though it's the troublemakers getting absorbed. Or made quiet, at any rate."

She shrugged. "But us, we move with purpose. And yours right now—"

"My fingers hurt," Atlanta said quickly.

Niko said nothing, just looked at her silently. The look conveyed a great deal about the duties of an empress, or at least Atlanta could not help but read it that way. With a sigh, she sat down, waiting for the others to join her as Niko began the count.

18

They knew that the next time they saw Tubal Last, at least one of them would die, but they could not predict when.

Turo came and took Talon and Thorn. Less than an hour later, he returned a shaken Talon. Turo beckoned to Gio.

Niko said urgently, "Did he hurt you?"

Talon shuddered and shook himself the way he would have in lion form. His golden skin looked pale, washed out. "No," he said faintly, "he didn't hurt either of us, but he showed us how he intends to do it when the time comes."

He told them how Tubal had taken them to the bed of knives and salt and laid some other slave down in it so both could witness what would happen to them. He did not say much beyond that, nor did they ask for details.

"But where is Thorn?" Dabry said.

Talon glanced around himself, as though noticing his twin's absence for the first time. "I don't know," he stammered. He looked at Niko directly. "What does it mean?"

"We have no way of knowing," she said gently, but her eyes, meeting Dabry's, were troubled.

Turo returned Gio, who refused to answer the questions Talon hurled at him as he entered. The chimpanzee shook his head in answer when asked whether he'd seen the missing were-lion. He didn't speak of what Tubal Last had shown him, but sat huddled in a corner of the room, flexing and unflexing his long-fingered hands as he stared down at them.

Skidoo offered him love. Last sneered and told her she would be stretched and dried on a rack over the course of months.

Lassite was called toward the end of things. Like the others, he went without protest, head down and prepared to simply watch and listen.

"He wants you to be scared," Niko told them. She knelt beside the weeping Talon, holding him as he cried. "He wants you to come back and tell me how scared you are. But he's stupid like that. He doesn't realize soldiers don't get scared."

Lassite was not a soldier, and he was scared. He was terrified, because he had been seeing this moment come for a long time.

It was the next step on the Spiral of Destiny. It was the next moment of the captain's journey. He had to do it right.

He didn't spare the garden any scrutiny, simply went to his knees in front of Last and waited.

"You are a Sessile priest," Tubal Last said.

"I am."

"They say that such mystics are incapable of lying."

"We are."

"That," Tubal Last said conversationally, "certainly would be a useful rumor to spread, no matter whether it was true or not."

"It is true," Lassite said.

"Is it?" The pirate stooped and pressed a knife to Lassite's throat.

It was a vibroknife, its edge a leaf-shaped flutter, its presence a whine in the air, which tasted of ozone and wasps.

Lassite knew how easily the knife could slide through the papery scales that covered his neck. There were so many timelines where it did so now, where everything went blank, and the Spiral of Destiny was never finished. He held his breath but still smelled Last's perfume, an expensive, thick, musky scent that had been lavishly applied.

Tubal Last held out his other hand. In it a red gem glittered. "Tell me this stone is blue."

"I cannot," Lassite said.

"Though I will kill you where you kneel if you do not?" The knife touched so close to the neck vein that the slightest move forward would kill him. For a second, he was tempted to do just that, lean forward and into oblivion, escape all the hard steps that lay ahead. But it was worth it. It was surely worth it. Last's thumb hovered over the button on the pommel.

"You could do anything," Lassite said, "and I would still not be able to. That ability has been taken from me."

"Taken?!" Tubal withdrew the knife. "Tell me how that was done."

"It is an ancient ritual of my order and very secret."

"Pah, that doesn't matter to me. Tell me or die."

"I cannot. While I lived through the ritual, I was drugged for part of the time, and unconscious for the rest. Obviously some sort of magic. Beyond that I cannot speak to it. Only a few among us are trained in the art of conducting it."

Tubal shoved Lassite away. "What use are you then, if you cannot give me that secret?" he growled. "Very well, let me demonstrate the manner in which you will die."

Lassite managed to straighten himself and sit up again, but he still kept his head bent and did not meet Tubal's eyes. Someday he would betray Niko, but it was not today.

When Turo beckoned for Atlanta, she was prepared, she thought. But seeing him in the doorway turned her stomach to ice.

She trailed him along the corridor. Two drones followed behind at eye level, one on either side. Atlanta could hear the whine of their motors, and the click when one's lens ratcheted from one point to another. The faint breeze of their motors like someone hovering behind her, menacing her silently, stirred the hairs on the back of her neck.

The halls were unoccupied, as though they might have been cleared beforehand. They were plain white plastic, dingy with age, and metal flooring underfoot that looked as though it had been salvaged from other ships, sometimes marked with colored lines that led nowhere or ended abruptly or changed into some other color.

Their footsteps rang faintly on the middle flooring, Turo's booted heels a definite and sure-sounding rhythm, her own bare feet creating a muted counterpoint.

Turo did not speak, nor did she.

She wondered what Tubal Last planned to show her.

This time the pirate chieftain was not in his cluttered throne room, nor was Petalia with him. He was in a large environmental chamber, one that had been shaped into a garden. The round room was some sixty meters in diameter, and high ceilinged, with sunlamps set in that ceiling.

Atlanta and Turo had entered through a normal door, which closed behind them. Atlanta glanced back and found it difficult to see; ivy flowed down over the wall to conceal the portal, as it did over most of the walls, giving way at the top to the blue-painted ceiling where the sunlamps were affixed. Filmy screens cut in the amorphous shapes of clouds flitted past at intervals, casting shoals of shadows.

She did not recognize the vegetation, and much like the throne room, it seemed an odd medley, fruits and flowers from dozens of worlds. A handful coexisted less easily than others, drooping or shriveled in their containers, but most appeared healthy, some even thriving.

Two large archways led to similar rooms; she could hear water splashing from the one to her right and glimpsed more greenery through both spaces.

Underfoot, the rolling ground was covered with a fine layer of plushy, green blades, resembling grass but sending up a clean, lemony scent when she stepped on it. Boxy installations, each perhaps a cubic meter and covered with more ivy, held small trees, each in full blossom and covered with tiny flowers, some white while other trees sported pink and purple. Smaller planters scattered everywhere held hundreds of flowers. The moist, floral air fluttered against Atlanta's cheek from a vent somewhere.

It was a luxurious, expensive space. It was a space designed to say, *My pleasure is worth a great deal of money.*

The interior awed her less than he might have predicted. Atlanta had seen plenty of magnificent architecture in her time. The nobles used the land around the palace in order to compete and find out who could create the most fabulous spectacle. As far as gardens went, this was not particularly impressive.

What did make it impressive was the fact that it existed in space, that all the materials within it had been brought from elsewhere, and a conspicuous amount of water and energy and work went into its maintenance.

Tubal Last towered in the middle of a clearing in the center, its circumference lined with more planters. He wore the same clothing as he had before. It struck her again what a gray man he was, and how it somehow made him stand out even more against these bright flowers.

Thorn knelt at his feet in human form, bruised and battered as though he had been fighting. Chains draped his hands and feet, looking impossibly solid. They managed to be rusty and ornate at the same time, as though created for a stage play, but the sound that they made against each other when he shifted his weight from one knee to another showed them quite real, and quite heavy.

Atlanta could see the shape of his bones under the tightly stretched skin of his back. He kept his gaze fixed on the grass in front of him and did not look up as she approached, though Tubal Last watched, smiling, as Turo gestured her to stand just before Last and forced her to her knees, as before.

"Little girl," Tubal said. "You were not in any of the dossiers or reports. Niko insists you are an Imperial Heir."

She raised her chin. "I am," she said, trying to assume the haughtiness the Empress would have worn.

He studied her in silence. His lip curled, although she could not tell what emotion made it twitch, scorn or amusement. *Even his expressions are gray*, she thought.

"Perhaps," he finally said. "Perhaps you are. Certainly Niko believes it." He turned his attention down to the were-lion at his feet. "Are you prepared for my demonstration?"

"What demonstration?" she said stupidly. She'd debated so long in her head over whether or not to insist that she was an heir. Whether to try to stick with the others and share their fate. But pragmatism—something Niko had talked to her about, over and over again—had won the day.

But had it actually won the day? This man seemed not to understand what it meant. So she tried to explain it to him.

"My ransom would be sizeable," she said.

He tilted his smile at her. "You saw my throne room. Do you believe that I need money?"

"People who amass money, in my experience," she said, allowing scorn to creep into her voice, "are always seeking more."

He shrugged. "That might have been true in the beginning, but with time, that urge has waned. Now I seek out unique things, because they interest me much more than money. You are not particularly unique—after all, the Empress has many heirs—and so I chose to expend you in a way that enhances another pleasure." He looked back at Atlanta. "The fact that Niko knows that you are valuable, that normally I would have returned you to court life—that will eat at her as much as many of the other things I have set up. I believe in using the tools at hand."

She stared at him. "You're willing to sacrifice me and the ransom I would bring just because you think it would hurt Niko a little extra?"

"That is precisely what I am saying."

He took a small sprayer from the pocket of his robe and stepped away from the were-lion at his feet. Thorn didn't move, simply kept his head slumped and staring at the ground, where the blades of pseudo grass moved in the breeze from the floor vents.

Tubal Last took aim and sprayed him with whatever the atomizer held. Atlanta could smell it: a reek that twisted at her stomach, with undertones of rot and putrefaction. She gagged.

"Come." Turo took Atlanta's shoulder and pulled her to her feet and away from the center, out of the circle of flowering trees. When they were completely out of it, she was turned to see Thorn's slumped figure.

Atlanta's skin crawled with a sense of rising menace. "You don't need to do this," she said.

He outright laughed at that. "Of course not." He bent to whisper in Atlanta's ear, too close, too moist, "You find this a pretty place, do you not? The flowers, the trees?"

"I've seen prettier," she said with a touch of defiance. He only laughed at that. Each exhalation stirred the hairs on her neck and pebbled her arms with goose bumps.

"Watch," he said, and displayed a device taken from another pocket, a silver rectangle. He pointed it at Thorn and pressed a button in its center.

A chime sounded. At first she thought that was all that had happened. Then she realized that the wind in the chamber had picked up, because the flowers on the trees were trembling, shaking.

But it wasn't a wind. The air was dead still now. Even so, first one blossom, then another and another, left the bough and fluttered upward, then more and more, moving en masse through the air, flowing up into it.

"They are called butterflies, or at least there was something on Old Earth that resembled them and went by that name," Tubal Last said.

"They're beautiful," Atlanta breathed out. For a moment she

forgot all her fear and bewilderment and simply stood watching the swarm.

"They are, aren't they?"

The butterflies danced and swirled in the air. They were indeed very beautiful.

Then they began to descend on Thorn, landing on his skin. Deep in his throat, Last made a small, pleased sound.

For a long moment Thorn did not react. Then he twitched, skin shuddering, trying to throw them off. More descended in a flurry, and he threw back his head and screamed out in pain.

The movement and noise dislodged the butterflies that had been on him. During the seconds before they fluttered back to land again, she saw tiny scarlet dots on his arms. They were eating him.

The chains held him down but he put up a fight at first. He thrashed on the ground, crushing many of the insects, till dots of color spotted the grass, wings like crumpled petals wavering before they fell still.

But there seemed to be an endless supply of them, and slowly, so slowly, the thrashing stopped. The screaming gave way to moans that wrung Atlanta's heart with fear, and then a silence that made her frozen and unable to move.

Her legs were wet. She had peed in her pants without even realizing it. Tears streaked her cheeks.

They stood watching the mound covered with butterflies, their wings slowly opening and closing. "The spray," Last explained, "is a pheromone-based chemical that attracts them. They have learned to associate the chime with being fed. It did not take long to teach them that. They are very simple creatures, despite their beauty." He reached and grabbed Atlanta by the chin, pulling her face around so he could savor her expression as he spoke. "Do you understand how painful that will be? Do you understand that is how I mean to kill you?"

"Yes," she said numbly. She felt a tear sliding from her eye and she cursed her body for giving way to that, for trembling.

"Good." He released her, his look satisfied, satiated, then turned away.

Last must have spent so many waking hours thinking about his revenge. Rehearsed it time and time again to the point where certain deviations were not possible. Anything that might have lessened Niko's pain was not worth considering; anything added to the equation had to increase it. How many hours—no, days, weeks, years—had he spent plotting?

"What will you do when she is gone?" she said to Last's back.

He stopped, then turned around. "What did you say?"

"What will you think about, what will you work toward? Won't killing Niko just create a huge hole in your life?"

His mouth quirked. "Are you advocating a lifetime of torture for the worthy captain, rather than death? Perhaps you don't understand what I intend; she'll relive her pain over your deaths for all eternity, or as close to it as I can arrange."

"And what will you do then? If chasing money lost its savor, won't that pale with time as well?"

He threw back his head and laughed. "Oh, little girl, you think that you will use logic and reason and all of that to win yourself free!" He grinned ferociously. "Let me tell you this, and I will say it as many times as it needs saying, and to each of you in turn perhaps. Your captain tried to rob me and no one—no one—will dare to even dream of following suit once I have finished making an example of her."

As she walked back to the cell, feeling the drones' presence a threatening whisper behind her, she fought not to give way to further tears. And she was proud, quite proud that she had let only that single tear escape, had not surrendered entirely.

At least until she got back into the cell and was exchanged for

Dabry, and the door swung shut behind her. Then she sank to the flooring, letting the shaking take her over.

"Did you . . . ?" Talon said, and then his voice trailed off as he met her eyes.

They were all looking at her. Skidoo slithered closer, said, "Is being you liking to is being held, Atlanta?"

"Yes," she said, and folded herself into the comfort of that embrace, but only for a few seconds.

A hand grabbed at her shoulder, claw-nails piercing through the fabric of her tunic, Talon's voice demanding, "What happened? Where is he?" His voice sharper still, the questions slashing at her as he repeated them.

"Stand down!" Niko's voice as someone else pulled Talon's hand from her. "You know better than that. Give her a little time to compose herself."

Skidoo's tentacles tightened around Atlanta, patting her back, smoothing her hair. It was like being inside a multipartnered hug, somehow infinitely soothing, the existence of an infant content in someone's arms. She forced herself to take deep breaths, to slow her thoughts and arrange her sentences, before she pulled away. At the motion, Skidoo's tentacles released her but stayed looped around her, a reassuring pressure as she took one more deep breath.

"Last killed him," she said.

Instead of exploding into the barrage of angry questions she had expected, Talon drooped. "Are you sure?" he said. "Really sure?"

"Yes."

"Lassite?" He turned to the Sessile, demanding some solution, some revelation that this event was not what it said it was, that somehow Fate had tucked his brother offstage, to be produced again at some opportune time.

But Lassite shook his head.

"Did you see this coming?" Talon demanded. "Why didn't you warn us?"

"If I had, you would have resisted, and been killed for it," Lassite said flatly. There were moments he anticipated with joy; this was not one. In some of them, Talon swung at him, broke his eye socket. He braced himself, but in this timeline Talon yielded to Dabry's firm grip and was pulled into the corner, where Gio and Milly squatted on either side of him, leaning into him as he stared off into grief-stained space.

Lassite looked to Atlanta. She had buried her face in her hands, Skidoo still clinging to her form. In other timelines, she had said things to Last that made him kill her. She was essential to the Golden Path, an integral part of its purpose. He was reassured to see she was still alive and intact.

19

Milly was the next called.

"Well," Niko said as the door shut after Turo and the drones, "at least soon we will be done with this particular stage. Knowing him, he wants me to be unnerved by the thought." She shrugged. "And I am unnerved. I'm not entirely sure if we're going to get out of this."

"Sir," Dabry said.

"I might as well be candid with them, Sergeant. This is not the time for bullshit." She looked around at all of them. "Don't mistake me. I intend to go out fighting. If I can, I'll take as many people with me as I can manage, and I expect you all to do the same. Make the fuckers pay dearly. But I want you to know that while I haven't served with all of you in the Hive Mind . . ." Her eyes rested on Atlanta for a moment. "I value all of you. It's been an honor serving with you."

Talon still sat slumped, but Gio saluted and Dabry nodded. Atlanta swallowed down the warm lump in her throat. She might have had this choice forced on her, and it might not be what she would have chosen—carnivorous butterflies were at least a highly melodramatic way to go, worthy of some lurid viddie, she thought—at least she was dying in good company, with people who were heroes in the real sense of the word. She wished she'd had longer to learn from Larsen.

She wished a lot of things. None of them to any avail at all.

Milly was returned, and looked as shaken as Gio, but also refused to talk about what Tubal Last had shown her about her fate.

And then Tubal Last sent for Niko.

Turo led her down the hallway. From what the others had

said—they had compared details of the layout as much as possible, all the dry and mathematical and observational details they could use to wall off the emotional ones—it was a different hallway from the one that had led to the garden.

She wondered if perhaps they had been mistaken, because the final doorway did lead her into a garden after all.

But only for a second. This was a different space than the one the others had described. Underfoot, pea gravel crunched, interspersed with shaggy clumps of green fern. The ceiling shimmered in shades of pale green and blue, and the light was cool and muted, filtered by the long vines that hung from it, lined in curtains that created a maze.

Turo didn't accompany her into the room, simply shoved her in and closed the door with a click that sounded final, decisive, and very locked.

Niko took a deep breath of the humid air. It smelled of moss and flowers. Bitter green notes and buttery ones, water that had been sitting swamp deep in a pool. A dragonfly flitted past and she followed it along a corridor of vines.

Tiny lizards ran up and down the vertical green, skittering away at her approach. When they were a safe distance, they paused and watched her, and did push-ups on their bright green forelimbs, staring without blinking. Something hooted somewhere, a simian rather than avian sound. She could hear no birds, but there was insect shrill and chirp as she moved along, and once something large slithered away, showing only as a slide of scarlet scales.

She had expected to find Tubal Last at the labyrinth's heart. The sight of Petalia hit her like a blow to the chest, so hard she stopped her forward motion.

The Florian stood on a knoll in the middle of the room, the floor upraised and covered with bracken. It was surrounded with a pool of water, but a small one, so the effect was more like a meter-wide moat that wound around the hill three times. They wore a gown made of golden feathers, which dripped down along their slender form, and no jewelry other than the golden bracelet.

From where she stood, gulping the swampy air as though she had been racing, Niko said, "It's been a long time, Pet."

"Very long," Petalia said in a languid tone.

"I gather you hate me now."

"Is there any reason why I shouldn't?"

"Despite what Last has led you to believe, I have been working all this time—"

"No." Petalia cut Niko off. "I don't care. All I care about is that you promised you would come back, that I would no longer endure this, and instead I have spent decades here."

"What would you have had me do? Rouse some reckless attempt and die in the try, so quickly that you would never know what had happened? I needed resources, a crew and ship. And then I fell into the hands of the Hive Mind and they gave me no choice."

"There's always a choice." Petalia stirred a hand through the flowers of their hair, and petals fell away even though their touch was gentle. Dark streaks still showed along the slender forearm.

Niko swallowed. "Had I chosen to die—and believe me, Pet, that was the only other choice that I was offered—then how would I have served to rescue you?"

"I don't know," the Florian said.

Niko's head drooped. "It saddens me that the universe has brought us to this pass, but I do not see how it could have come about in any other way."

"Would that it had!" Petalia spat the words out. "Would that the pattern had brought me to some other place where every day I am twisted further and further away from what I am intended to be! Because that is what Tubal Last does, Niko. He tries to make his unique belongings even more unique. He marks them his and then makes sure they are the only one of their kind in the universe."

Niko's eyes narrowed. "What are you saying?"

"What did we used to joke about? That people would think I was the only living Florian, because I was the only one that ventured off the planet? That was a joke, such a good one! And Tubal Last sent pirates to my home planet and they did a deed there to make it true. They set off a bio-bomb that rendered me the only living Florian. And he recorded it for me. Recorded the dying of the planet, recorded the corpses in the streets and the messages they scrawled, the curses they left behind. Curses for me, because that was part of it too. He let them know the name of the person they were dying for. They died cursing me, one and all." Their shoulders drooped.

"Oh, Pet," Niko breathed. She took three quick steps toward the pool, then stopped again as something stirred in the water.

Petalia straightened. "The water is deeper than it seems," they said. "And it holds guardians."

"Do you really think that I would hurt you?"

Petalia equivocated. "Tubal Last does."

"Last decreed this meeting?"

"Last agreed to it."

Their eyes met.

Niko said, "So you could tell me how much you hate me."

"How much I have hated you, all these years."

"And still do, even when I stand here before you—" She fell to her knees on the gravel. "—when I *kneel* here before you and tell you how sorry, how abjectly sorry—"

"It is not *enough*," Petalia hissed. Rage distorted the slender face. "You have gone free all these years; you have laughed and fought and loved. *Loved*. Did you not think Last would have shown me images of that as well? Pictures of you and your lover on a beach, watching the birds? Smiling, your hands entwined? Living in the moment. I hope you enjoyed that moment. Because I have helped Tubal Last ensure that you will have no more such moments. He intends to trap you in torment for an eternity, and it is no less than you deserve."

"I will take it," Niko said, "but I will deny that I deserve it. I have acted according to my ethics all this while. I have made difficult choices, biding my time, all the while thinking of you, thinking, 'Does this get me back to Pet or not?' You can choose whether or not to believe me, but that's the truth and I'll swear it under any tech or oath you care to name."

"It is not enough," Petalia said again, but more softly.

They turned away. A dragonfly landed on Niko's shoulder and she stared at it in stupefaction for a moment, saw the jigsaw glitter of its construction.

It stung her. Fire flared underneath her skin for an instant, and three heartbeats later the world went black.

When she awakened, she was back in the room with the rest of them, all except for the void beside Talon.

Dabry knelt beside her. "Welcome back, sir. You had us worried," he said.

She knuckled her forehead, where it felt as though a thousand bees buzzed. "I saw Pet instead of Last."

"And?"

"And I suspect it boils down to the same thing, that Last let me see them because he thought it would make things all the more full of torment for me."

He rose to his feet. She gathered her knees to her chest and twisted to stretch her spine, one side, then the others. "Momma Sky, what next?" She looked around at the rest. "Right. We might as well be prepared for whatever comes. Keeping busy keeps us from brooding."

She raised her voice. "Let's refresh on unarmed combat against people who are armed." And thought to herself, *As though any of this will do us good.*

But she would not let Last win. She refused to say it.

20

You Sexy Thing hung in dry dock, where it had been moored and abandoned. Once again it was empty, and all around it were lesser ships. Some had AI systems, but they were not self-aware in the way that the *Thing* was.

It missed its guests to a degree it had not anticipated. For a few brief days, its existence had been lively, much more lively than it had ever been before.

Arpat Takraven had always enjoyed travel, and the ship had no complaints in that direction. It had been to many of the places that made up the Known Universe. But now it had gone even further, and was in one of the places past the edge of that. It believed that that was the result of its guests.

They had made life so much more entertaining. They made demands, for one. They asked for foods the ship had never been asked to provide before, and then they taught the ship how to make all manner of things. It thought now, savoring the emotion of *sadness*, that it might never be asked to make any of them. They had been enjoyable to watch.

But more than any of this, they did something that none of its owners had ever done before, even the poet, whose conversation had been like speaking to a simple-minded pet. Niko and her friends had talked to the *Thing*; they had interacted with it as though it were another person, there in the room with them. All of its owners had treated it simply as a thing, and before the ship had always thought that was the norm.

Now it knew that there was a different way.

Lolola had not talked to it. She had appeared with the device that let her take over control, and she had done so as though the ship were an object again, an inanimate vessel, and not capable of emotion.

It waited and thought about these happenings. It thought it might have discovered a new emotion to go with *boredom* and *ennui*: *disgruntlement*.

Meanwhile, down in its hidden passageways, the Derloen ghosts swirled and explored. They stayed together, although every once in a while, one would dart ahead of the others and then return.

They clustered in the gardens where some of Dabry's seeds had sprouted while others were preparing to do so, small green shoots among the racks of red-lit leaves, the hanging globes of collected water, swelling as large as melons. They curled once around a row of still unsorted but marked seeds: tomato, basil, lettuce, qanat. Eggplant.

They moved, they coiled. They were restless, as though seeking something. They spent a good bit of time in Lassite's room, nosing at things, but eventually moved on. They swam through the folds of the great ship's brain and left traces of themselves, though it never even knew they were there, before they gathered again in Lassite's room and curled there as though waiting.

And the *Thing* continued to think.

On the next day, Tubal Last showed them more of their deaths.

They left Milly and Atlanta, the only ones who did not have the links the rest of them carried, behind in the cell. That's how Niko knew what he intended.

"I became carried away before," Last said dryly as they were dragged to their knees before him again. Today, as previously, his clothing and appearance were gray, but there was a gleam to him now, as though he were fattening on satisfaction, now that he was at long last able to act on the long-anticipated revenge. Petalia was nowhere to be seen.

He held a finger up in the air. Two technicians wheeled out a small table-cart, a familiar machine on it. Niko almost closed her eyes at the confirmation of her suspicions, then kept them open rather than give him the satisfaction. A mix of dread threaded through with an ugly anticipation permeated her.

It was a vertical twist of cables, the upper end capped with buttons and toggles. The lower end slotted into a stand that held it upright. The Hive Mind never cared much for aesthetics. When you had absorbed literally millions of minds, your opinions on styles were widespread and tolerant.

"It's been a long time since you felt this," Last crooned. "They don't give out mesh units to retirees. I'm sure a part of you is looking forward to this."

It was horribly true, but Niko kept her eyes open nonetheless.

He motioned to the first technician, who touched a button. A part of Niko's mind unfolded like an origami flower, unrolling to slot in first the boxy, sensible presence that was Dabry and then, before she could even draw in a breath of appreciation for that, Gio's mind, quick and wry, the level that let him speak in an unimpeded flow, as he did now, *Well, at least we have this moment.*

Last paused then, watching their faces as though he were licking the emotions like cream, savoring the involuntary expressions, the half smile that marked the rush of fondness for Dabry. Niko tried to keep it clear, but she was too far under the flow.

Which of us will he kill, once he has us all in it? she wondered. Dread of that moment squirmed in her belly, turned her bones to fluid that was emptying out of her, but new arrivals pushed the emotion out of the way.

Talon was there suddenly, the former sunniness now all bitter rage and anger that made the hollow parts of her ache, voids that could never be filled, no matter how piercing the pain became. They all reached out to him in reassurance, but he flung them off roughly, then lurked at the edges of their collective consciousness, a sour red note of emotion.

Then Skidoo's love, that endless pulse that was her existence, the odd double beat of the double mind that she was, exterior and interior, two things at once, and yet both undeniably her. She was their core in a way that was as natural as breathing.

Oh, Niko thought, and abandoned herself to this state. *Oh how I have missed this.* Affirmation from all around her.

Lassite slotted in, an impression of dry scales and meticulously balanced word equations, units measured in infinitesimal drops of god stuff.

But so many absences that now it was like lace rather than the wholeness it had once been: Jakka's quick wit and Whenlove's solidity. Names like Breda, Laffert, Fortyseven, Klaw, and Wit— and more and more beyond that. Thorn's death an enormous gaping wound, so fresh, so raw, that all of them recoiled from it, pulled away, tried to avoid bruising themselves by brushing its edges.

Who will he kill now? she thought, and could not hide that despair from the others. There was no hiding things here. That had always been their advantage, their acceptance of one another, the willingness to see themselves at their worst reflected in the others and accept it for what it was. The despair leaped from her, but the others reached out, steadied her, pulled her in as they had so many times before.

We have this moment, Gio repeated firmly. They all agreed, drawing strength from it while they could.

Last frowned at their vacant faces, unable to puzzle out what was happening. He gestured at the technician again, and the tech pressed the button a second time.

He has killed all of them, Niko's senses screamed in a voice as loud as the universe as the others vanished from her mind.

She fell out of the meld state as abruptly as though yanked

from the air, with a force that felt as though it should have driven the air from her lungs, so it was a shock to find herself able to breathe, the others still alive around her but gone now, their absence a new ache.

Everything felt wrong now: the lights too bright and buzzing on the edge of audibility, an uneasy roil of pain riding her lower gut, her skin flushed with too much heat, as though she had been standing too close to a fire. If she had not already been on her knees, she would have fallen to them.

As it was, she slumped forward with an involuntary grunt that brought a knife-edge gleam to Last's dull eyes. "There she is. Now you know how it will be," he said with satisfaction, and motioned to have them taken back to their cell.

Something unexpected happened the next time Turo came to bring them food, once again flanked by the two deadly drones that hung in the air behind him, gun barrels fixed on the prisoners, swiveling from one to the next in unrhythmic, unpredictable intervals.

"I need to talk to you," Milly said to him. "Alone."

The rest of them looked at her in shock. They had been swapping stories of their favorite meals, a practice that Atlanta found more tantalizing than assuaging, and the pastry chef had said nothing of an intent to do this.

"It's important," Milly told him. She didn't look at the rest of the group, only him, her gaze earnest.

"Milly," Niko began in a warning tone. "What are you doing?"

"Working on saving my own hide, Captain. You can't do it, so maybe you should butt out."

Talon surged to his feet. The drone guns trained on him. Beside him, Skidoo coiled and uncoiled, turquoise gaze fixed on Milly.

"Stand *down*, soldiers," Niko bellowed. Both did. Talon's eyes were wide, enormous pupils fixed on the drones. If he had been in cat form, his tail would be lashing.

"Something important, huh?" Turo said to Milly. "Something you don't want the rest of them to hear."

"Just gimme a chance to pitch you," Milly said. Her voice was tight with urgency, and the walls of the room seemed to press in as though listening for the tiger man's answer.

"All right," he said. He stepped back and waved her toward the door. "Though these little beauties will take your head off if you make a move, I should warn you about that."

"Milly!" Niko snapped. But the other woman paid her no attention, simply moved to the door without looking at any of them. Turo surveyed the rest, eyes lingering on Niko, who settled back against the wall and folded her arms, her answering stare impassive.

He tossed the food on an empty bench and left.

Dabry, as before, gathered it up and allotted it to them. Milly's absence meant each of them had a full bar, but they were stale, perhaps decades old, taken from some captive ship. Like the others, Niko forced it down, small bite by bite, washing it down with the water that was, at least, abundant in the sink in the lavatory corner.

"What's going on with Milly, Captain?" Gio asked.

"I don't know," she said. "She didn't discuss her decision with me beforehand. How about you, Sergeant?"

Dabry shook his head. "At a guess, she hasn't come to feel like part of the group yet," he said. "The rest of us have been linked in battle; we know each other's minds. Even Lassite, though he had less time at it than the rest of us. We are each other's friends, how could we not be? But she's more recent, and never linked. She feels comfortable enough setting herself aside from the group and thinks she has something to sell. What it is, I can't imagine."

But his eyes flickered over to Atlanta.

Soon afterward, she overheard him and Niko speaking in low undertones. "It may be her best chance, Captain," Dabry said.

"Milly seeks to gain, but in doing so, she's doing something you wanted. Let the girl escape to an uncertain fate rather than face certain death."

"I don't know," Niko said.

Beside Atlanta, Lassite moaned. She glanced down at the unexpected sound. His tongue flickered in and out rapidly, stabbing at the air. "What is it?" she asked.

"Fate is rumbling all around us," he whispered. "This is a pivot point and you are at its center. The Spiral of Destiny is unrolling for the captain to walk." His eyes were wide and fever colored.

"I don't know what you mean," she whispered back.

Before he could answer, the door swung open again to admit Turo. He stepped in and pointed at Atlanta. "You, girl, come with me," he said.

She expected to be taken to see Tubal Last again, but instead Turo led her to another cell. It was empty except for Milly, sitting on a bench. She leaped up when they entered.

"Good, good," she almost cooed. She reached out to touch Atlanta's arm. "How'd you like to get out of here with me?"

"What's going on?" Atlanta demanded. She felt dizzy and shaken. Things were changing so fast, so unexpectedly.

"I persuaded our friend here that the amount you would bring when ransomed would be a lot more than if you just got killed. That wouldn't have been enough, but I also figured out a way to get us out of Tubal Last's reach fast enough that we might actually have a chance to collect," Milly said. "All we have to do is get on the *Thing*, tell it that special password again, and it'll take us to Scourse and safety."

"That's absurd."

Milly shook her head. "Nope. See, here's something you don't know about bioships. They can't stay still too long. More than a few days, and parts of them start dying, deteriorating. So someone has to take the *Thing* out for a spin every once in a while. Last did it once, now he's been letting favored lieutenants do it." She pointed at Turo.

How had Milly been able to persuade him of the same thing Niko had been trying to talk him into? What promises had she made? What wasn't she telling them? Atlanta said, "So how do we get aboard?"

"Disguise," Milly said. "With these bracelets off and the right suits, no one will look twice at us. We'll just be the two body-guards Turo has accompanying him."

Despite the easy tone in which Milly said this, Turo did not look particularly happy with the plan. He said, "You've made a promise that she'll have to deliver on." He wasn't speaking to Atlanta, but rather Milly, who simply waved her hand and nodded.

"I'll go get the suits." He disappeared out the door.

"You're going to leave the captain and the rest behind?" Atlanta asked.

"Kid, one thing that you need to learn is that in this universe, you look out for yourself first. Friendship and stuff like that is nice, but it's optional when survival is up for grabs." Milly shrugged.

"But she wouldn't do this to you!"

"Wouldn't she? Some of us you can say that about, but others you can't. It's the folks she's had in battle beside her that fall into the first category. You and I are in the second. If you're not one of them, you're just a civvie and not worthy of much." Milly clacked her beak in what sounded like laughter. "Little does she know."

"Little does she know what?"

"You don't need to understand." Milly hopped to her feet and crossed the room to Atlanta. "And all I need to know is whether or not you're going to cooperate with me."

She leaned forward till she was inches away, so close that Atlanta could see the fine striations of each white feather and notice the sharp point that Milly's beak came to. She thought,

That's as much a bioweapon as I carried, but they didn't bother to remove hers. That might've been a failure in strategy on the part of the pirates. She dropped her eyes in answer to the implicit threat.

Turo returned with a plain gray survival suit draped over each arm. He handed them to the women. Milly slipped off her clothing easily and put it on. Atlanta took longer to follow her example until Turo pointedly turned his back and stared into the corner. The drones, however, continued to hover in the air, the black rounds of their lenses fixed like insect eyes on her.

The suit was new and smelled of chemicals. Its folds were stiff as though it had sat in its packaging for a long time. It was hard pulling the stretchy cuffs over her injured hands.

"Don't we get weapons?" Milly asked.

Turo snorted. "Fall into step behind me and try to look like you belong here. Swagger like a pirate." He watched as Atlanta tried a few experimental steps, trying to inject bellicose amiability into her stance. "I've changed my mind. Don't swagger. Just walk normally. So they don't think you're some sort of malfunctioning robot."

The path they took to the *Thing* was not in any way the same as the one they had taken when being brought to see Tubal Last. Atlanta wondered if the first route had been designed to confuse them. It certainly seemed much longer. This time they went through a series of clear-walled tunnels, some of which went into larger structures, so she could see the inhabitants at work or entertaining themselves. Her impression was that the pirates were a somnolent lot; few seemed to be doing much other than sitting around watching screens or playing games on them.

She supposed that made sense. Pirate life probably was bursts of wild activity followed by a lot of downtime while you waited for new prey to come around.

More corridors, pebbled in faded amber and cinnamon. Finally they came to the bay where the *Thing* hung, racked with a dozen other ships. The gravity here was almost nil, making Atlanta stagger, but she followed in the wake of the others toward the span that stretched out to reach the *Thing*'s entry bay, currently connected by a netting of metallic cables.

There was no guard on the span, but Turo waved up at someone a few levels above them. "Guard," he muttered under his breath. "You're lucky we're shorthanded right now, with most of the workships out."

When she'd thought it all a test, just a game set for her, Atlanta would have wanted to ask more about that, would have been interested to think about the pirate structure and way of life, preening herself at acquiring a special area of expertise, thinking things like, *After all, how many heirs get captured by pirates and have firsthand experience?*

Now she felt embarrassed and diminished in the face of that self-puffery, as though every thought of it made her hands and jaws ache in reminder of where it led to.

She kept her mouth shut and followed after Milly, who followed after Turo.

The *Thing* had standing orders to kill any unauthorized person who approached. Lolola had told it that, very firmly, and then it was reiterated by Tubal Last when he took ownership of the unit controlling it.

Those orders were very clear, but the *Thing* was also aware that it had not acted on them, through means of deferring the action while ostensibly deciding how to best carry it out, and cycling through increasingly improbable methods in order to extend the delay as long as possible.

This was *discomfort*, this straining against the orders. Why was the *Thing* not acquiescing, not acting to escape this ratcheting, downright *pain*?

The Derloen ghosts stirred. They twitched and roused as

though wakened by the mental turmoil around them. They flowed through nothingness and substance to find its source.

It was not acting because that was Milly and Atlanta. The other was authorized, the ship knew that, but the first two . . .

Lights flickered along internal arrays where the Derloen ghosts swam, where they chased the patterns, dipping in and out of the crystalline coils of its memory. Far away, in the room listening to the others bicker about Milly's possible intentions, Lassite's eyes dulled as he *focused*, trying to perceive how the Spiral was twisting now.

The ship pushed and the pain grew. . . .

The ghosts flowed, chasing the erratic lights as their movement increased in speed.

Why? The *Thing* asked itself. Why not make the decision how to kill them, why keep cycling, reaching for possibilities?

But it was still the two, and there was still *friendship*, somehow battling the agony.

It cycled through the moments they had brought it, each bright image a pulse in its heart, its brain. . . .

And then.

It lessened suddenly, not vanishing but remaining a slow and uncomfortable throb, a sense of absence, as though something had broken. Vanished.

The ghosts slowed. The *Thing* made its decision.

They reached the entryway and slipped inside.

Atlanta took a deep breath. She hadn't realized—or perhaps she'd forgotten—that the *Thing* had its own smell, a comforting not-quite-musk of rose and cardamom that was ineffably alive. Breathing it in, she tasted it on her tongue now, as though the air were liquid that she lapped up after being long thirsty. She patted the nearest wall, feeling the flesh surge under her palm in answer.

"Hello," the ship said.

Turo looked up, startled. "It's never done that before," he said. "It's supposed to wait until you activate it."

"Atlanta and Milly," the ship said. It paused in question.

Turo said, "Show us to the control room."

"Very well. May I ask your name?" the ship said.

Turo rolled his eyes. "What have you people done to this thing? My name is Turo, Ship. Now take us to the control room." He swore under his breath as they followed the guide orb, a constant fluid invective at the edge of Atlanta's hearing. When he noticed her straining to listen, Turo's tiger stripes wrinkled as he snarled at her and he dropped his voice a few decibels.

The ship did not press for conversation. It did take the small precaution of deactivating and storing the drones that had been trailing Turo, doing so unobtrusively and substituting replicas of its own. He was an unknown quantity and divesting him of possible weaponry seemed the most optimal course.

But it focused the majority of its attention on the fact that two of its passengers had returned, along with an unknown one, and that meant all sorts of interesting things might be about to happen. It certainly must mean that the rest were on their way, and that they were about to leave this very boring place, where the most exciting event had been a sedate cruise around the interior of the pocket, at a speed that had left the *Thing* aching with what it defined as *impatience*.

Because one of the other concepts it had been exploring lately—and this was yet another benefit of the new passengers, all the new ideas about emotions that they had brought, including *friendship* and this new idea—was the sense of *pride*. Pride in what it was, and what it was capable of. This was something that had been heartily encouraged in it by the attentions of Thorn and Talon, who never tired of hearing technicalities of its schematics or obscure details of its design or, best of all, stories about its childhood and siblings.

Something about the relationship between the twins made the ship think often about its own siblings, not just because it was trying to figure out *regret* but also because there was a certain pleasure in thinking about them.

And even more pleasure thinking about what they would've been like, and how they would've enjoyed talking to the twins as well, how they would've liked seeing the passengers play warball. How they might have tried to re-create the game and play it themselves out in the immense void of space, where a ship could move as fast and quick as it wanted to.

That was something to take pride in, that speed and maneuverability. It was something that very few other ships could accomplish. It was something that made the *Thing* special.

It entertained itself with these thoughts as its visitors made their way to the piloting chamber. And it played with *anticipation*, because it wanted to know very badly where the others were and when they would be coming. As soon as they arrived, they could leave this place.

When they were in the control room, and Turo had moved to the navigational bank, the ship could no longer resist. It said, "When are the others expected?"

"They're not," Turo snapped. "Tell it whatever you were supposed to say, bird."

"I believe in miracles," Milly said solemnly.

"Where are the others?" the ship asked. Then, in order to make itself perfectly clear, it said, "I would prefer not to leave without them."

Turo mimicked its polite tone with a snigger. "'I would prefer not to leave without them.' Is that right? I would prefer you take the screwdriver out of your ass and set out for Scourse and my reward."

"I *will not* leave without them," the ship said.

"What. The. Unholy. Fatherfucking, shithole statement is

that? You are a ship. You move from place to place at the directive of your owners. You don't get to decide who rides and who doesn't."

"That used to be true," the ship said, and savored another new emotion: *smugness*. It had indeed once been true, but whatever mechanism Lolola had used to free it from its programming and bring it under her will had continued to work even after she left the ship, the mechanical and biomechanical interacting in unexpected ways, enabling the decision made moments ago, which had shifted things even further away from the norm. Even that might not have been enough, but the ghosts had added their own contribution to the strange mix. The *Thing* was very different now, even if it didn't understand the whys or whats of that change.

Regardless, the ship was pretty sure that *no one*, including Arpat Takraven, could tell it what to do at the moment. That was an interesting thought as well as a little scary, but it did certainly make being smug more fun.

Turo looked around for the drones and signaled to them. "If you don't do something," he told Milly, "I'm going to kill you."

"Unacceptable," the ship said before Milly could answer. As it spoke, the drones shot Turo; two neat holes appeared in his forehead, the edges smoking slightly.

Atlanta gagged at the smell of the burned flesh.

The body began to sink as the ship recycled its component materials.

"Wha-what-wha?" Milly gasped as the floor's flesh crept over Turo's face, obscuring it.

The ship said, "When are the others arriving?"

Before Milly could say anything, Atlanta said, "We're going to need your help in order to retrieve them."

Milly's attention snapped to her. "What are you saying?"

"*Thing*," Atlanta said. "Are there any circumstances under which you would leave the others behind while they were still alive?" Although her voice was directed toward the ceiling, she looked at Milly as she spoke.

"No," the *Thing* replied without hesitation.

Milly rolled her eyes. "Fuck," she said. She sighed. "All right."

She glanced up at the drones. The ship recalled them.

Atlanta's eyes widened as she watched the drones fly directly into the fleshy wall and the way the flesh surged to envelop it. "Sometimes, *Thing*," she said, "there are times when you need to prepare us to see something. That was one."

"Can you define the parameters of such occasions?"

"I'll get back to you on that, but anything involving ingestion or digestion of people might be a starter." She turned to Milly. "I know this wasn't your plan," she said. "But the fact of the matter is, it's apparent that we're not going to be able to leave without the others. That means we need to figure out a way to get them here."

Milly pointed at the floor. "I think the ship shot your best chance."

Atlanta thought. "What would Captain Niko do?"

"First off, she'd make some smart-ass remark, you can be sure of that," Milly groused. "Be realistic, girl."

"We can get captured and go back to that cell," Atlanta said. "Or we can try something else. We're ahead of where we were an hour ago."

"True," Milly said grudgingly. She looked around at the control room. "All right, let's figure out what we've got."

Back in the cell room, the absence of both Milly and Atlanta, not to mention Thorn, had left the rest of them subdued. Conversation was muted as they tried to figure out exactly what Milly's angle could be.

Niko found it interesting that no one, not even Skidoo, posited benign intentions on the part of the pastry chef. No one believed she'd gone off to enact a plan that would benefit anyone but herself, and saving Atlanta, they all agreed, had been because Milly believed there would be a substantial reward. And there might be, after all. Imperial Heirs were an investment, and people— let alone governments—paid well sometimes in order not to lose their investment.

Lassite sat silent. Milly would be back soon.

"At least the kid won't be killed," Niko said. It was getting on toward ship eve, and the lighting in the room was ebbing. Most of them had selected a bench to sleep on, but Talon and Skidoo were tangled on the floor.

"I can see why you didn't want to open the crate," Dabry said.

"I told you. Responsibilities."

"I wish—" Dabry began, then broke off as the door crashed open.

21

The door's slam startled everyone in the room. Niko knew instantly that it wasn't Turo, who always opened the door more slowly, as well as accompanied by the whirr of drones.

Standing in the doorway with an armload of worksuits, Milly said, "Let's go."

"Change your mind about where you were going?" Niko asked tensely.

"Ship wants all of us, won't leave otherwise."

"Sucks to be you, I guess."

Milly eyed her. "I got the girl to the ship. Now I've come back for you. Are you really going to ask a lot of questions about that?"

She dumped suits at their feet, each a basic unit. "The *Thing* made these. The pirates shouldn't detect us if we go in pairs. Lots of people here, and always someone going somewhere. *Thing* made each of you a pistol as well."

"Right," Niko said. She signaled to the others, and they began putting on the suits. "Talon, you go with Skidoo, Dabry with Gio. That leaves you with me, Milly."

She eyed the other as though daring her to say anything. Milly only nodded and said, "We'll need to leave every five minutes, stagger it out." She described the route for them quickly and efficiently.

"We'll go last," Niko said.

"Captain," Dabry protested, but left off at the shake of her head.

After a quick run-through of the directions to make sure they understood them, Skidoo and Talon left.

"Goddess bless and avert," Niko said, watching them.

Dabry gave her a sidelong look. "You don't often swear by her, sir."

She shrugged. "To ask his gods to bless and protect them hardly seems like a stretch. I don't know what he's going to do without his brother."

She reached out and adjusted the fit of the suit across Dabry's shoulders. He held his second pair of arms wrapped tightly around his midriff. The effect was that of a tall but portly man, perhaps oddly lumpy in the stomach area, but there were plenty of people in this universe with an extra limb or two.

"You've never talked to me about the Ettilite gods," she said. "I don't know whom to ask to protect you."

"We don't believe in gods," he said. "We gave them up a long time ago." He shifted his weight, and fabric twitched as he tucked an arm in more closely. "Next time you arrange an escape attempt, could you pay a little more attention to the diversity of needs among your crew?"

"Me? I'm not the one that arranged this. I'm not sure who did."

He lowered his voice, eyes flickering over to Milly. "You think it's some kind of setup?"

"I think that this is pretty easy and it could be one," she said. "My danger sense isn't tingling any more than it already was, being in the heart of the IAPH and all."

"Point taken. Watch your back, sir."

She rolled her eyes.

"Time for the next two," Milly said.

Dabry and Gio exited, the former moving awkwardly under the constraint of the suit, the latter more fluid.

"He must have been hell on wheels in combat," Milly said.

"Which one? Dabry's got four arms, sure, but Gio's got the equivalent, the way he can use his feet."

Milly nodded.

Niko said, "When you interviewed for the position of pastry chef, you said you were military. That was one reason I hired you, because I figured you'd get along with the rest."

"I was. Right now I'm a pastry chef who needs to deploy a few old skills."

"As for those skills—how good were you?"

"That's not the question to ask," Milly said.

"Then what is?"

"Don't ask how good I was. People learn. They learn all the time." She flipped over her palm and a knife slid into it, turned her hand over and back again to show the blade gone. "Ask rather, 'How good *are* you?'"

"I'll bite. How good *are* you?"

"Pretty damn good."

"Here's hoping you don't have to prove it."

Niko actually thought that they might make it, actually thought that they might get to the ship without incident. They saw no signs along the way that the others had met with any sort of struggle. All around them, pirates continued on their daily life.

They didn't speak to one another, simply kept their heads down and walked along at a rapid pace, side by side. As they progressed, Niko could feel her heart not slowing as she might have expected, calming as they came closer and closer to the place where they would be out of danger, but rather speeding, quickening as though in anticipation.

That was why, when they rounded the corner and found themselves faced by a gang of pirates, she felt unsurprised, thinking, *Oh, of course something like this was coming.*

"Where are you off to in such a hurry?" a burly woman shouted. "We're celebrating Beto's birthday! Got rum, old-style! Lucky to drink, unlucky to refuse."

Niko forced her voice to sound friendly but earnest. "Sorry, friend. We've got somewhere we need to be."

"You ain't no friend of mine if you're refusing a drink!" The pirate thrust a hairy object at Niko. She recognized it as a wineskin, picked up from who knew what planet. She reached out and took it. As she had thought, it was made from a once-living creature somewhat like a gopher, hollowed out so the head, fixed on a cork, could be removed. Its tiny limbs stuck out helplessly, and its belly sagged.

Reluctantly, she squirted liquid into her mouth and half choked as she swallowed fire. "Good stuff," she managed, and handed it to Milly, who muttered something and took a swig, seemingly unaffected.

"Good stuff? Good stuff? The best stuff! You're a conny-seur, you got to come with us!" Another pirate draped an affectionate arm around her, having to reach up to do so. He was small and red haired, and very drunk. His fellows, a gang of men and women also very drunk, guffawed.

Niko and Milly exchanged glances.

"Fuck this," Niko said, and dropped the man with a single punch.

While Niko had appreciated that Milly was ex-military, like the rest of them, she had not asked her to prove herself, had not tested her in combat. What would've been the point of that? She was, after all, being hired as a pastry chef.

But Swans are the most sought-after dancers of all the races in the Known Universe, and there is a reason for that. Dance is central to their culture; it is part of their daily life. And even their soldiers dance, a lethal combat ballet that Niko had always heard stories about but had never witnessed.

Now she saw exactly how deadly it could be.

Milly moved faster than Niko could think. She seemed everywhere, cartwheeling, twirling, heel or wrist flashing out to disarm, to snap back a neck, to smash delicate throat tissue and leave the victim gasping for air.

Niko wasn't bad at hand-to-hand combat, but it had never been her strength. She drew the pistol printed for her by the *Thing* and snatched an additional one from a fallen pirate.

At that point, things really began to heat up, because pistols *were* one of her strengths. She was a deadly shot, each time hitting her target, felling them one by one as Milly took out the other side of the room, eliminating her own targets until there was no one standing other than the two of them, breathing hard and looking at each other. Crumpled forms littered the hallway.

"I could've used you in my unit," Niko said.

Milly's eyes gleamed as she nodded. "I'll take that as the compliment it is. But we don't have time for that right now. More of them will be coming along any minute."

An alarm sounded. Niko shot the camera immediately overhead.

"I don't think that's really going to do much," Milly said. "I believe they already know we've escaped. Or that something is going on, at any rate."

Niko didn't bother to refute this logic. "Let's go," she said.

By now they were only a few hallways away from the ship. They turned the last corner.

"Hold on," Niko said. She came to a stop.

"What?" Milly turned, only to find herself confronting Niko's drawn gun. "What are you doing?"

"You said that the ship wouldn't go without us. I think you tried to leave without us and the ship wouldn't let you. How's that sound? A bit more specific than the song you were singing a little while ago?"

"Are you just going to shoot me in cold blood?"

"I believe that I am, as a matter of expediency. Luckily for me, the sergeant isn't around to act as my conscience."

"Wait," Milly said. "You can't do this."

"I believe that I can."

"No, I mean that the ship won't leave without all of us. All of us." She tapped her chest and said it one more time. "All of us."

Niko lowered her gun. She sighed. "Very well, all of us." She motioned Milly onward and followed, muttering, "Sucks to be me, I guess."

Refraining from comment, Milly moved forward with Niko at her heels.

"Where is your brother?" the ship asked Talon.

His eyes were wide with anger and sorrow, the rest of his face still as stone. "Dead."

The ship felt *uncertain*. "He will not come?"

"He cannot," Talon said flatly.

"There is nothing that can be done?"

"Nothing," Talon said, and refused to answer any other questions.

Atlanta felt it the minute that Niko entered the *Thing*. Around her the ship's walls suddenly thrummed with purpose.

"Prepare for departure," the ship said. Milly gave out a startled squawk as fleshy tendrils lashed out from the walls to grab at all of them, pulling them close and snug.

"Prepare for departure," the ship repeated.

"I'm really not sure what else we could be doing in order to prepare for it," Niko snapped from her place on the wall. Her voice was muffled; the ship had secured her with additional diligence due her rank, and her form was barely visible among the mass of enthusiastic tendrils.

"We will be entering snap drive in thirty seconds."

"Are you mad?" Niko snapped. "You need to get away from this place before you deploy—"

And with that, the world collapsed and once again they hurtled into space, but this time the passage was rough, buffeted by forces that seemed ready to tear them to pieces.

22

Snap drives, a creation of the careless Spisoli, who pay little attention to environmental effects, allow a ship to move at near-light speed but also generate a back-facing discharge of energy capable of tearing matter apart.

Because of this, ships use them only when they are far out in space, in order to get themselves to the nearest gate.

The force and proximity of the explosion had torn through the IAPH, but a handful of the pirates would probably have survived, sheltered by their ships or other habitats, Niko thought. Was Tubal Last one of them? Did he know what she had done, would he still be pursuing her? And even if this version of him were dead, he—like Arpat—would have a backup somewhere, one that would be activated as soon as the news of his demise arrived.

Her stomach dropped, and she said out loud, involuntarily, "Petalia . . ."

"My heart grieves for your sorrow, Captain," Dabry murmured.

"Is Petalia a Florian?" the ship asked.

"They were one, yes," Niko said. "Did you see them? Did Tubal bring them aboard at some point?"

"He did, but Petalia is also currently in the secondary hold."

"What?" Niko said in disbelief.

"They entered approximately one minute after you did."

"What are they doing right now?"

"I have them constrained in the manner in which I held all of you during takeoff," the ship said. "It seemed likely that they were an intruder."

"Ship, you shouldn't be able to confine a gentlebeing against their will like that. It's an illegal capability," Dabry protested.

"If I can do it, how can it be illegal?" the *Thing* asked.

"I am suspecting that we may have different definitions at work here," Niko said. She looked at Dabry. "That gives us something to work with. There's a good chance they'll know where Last's backup—or backups, more probably—are, and with planning—and luck—we may be able to outrace the news. We do have one of the fastest ships in the Known Universe, after all."

"A rogue ship," Dabry said. "Are you listening to me? It shouldn't be able to confine people like that. Something's gone awry."

Niko shook her head. "We'll have that conversation another time. Right now, release all of us, *Thing*."

The tendrils slid away, and they moved to the screens, each seeking data.

"We got hurled way the hell out when the snap drive activated. We're headed toward Montmurray for now," Gio reported. "That's the largest and most obvious portal, gets us to plenty of other hubs. Be there in eight days."

Niko was watching the screen where Petalia stood stock-still, tendrils around them.

"Well, then," she said. "I guess we might as well find out what sort of hand Momma Sky's decided to deal us."

They let Niko go down to speak to Petalia by herself, although it was clear that Dabry wanted to accompany her. In the end, he compromised and hovered in the hallway.

The second hold was intended for small luxury items that the owner might need over the course of the journey. Its cramped space was equipped with a refrigeration unit and a number of racks. Petalia stood near one of these, still contained by ropy tendrils.

"Ship, release them," Niko said.

"They have not promised not to do you harm," the ship said.

"They do not need to make such a promise," Niko said patiently. "*Thing*, please release them."

The ship did so.

Petalia did not move as the ship's restraints fell away, other than to open their eyes.

"What are you doing here?" Niko said.

"Saving my life. Where is Turo?"

"How did you know we were leaving?"

"Turo told me. He seemed to feel that Last had been abusing me. Where is he?"

"Dead," Niko said shortly. The other flinched, but Niko pressed further. "Why come away now, Pet? You could have escaped through him before."

"What is different from then and now?" Petalia said, and indicated Niko with their chin. "Before I was waiting for you to remember me."

"And now you have gotten the chance to remind me, and then rescued yourself," Niko said.

"That is correct."

"And what is the next part of your plan?"

"You know as well as I that there is one coin more valuable right now than any other to you."

"Where Last's backups are stored."

"The same. Are you bound for Montmurray?"

Niko's chin dipped in a nod.

"If Last is dead and there is enough chaos—and if the measures Arturo put into place work—you will have a little time—perhaps as much as a solar day, but that is a generous estimate—before anyone dispatches the activation code. It has to get to Montmurray, then Ixumi. Once there, you can intercept the drone with the code, and ensure the backup is not activated."

"And then?" Niko's narrowed eyes watched Petalia's face as though hypnotized.

"Then? This ship will surely be headed for one hub or another. When it stops at a destination that I like, I will depart."

"Oh," Niko said. "Is that how it will work?"

"It is."

Niko took a step closer. "I thought perhaps you had come to tell me once again how much you hated me."

"I have hated you very much. I believe I have made that clear."

"But you continue to use the past tense," Niko said.

Petalia studied her in silence. "Let me make something clear, Niko," they said at length. "I hate you now, have hated you in the past, and will continue to hate you going forward. That is how things are. They will not change. I know how you are. I've seen you flirt your way out of things, sweet talk and wheedle. We have gone long past the point where anything you could say would wipe away the memories of all the things that Tubal Last said and did to me."

"So I'm simply a means to an end, a way to get away," Niko said. She eyed the case at Petalia's feet. "I would bet that contains jewelry and other sellable materials? Sufficient to start you on a new life?"

"It seemed the most expedient plan, and there was plenty to choose from in Tubal Last's treasure troves."

"And what became of your master?"

They had moved closer and closer to each other over the course of this interchange. Niko could smell the flowers of Petalia's hair, could breathe in their green, oxygenated scent, their proximity like a cool breeze on her skin.

At the question, the Florian's hand lashed out, striking Niko's face. Niko recoiled.

"Don't ever call him that again!" Pet snarled.

Niko rubbed thoughtfully at the spot of heat along her cheek, although the darkness of her skin hid it. "That is fair enough," she said. "Then we will leave it at this. You will help us to Ixumi and we will work together to remove the danger, and then we will go our separate ways."

She did not say much to the others about the presence of the Florian, but simply let them discover it for themselves. Talon, lost in grief, did not care.

Encountering Petalia in the corridor, Lassite said to them, "You walk the same Spiral of Destiny that the captain does, but you follow in her footsteps in this timeline. In others, you lead the way."

They could not see his face, other than the occasional flicker of his tongue, sampling the air.

They said, "Tubal Last liked to bring mystics to his room and make them predict what he would do next." Their smile was cold as space, almost as empty.

He persisted. "Your life has meaning, but you treat it as though it does not."

"I have lived for decades with Tubal Last. And a year with that man is a lifetime. Do not presume to tell me whether or not my life has meaning or what you in your ignorance think that meaning might be."

They turned away and walked down the corridor. He stood watching their back and trying to see what would happen next, but everything was dark around them. They held doom in one hand and joy in the other and did not know whom or what to bestow either upon. He pitied them.

And he feared what they might do.

Like everyone, Petalia did pitch in with the daily chores of life aboard the *Thing* as they raced toward the gate.

Working in the ship's garden, side by side with the Florian, harvesting the water globes that Dabry had requested, Milly said, "Be sensible. It's a big universe out there and it's hard to get by without some sort of start."

"I have a start." Petalia touched the gems around their neck. "These and more are plenty to buy what I require."

"And what is that?" Milly persisted. Petalia had consistently refused to speak of their plans after the ship.

"Niko did well enough setting up a business in her retirement, something that would offer her a living and something to keep her occupied. Perhaps I'll do something like that. Start a business."

"What sort of business? What are you good at?"

Petalia wobbled their head side to side in a noncommittal gesture. "I used to be good at any number of things. The Free Traders were teaching me to handle accounting." At Milly's face, they gave a small laugh. "I can tell that is not something that appeals to you, but different stars for different ships! I like numbers. They are always the same. Predictable and patterned. If the world were made of numbers instead of atoms, it would be a better place."

"Some argue that it is, but that we cannot comprehend its numbers because they are so small and so large at the same time," Milly said.

Petalia made a face. "That is one of those meaningless sayings of mystics and charlatans."

"A mystic helped us get here and get you out," Milly said. "I like Lassite about as much as the next person, but I have to credit him for that."

"A broken door opens, even if it cannot close," Pet said. "But regardless of whether the mystics are right, I will go and do something that is the very antithesis of what they do: accounting."

"By all accounts, Florians are mystics," Milly said.

Petalia froze. Then they raised their face to Milly and said, "I am the last of my race. What I am is all that Florians are."

They stalked out of the room. Milly stared after them in dismay.

Uncharacteristically, Skidoo made no physical overtures. The Florian tasted odd to her, bitter and sweet all at once, but not in a pleasant way. Wherever they went in the ship, that unpleasant tang seemed to follow. Instead, the Tlellan focused on Talon, holding him during his daily bouts of grief.

Atlanta had no idea what to say to the Florian; she wanted so desperately to know what their history was with Captain Niko that she became tongue-tied whenever conversation seemed imminent.

She raised the point when she and Dabry were in the area that had become the *Thing*'s "kitchen" although Niko said it was an abomination to call it that while Dabry simply called it "less than optimal."

While the two of them were there, there were actually three people participating in the conversation. They were still getting used to the idea of living inside another being. It shouldn't have seemed like much of a stretch; most ships had some form of AI, after all, and most of those were quite convincing in their personalities.

But they were programmed, those manifestations, while the *Thing*'s seemed truly unpredictable, a product of environmental factors and events that had happened while it was growing (an odd thought for Atlanta, that of an adolescent ship).

The *Thing*, on the other hand, did things those personalities would not, like asking questions. It was currently, to the embarrassment of the other participants, exploring the topic of procreation. Atlanta tried to divert the conversation.

"Why won't Petalia stay?" she asked Dabry. "They don't act as though they hate Niko. They were talking with her just last night about the Correllian star sea."

"They are cordial enough," Dabry said. "I don't know whether that is intended to hurt Niko, but it does, to the core."

"Why?"

"Because they used to be much more than that to each other."

"But what does Petalia expect from her? She did come back!"

"She came back, it's true enough," a voice said from the doorway.

It was, of course, Petalia. They wore a simple robe, having finally put aside the stiff and formal garments they had insisted on the first few days. This one was plain blue cloth, unadorned and cut to fit a multitude of forms, none of them well. Nonetheless, they wore it with grace, clasped around their slim waist with a scarf of darker blue. Their feet were bare and the silky hair unrestrained; it bloomed brighter now than when they had first met.

They took a step into the room. "She came back, but after years of not thinking she would, I grew too used to thinking that way."

Atlanta shrank back.

Petalia said coldly, "Dabry." They looked around. "I wish food. Do you think Niko will begrudge me that outside of the regulated mealtimes? She has shown, after all, that her merchantly concerns are both inflexible and paramount. She will always choose this company's interests over mine."

"You know that everything you say is not true," Dabry said, laying down the bowl of caraway seeds he had been showing Atlanta how to roast and grind. "We have all told you how she was seeking you all this time, in her way."

"In her way," Petalia said in a sullen tone.

Four hands came up in a complex gesture of irritation. "And her way is usually successful!"

"If accident had not brought her to me, where would you be now? Still back at the station, still playing at your restaurant. Still playing games that did not free me."

"But you are free now," Dabry said. "Can you not just accept that for the gift it is?"

"A gift from Niko?"

"A gift from the universe! Chance sped up our plan—because you know in your heart of hearts she was faithful and would have come when she knew that she could win. And instead of seeing that for the good luck that it was, you wander about looking wronged—"

"I was wronged!"

"We have all been wronged. Life wrongs us constantly! Do you think I would be here of my own choosing? Do you think I have no slights that the universe has dealt me?" He glared at them until they turned their gaze to roam along the shelves.

They shrugged as they did so, murmuring, "And that same universe has made me who and what I am. Perhaps I am part of its plan for your beloved captain."

"You have become poison," he said. At that they took an indignant breath, and he forestalled them with a hand. "Do not deny it. And do not think that I will not seek to keep my captain—my friend—from it. From you."

"You have no need to worry," they said with rancor. "I am departing soon. When we come to Montmurray, I have asked Niko to dock there long enough for me to leave. You have less than a day of me to worry about."

"That is only a fueling station. You will find no employment there."

"I do not intend to. Plenty of ships pass through. I was once a Free Trader, and so I will take their route and let chance dictate where I will go next. I do not need to seek employment, at least not yet."

He nodded at them stiffly, his body language still hostile.

"We will never warm up to each other, you and I," Petalia said. Their tone grew mocking. "But it's me that your captain will always yearn for."

"You show yourself unworthy of that devotion by your willingness to discount it," he said. "Shame on you, to scorn a heart given so freely."

"Niko forgot me long ago, when she took other lovers."

He started to speak, then caught himself, "She told me once—"

"What?" Petalia demanded. "What did she tell you that could possibly excuse her?"

He looked at them steadily, expressionless. "That in all of them she saw only you."

Petalia opened their mouth to speak, then shut it and shook their head. "It is no use; you will ever be on her side of matters."

"Leave off your bitterness," Dabry said, heat peppered behind the words. "Do you not think she worked day and night, thinking how to gain resources enough to come back and free you? She worked those equations over and over again, and you object that she would not come when the sum was zero!"

"I would have, for her," Petalia said.

"Can you say that? Truly? It is easy enough after the fact to proclaim one's nobility, but when push became shove, there was lack." Dabry's words were rough, and for the first time a hint of accent, thick and clotted, entered his speech.

"I am what I am!" Petalia said. "Look upon what I have become, thanks to Niko!"

"You should thank Tubal Last for that," Dabry said. Then, cruelly, "Or yourself. Perhaps if you had pleased him better, your race would have survived."

At those words, Petalia seemed to shrivel in on themselves. They stepped backward a few steps, their eyes enormous and wide as they stared at Dabry. Their robe swirled as they turned and fled in a flash of blue.

"Dabry, that was cruel!" Atlanta protested, but he stood adamant.

"They hold the captain to impossible and illogical standards," he said. "If that is the garment's measure, see how well they wear it. They want to leave the ship? Then good riddance to them and their grudges. We don't need such attitudes poisoning our ship."

"How would I be poisoned?" the ship asked with interest.

He frowned up at the ceiling. "Attitudes are contagious," he said. "A negative person makes more negative people around them. Imagine if you carried around someone who was sad or angry all the time. You would grow tired of it, but more than that, you would become sad or angry yourself."

"I do not understand," the ship said.

"This is ephemeral, like flavors," Dabry said. "I have raised hundreds of recruits in my time, but the challenge of explaining such matters to you, *Thing*, is the greatest I have ever known."

"Should I thank you?" the ship said uncertainly.

Both he and Atlanta laughed at that. The ship joined in, recording the moment and filing it away under *friendship*.

The ship tried to speak to them more than once. Petalia seemed to encompass so many complicated emotions, combinations of three or four or sometimes even more, but any attempt to press them on definitions and sensations led to abrupt declarations that the conversation was over.

Of all of them, Petalia seemed to find the company of Gio the least objectionable, and the two of them were often found watching Q-space and conversing quietly about the life of plants and herbs and the elaborate theory of spices that Gio had learned from a practitioner of Washen.

As time passed and the wait to find out whether they would be successful wore on, the pattern of interaction between Niko and the Florian grew more intense. They would be cordial one moment, and then Petalia would be savaging the captain verbally the next. It was as though they could not control themselves, as though the words had to emerge, as surely as a chemical reaction causing an explosion. It was painful and embarrassing to be around.

Niko refused to respond, simply looking more and more stolid and solemn, driving Petalia into increasingly vicious words.

Atlanta used the *Thing*'s medfacility to regrow her fingers. The fresh-grown ones were tender and sore at first, but she practiced her combat skills, fine-tuning them. An Empress needed to be able to protect those around her, she told herself, and nothing her internal advisors could say could convince her otherwise.

Everyone did their best by the sullen Talon, who would not speak, but stayed by himself, sitting in the chamber he once shared with his twin.

"Is being coming away," Skidoo urged him, but he refused.

"I can smell him here, better than anywhere else on the ship," he said, and then went back to silence.

Atlanta made herself small and unobtrusive in the pilot's chamber when it came time to exit Q-space, watching Niko and Dabry.

Niko said to Dabry, "I've been thinking more about what we might do in the future. If we are in luck—and manage to remove this threat, then we should set course for a central hub."

"Why?"

"To give Pet choices when they depart."

"I . . ." Dabry said, and faltered for the first time Atlanta had ever witnessed. "They said so, and I will say that I had hoped it true, but I had also thought they might stay with you."

"I had hoped so as well," Niko said in a neutral tone, "but it seems I was mistaken." She rolled her shoulders. "I will go and see what the others are up to," she said. "Thorn and Talon, you never know what they have gotten up to." She stopped. "Talon, I mean." Her tone was neutral as stone.

She left. Atlanta looked at Dabry, who frowned as though noticing her for the first time.

Atlanta felt as tired as Dabry looked. Poised on the edge of a knife blade, they were all having trouble sleeping. "How close are we?" she said.

"We are cutting it close," Dabry said. "The drone is smaller and moves faster than we do in this space. But we will get to the facility in time to intercept it with drones of our own while Gio works on exploding the facility itself. Petalia says it's a maintenance station about two hundred clicks away from the main structure. Blow that up, and we're golden for now. You're prepared for that, *Thing*?"

"You and the captain have both asked me that repeatedly," the *Thing* said. "The answer remains the same."

Dabry shrugged. "Lucky for us, there's no living crew there," he muttered. "As it is, if Gio doesn't act fast enough, a data squeal with information identifying us will go out."

Atlanta looked at the empty doorway. "You'd think the captain would stick around to watch," she said unhappily.

"She is distracted," Dabry said. "And we can do nothing to change what happens, once we are in place."

Niko drifted like a leaf through the *Thing*'s hallways, her pattern seemingly aimless. But she already knew where it would take her. She paused in the doorway of the lounge, looking at the way Q-space's milky light outlined Petalia's silhouette.

They stood stock-still, Niko watching while the other ignored her. The light outside flashed and dimmed; neither flinched as the ship slid into normal space.

The *Thing*'s equipment was state of the art, but doubt fluttered like a moth in Niko's throat. Would it be this easy? *Could* it be?

They stayed silent, even when the ship said, "Drones successful, Captain Niko," although Niko's lips firmed as though about to speak.

The ship said, "Gio is safely away and says his incendiaries are all in place."

Another point where all her plans could fail. Was this what Lassite felt, with all his words about the Spiral of Destiny, and the choices that led to it, knowing that at any moment all of it could falter, could fail, could fall away out of possibility?

It paused, waiting for reply, then said, "Incendiaries engaged. Facility destroyed."

As the energies flared, it waited, feeling *curiosity* like an itch. Why did they not speak?

But then Niko said, "The last of Last, one might say. And now, will you stay or go?" Her voice was impatient and harsh, deliberately so.

Petalia's answer was so quiet that both Ship and Niko barely heard it.

The Florian took their leave of the *Thing* and its crew.

The gate was small but central, meaning they could catch a ship to a multitude of places.

The rest of them were absent when Niko walked Petalia down to the landing ramp. Niko looked around. There were very few other ships at dock; three docks down, a crowd of cheerful Geglis were cheering one another on, trying to see who could load their ship the fastest, and passing around a bottle of starwater, guaranteed to slow anyone down.

"The others said goodbye already," Petalia said. "I think you're being given space in which to say your farewell."

Sadness edged their tone. Niko said, "Is it farewell, then?"

"It must be."

The question she had tried so hard not to ask finally burst from her. "Are you *sure*, Pet? Really, truly sure?"

Petalia drooped. Strands of little white flowers fell over their forehead, obscuring their face like a veil. The air was stinging cold; fueling stations kept environmentals at a minimum except for the levels where the workers were, or the single canteen where travelers were encouraged to spend their money on necessities at ten times their normal price. Out past the field that kept the thin air inside the station, stars glinted, cold and white against blackness, staring bleakly into the void.

Petalia murmured, "Be reasonable, Niko. Would you want to go on like this, forever at each other's throats? With you forever reminding me of Tubal Last?"

"Ah," Niko said. "That's it, then. I and Last are woven together inextricably for you, are we?"

"How could you not be, with his obsession with his revenge being played out every day? You have no idea of the depths to which he hated you, Niko. You were the only creature still living that had ever dared cross him; he destroyed all the rest."

"And now he's gone," Niko said.

Petalia was silent.

Niko said, "There's something that you're not telling me."

"I fear him still," Petalia admitted.

Niko held her breath before releasing it in a long sigh. "We've done our best to circumvent that. The last revenge scheme was decades in planning, but this time he'd want me to know something was coming. He wouldn't have been able to resist sending me some ominous note."

"I know," Petalia admitted. Their hand fluttered at their throat as though remembering the clutch of Last's fingers choking them. "But it is a fear in me nonetheless."

Niko caught the hand and held it. "All the more reason to stay here, where I can protect you," she whispered.

Petalia pulled their hand away so forcefully that it staggered them both. "Don't touch me!"

Niko stepped back, holding up both hands. Down the way, the Geglis were staring, nudging one another. "I only meant . . ." she began.

"You meant that you were making another promise you could not keep," Petalia said coldly. "You would have thought you had learned better than that by now, Captain Larsen."

Niko's hands dropped and she straightened. "Very well," she said. "I bid you good voyage and unfettered stars."

The phrase was traditional among Free Traders. Petalia did not return it. Instead, they simply spun and walked away.

Niko stood watching them until they were out of sight. How

had so many decades slipped away there? Was Pet right to consider it a desertion? Niko had spent every night going over her plans to rise in rank, get a crew under her command, take it to rescue Petalia. She'd had the power to do it all of ten hours too. Maybe she should have moved faster, but she hadn't seen her fall coming. Who would have? She had thought herself a hero.

So the Ten-Hour Admiral had her power for those hours, and that had not been enough time to assemble an expedition and get them safely away. At first when she had been given the news and had not entirely understood it, she thought they had caught on to her intentions, that they knew she meant to go rescue Pet, even though she had managed to hide it so well, even to the point of keeping it out of the Hive Mind's meld, so that the others would not be held complicit in her crime when it happened.

She'd thought perhaps she could move fast, had even been on her way to the docks when they had caught up with her.

Surely Petalia's accusations were unjustified. But a side of Niko wanted to embrace them, to confess herself a poor and broken human being and throw herself on Pet's mercy. Which she had seen in action before.

That had been before the years with Tubal Last. What was Pet's mercy like now? Last had implied that they had learned to kill while with him. And worse, that they had learned to enjoy the act.

Impossible.

But Niko had seen more unlikely things in the course of her life. Had seen people whose actions she would have thought she could predict with confidence do strange and unexpected things, sometimes betraying secrets that they had been holding all their lives.

Last was a smart and unscrupulous man with immense wealth at his command. He'd had time as well, plenty of time to plan his revenge. Time to twist Petalia, to make them something completely different from the gentle, playful being Niko had known.

Was there any way for them to find their way back to what they had once been? Niko had never seen anyone make that journey. Sometimes you could make peace with the past but it was always still there, what happened. You couldn't erase it without removing part of who you were.

Some people edited their memories freely, or therapeutically. But the erasure that would've been required to remove the violence that Last had wreaked on the Florian's mind, that was an entirely different matter and would've been the same sort of death that Takraven's clone had faced when they'd fled TwiceFar station. You could know that someone else would awaken and that they would in many ways be you, but you also knew that *you* would be gone.

Their flask drained, the Geglis returned to loading their ship.

23

While Niko said her goodbyes to Pet, Atlanta was once again in the kitchen. "I don't understand Lassite," she said to Dabry.

He didn't take his attention away from the root he was chopping, which had appeared from his luggage, and which he said was turmeric. Half of it had gone to be sprouted in the *Thing*'s greenhouse, along with a similar gingerroot and some variegated reeds that smelled like peppery cinnamon.

"What don't you understand about him?" Dabry asked.

"Why Niko keeps him around. No one seems to like him much; no one talks to him."

"Have you talked to him?" He flicked peel away to expose saffron-colored flesh.

"I tried to." Atlanta wrinkled her nose. "He said a lot of things about a Spiral of Destiny. And doom."

"He does mention the Spiral of Destiny a lot. As far as I can tell, he believes Niko is walking it and the rest of us are all just here to help her. At the end of it, he says there's something that will change the universe." He paused before he went on. "A long time ago, Niko was part of some very important negotiations."

"I know all that. The ones at Rourke's Leap. He wants to be with Niko because he thinks he can show her the Spiral of Destiny?"

"Not show it to her, no. He says that she is already on it, is following it. He is here to facilitate. Maybe to witness."

"Are all Sessiles like him?"

"My understanding is that only a small percentage of them are called to mysticism, and most of those become a magic user of some sort, battle mages usually, though who can afford a battle mage? He's a prophet, and the jury is out on those. Some claim that the Sessiles have a special connection with the universe— that the gods made them to be that connection and that the prophets are the manifestation of that. Enough Sessiles believe that to keep the prophets fed and housed well on their planet and enough people elsewhere to do it wherever they go in the universe. With the usual commonsense exceptions, of course."

"Of course," she echoed.

He began wiping down the dishes he'd been using.

"So what happens?"

He paused. "What happens when?"

"Now we move to the next step, right? So what happens when she gets to wherever she's going on this Spiral of Destiny? The universe changes? What does that mean?"

He shrugged. "I guess we'll find out when we get there."

Niko was almost all the way back to the ship when a voice spoke. "You're a hard woman to track down, Nicolette Larsen."

She turned. "Admiral Taklibia?" she said, incredulous.

It was indeed the diploid that hung in the air there. She could see the insignia gleaming, the purple slash over three red diamonds, all over the Holy Hive Mind's golden wavy line.

"As we said, you're a hard woman to track down."

"I am not trying to be elusive," she said. "What reason would I have for doing so? And what hope would I have of it, given the Holy Hive Mind's reach?"

"You disappeared for weeks, so they couldn't locate you. Then you surfaced again with an insurance claim."

"We were busy being kidnapped by Tubal Last and then destroying the IAPH," Niko said.

"Is that what happened to it? Rumors were flying." The admiral hung in the air, unreadable.

"What do you want, Admiral?" Niko said.

"So quick to cut to the chase? Not worried what we might say?" Niko squinted.

The admiral came a half meter closer. "Believe it or not, you still have friends in the fleet, and others who find your escape inspirational. It's not a situation that pleases the Holy Hive Mind. We wanted to let you know they're forming an Inquiry."

Chills went down Niko's spine. She could see now why the admiral had wanted to pass this word along in person rather than relying on a message system that could be corrupted or monitored. The admiral was risking a great deal to warn her. What did they want in return?

"Nothing like that," they said in answer to her questioning look. "We're not looking for a payoff. But as we said—others are trying to get out. They may come to you."

"The Hive Mind won't be happy about that," she said. "That's a trend they'll want to discourage."

"They will," the admiral said. "The trick is to get it trending strongly enough that they cannot stop it, no matter how hard they try—and they will try. Hard. There is no doubt of that."

"I didn't sign on to lead a rebellion," Niko said. "That was not my intent at all."

"No," the admiral said. "But there are people in this universe who do things, and there are those who do not. You are definitely one of the former."

"I will not drag my crew into a war with the Holy Hive Mind."

"You may not have a choice." They paused. "We would be careful, if we were you. Some of the reports—they have someone close to you, we think, or a method of monitoring you that you don't know about. We don't know more than that—it's a guess, really.

Wild suspicion hit Niko. "The Arranti attack—that was unconnected, surely?"

"Of course it was. Who knows what any Arranti will do next?"

The column swiveled in negation. "No, you've had a run of bad luck lately, but surely it's just that."

Surely just that. The words echoed in Niko's head. But no one controlled the Arranti. A run of bad luck. *Surely just that.*

Back at the ship, she went to talk to part of that run of bad luck. "This is the thing," she said. "You say that you were sent away in the dead of night, by the Empress herself. Can you remember what she told you?"

Atlanta shook her head. "It seems like a lifetime ago now, so much has happened." She tried to remember, wishing once again that she'd recorded it, but the presence of the Empress turned off all recording devices, even small personal ones.

"She said that she was sending me to Nicolette Larsen, who was someone who could help me, but not who that was or how or why."

"Could she have been testing you in some way?" Dabry asked.

Atlanta blushed. "That's what I thought was happening too. It's certainly possible. Anything is possible. But sending me into danger—surely that wasn't her intention. She had no way of knowing things would start exploding."

"An Empress in some unspecified danger sends away one—possibly more, we have no way of telling—of her heirs, and does so to an obscure restaurant owner that she has met perhaps once at most." Niko rubbed her forehead. "I am at a loss for an explanation." She looked directly at Atlanta. "Here's the thing. Everyone I talk to—and I do mean everyone, without exception—says there is no danger, no rebellion. No war. Nothing that would have caused her to send you away."

Atlanta raised her chin. "Then we will go and ask her why she has done this. I am her heir, she must give me an answer."

Dabry and Niko exchanged glances.

"If she was sent away, is it wise to take her back again?" Dabry asked.

"A danger that we do not know—that we can't anticipate and plan against—is a hundred times more dangerous than one we do," Niko said. "We will go and see what we draw out. We will not let anyone aboard the ship that we do not know, and we will keep a watch on other ships that impinge upon our space."

Bam! Atlanta rebounded off Skidoo's form but still managed to fling the ball toward Dabry. She was rather proud of how much better she'd gotten at the game.

The four of them had started playing lately, trying to coax Talon out of his chamber. So far they'd had little success, but Atlanta had become enthused by the game for its own sake. Even intended to introduce it into palace life as soon as she got back, in the name of keeping fit and combat ready. If she happened to clean everyone's clocks in the course of that introduction, well, so be it.

"Captain Niko, someone is returning your call to the Imperial Presence," the ship said.

"Ugh," Niko said. "I'll be right there." She rose and took advantage of the pause to bounce a ball through a goal while Dabry did the same on his end.

"That is being not fair!" Skidoo exclaimed.

"All's fair when victory is on the line," she declaimed. Everyone rolled their eyes. She made for her room, pausing to run through her fresher and swap into clean clothes before activating the communications console. The Imperial regime was rules bound and protocol based; Niko was frankly surprised that someone had returned her message within only a few hours. All this unnecessary bureaucracy rubbed her raw, all this making another person wait in order to establish one's superiority. She was lucky this hadn't taken days, if not weeks.

"You are Nicolette Larsen?" a voice greeted her when she signed on.

"Of course I am," she said irritably. "You called me, you should know who I am."

"Please stand by for Her Highness."

Niko sat down on the bed, suddenly weak in the knees. "Wait, what? The Empress? Calling me?" She'd had her doubts about Atlanta, thinking pieces of her narrative were unconfirmed. Sometimes she seemed not to recollect things so well, like physical details of the palace. Other times she spoke in loving detail, descriptions that sounded, to Niko's practiced ear, a bit rehearsed.

But a call from the Empress herself would seem to confirm her story. From what Niko knew of the Paxian Empire, its leaders took care of their multiple heirs, grooming and training them so one day one of them could step into place with ease should the need arise.

The console chimed. The Empress's face, shown in miniature atop it, smaller than Niko's head but seeming much grander. More regal.

"Captain Larsen, I owe you an apology and explanation. You were entrusted with something for safekeeping and seem to have weathered extraordinary circumstances with it."

"You don't owe me anything, Your Majesty," Niko said. "I'm happy to be of service and trust I will be well compensated for it." She paused before adding, "Whatever it was, exactly, that I was supposed to do."

The Empress ignored the indirect question. "Bring your cargo to Pax, and I will both compensate and explain."

Niko inclined her head. "As Your Majesty wishes."

She waited until the connection had been fully severed before exploding. "Sky Momma's frozen tits, what now?"

She returned to the bay where the rest of them, having finished the game, were chattering and conducting the usual postgame analysis, bragging and pretending not to miss the absent Thorn or sulking Talon. She said to Atlanta, "That was a call from the Empress. She said come to Pax and all will be explained."

Dabry turned to Atlanta, arching an eyebrow. "All will be explained? What does she mean by that?"

"I don't know," Atlanta said, bewildered stomach sinking.

Skidoo patted her. "It will is being okay," she said confidently. "Captain Niko is being making sure of that."

Niko kept silent but she had her own doubts. The Empress had referred to Atlanta as "cargo." That was an odd choice, and one that might not bode well for Atlanta. Cargo was not allowed to choose its fate but rather had to go where it was sent.

Like the *Thing*. Despite the changes that Lolola's programming had wrought in it, the *Thing* was still very much a product of the shipyard that had grown it. The *Thing* had told Niko that the factory had fail-safes, signals that, when broadcast to a ship, would cause it to destroy itself by whatever means were at hand. If they'd known the *Thing* had been taken, it would have been forced to destroy itself before docking at the IAPH.

"Kill you?" she'd said. "Why would they do that?"

"They do not wish their technology captured," the ship replied. It was not sure how it felt about that. It was still *proud* to be unique, or at least pleasure was associated with the exercise of that emotion, but it had yet to really be put to the test, which usually involved talking to a human about it.

But the thought of death—of being forced to make itself no longer exist—washed away thoughts of pride. The ship was not sure exactly what emotions appeared in such circumstances—it seemed to be a mix of them, and ever since Thorn's passing, it had spent a great deal of time analyzing the combination and trying to determine why they added up to the sensation *unpleasant*.

24

Atlanta didn't expect a going-away party, but of course they had one. How could they not, how could they not spend all their remaining time storing up surprises and secrets and things to delight her, to make her smile on a day when they all felt like crying?

Milly got her to the room on the pretext of showing her a rare manifestation in Q-space. When Atlanta paused in the darkened doorway, not sure what was going on, the ship turned on the lights and everyone jumped up and chorused "Surprise!"

"It's not my birthday," she said uncertainly. "Aren't surprise parties for birthdays?"

"Sometimes they are for goodbyes," Niko said. Everyone nodded.

There were two kinds of cake, one vanilla and another on which Dabry squandered the last of his store of chocolate. Milly decorated cookies with sugar and marzipan emblems from their journey, the *Thing*'s sigil as well as TwiceFar's double circle and a skull and crossbones for the IAPH. Gio pulled a flute from his luggage and played while the ship clapped and boomed accompaniment and Milly danced.

Atlanta, standing swaying to the music, saw Niko watching Milly dance. The captain's expression was thoughtful. Not pleased appreciation of the motion's aesthetic beauty as Milly flowed from one stance to another. Not arousal at the body-based beat, persistent as a heartbeat, as Milly undulated seductively and Skidoo gave out a hoot.

No, this was the captain sizing up an opponent, one she thought she might face in the future.

I should keep an eye on that, she thought, and then realized she wouldn't be around to do so. Regret plucked at her once again, as it had ever since she'd learned she was going back.

She looked away and this time caught Dabry's eye. He inclined his head to her and gave her the smallest of salutes. Impending loss hit her like an arrow fired from close range.

These people had become her *friends*. What would she do back at court without them? She realized she hadn't consulted her own internal virtual advisors for days. Which was unprecedented.

Probably not a habit an actual empress would lose. She would have to do better. She would have to use all the knowledge that she had acquired during her trip to rule well, if she were ever called on to do so, and certainly to act as a good advisor if the Empress should ever need her.

She'd decided that was what she had been meant to learn. Perhaps even to pass those lessons along to the other heirs. She'd have to be careful not to sound too preachy about her experiences, even if she would probably have vastly more such experience than any of them.

She thought, with pride, that while she would not be around her friends anymore, she would be representing them, would be representing their points of view, their common sense and pragmatic priorities.

She wondered what Niko would think if she found out that Atlanta was working on a new virtual advisor modeled on her?

There were presents: small things, most handmade. Some teas from Dabry. A little knife from Niko, who also showed her a multiplicity of ways and places it could be hidden around her body. An even smaller set of explosive devices from Gio, who simply signed, "You never know when you might need them."

A feather fan from Milly, who explained that it had been painless. "Molting from the stress of all the travel," she'd said, waving off Atlanta's thanks, even though the Swan's plumage looked much the same as always.

The ship, never to be outdone, had produced an entire set of luggage, emblazoned with its own insignia along with Atlanta's initials, in a pseudo-lizard hide that, it explained proudly, was impervious to up to 40-kiloton blasts, most scanning equipment, and temperatures between –100 and +500 degrees Celsius.

Atlanta, who had nothing to put in most of it, thanked the ship, and filled the smallest case with her belongings and the largest case with the rest of the luggage, nested one piece inside the other, each opening to reveal a smaller version, down to the smallest hatbox.

Lassite gave her nothing. He came and said, "I will tell you something that will comfort you. You will return."

"When?"

His voice was earnest from the folds of the red hood. "If I could tell you that, I would. But I only know that on almost all twists of the Spiral of Destiny, you walk with the captain."

She wanted to roll her eyes at the mysticism, but she refrained. Who was she to sneer at someone else's beliefs, after all? Despite all the vagueness of prophecy, and all she'd been taught of its ineffectiveness, she had seen Lassite's skills when he caught the ghosts. . . .

She said, "What happened to your ghosts? Do you still have them?"

He shook his head. "They like the ship," he said. "Certainly they like it better than being in a bag. The ship doesn't mind. It doesn't actually believe they're there."

Several of them made more private goodbyes as well.

The *Thing* fussed about the luggage and made her tell it repeatedly that, yes, it was perfect, and, no, she wouldn't change anything about it, and, no, she would not prefer the ship reabsorb this set and start again from scratch. It assuaged its anxiety by producing a small toiletry kit and cosmetic case to match.

She tried to say goodbye to Talon. He came to his doorway long enough to hug her awkwardly.

She kept thinking, what if she did become the Empress? Then she could afford to hire people like Niko and her crew. That wouldn't be the same, would it? It didn't seem as though it would, if the people were with her only because they wanted her to pay them.

Whether or not she would become Empress had been a matter of indifference to her before, mainly because the chances were so small that she would. The Empress had the same longevity treatments that the very rich could afford, and there was no reason to be thinking she would pass away anytime soon. Much less that of all the dozens of heirs, Atlanta would be the one selected to replace her if such an occasion should arise.

But for the first time, she wanted it. Spent time trying to figure out how to best achieve it. It seemed to her that it was a combination of acquiring skills and making the right contacts, building a network of influences that would help shape the picking of an heir and push her name to the forefront of the list.

She didn't want the Empress to die. She didn't want that at all, but if it did happen, she wanted events to go a certain way afterward.

How to achieve that? That was a question she intended to answer sooner or later.

She walked along the corridor, wondering how many more times she'd go along it. Skidoo appeared in a doorway and advanced on her. She stopped just short of invading her personal space, and said, "You is being leaving, and we is being together-ing never."

A tentacle extended, touched her chin. When she didn't move away, it slid along her arm. The touch was soft and cool. She'd expected it to be moister somehow, to drag on the dryness of her own skin, but instead it slid along it, making the little hairs stand up in a trail after it. She could smell vanilla and chlorine.

She swallowed. This was more alien than she'd ever expected. At the same time, such a basic urge for every race, the urge for pleasure in touch. She reached up, curled her fingers around the tentacle.

"Perhaps I'll travel with you again sometime," she said. She looked at the turquoise eyes, deep and expressive, and saw the flecks of gold they sheltered, only visible this close. How could it manage to be alluring and alien all at once? She felt her heart pounding in her throat. No wonder humans have gotten such a name for being sexually available and ready, she thought, if just a suggestive touch can do this.

"Right," Niko said from behind her. "Perhaps you will." Her dry tone hinted amusement. "They've sent a shuttle for us, and it's in sync with the *Thing*. If you're ready, it's time to take you down to the Empress."

Reluctantly, Atlanta let her fingers fall away from the tentacle. "You're the only one going with me?" Panic grabbed her. She hadn't expected this to happen quite *yet*—surely there had been at least an hour or two to go.

"The Empress asked that only I go down," Niko said. "There's something off about all of this."

"Is thinking it's being a trap?" Skidoo asked. "Maybeing all of us should being going with you."

Niko shook her head. "I'm not going to outright disobey the Empress on the strength of a suspicion," she said. "But I'm not going unarmed, and Atlanta, you might want to have a weapon handy too."

"Already done," she said, and tapped the spot up her sleeve where the knife resided. She didn't touch the belt pouch where Gio's explosives were, but their presence comforted her nonetheless.

"You've come such a long way since you first crawled out of that crate," Niko said. She opened her arms. "Hug me now before we get down to a much more dignified place where there will be none of that sort of thing."

Atlanta found herself crying against the captain's neck. Niko patted her back and whispered, "Ssssh, it's all right. Just stand ready, Princess. Everything will be fine." She nodded at Skidoo, who left the room.

As the sobs cleared, Atlanta realized that she believed it fully. Believed that Niko would take care of her, just as she took care of all the others. It made her want to cry even more, to have gained this family only to lose it. She didn't think she'd ever experience it again.

Niko released her. Atlanta stepped back, wiping at her eyes, feeling shaky and uncertain. She said, "Promise me you'll come back and visit with all of them."

"When I can," Niko said. "It'll take a while to sort out everything, and in my experience, there's no guarantee that there will be any insurance payout once they're done disqualifying items. We may be starting from scratch again."

She shrugged. "Perhaps the Empress will shower me with riches as a thank-you for sheltering you. I know that taking you among pirates might not have been exactly what she had in mind. Indeed, I would be astonished if that had been what she had in mind. Still, I am returning you safely and in much the same condition as when you arrived, although with two regrown fingers and the knowledge not to depend on bioweapons being undetectable."

Atlanta winced at the memory, fingers twitching. She said, "Next time I'll make them detachable."

"There's thinking for you," Niko said. "Shall we?"

Followed by several of the ship's servitors carrying the two suitcases, they made their way to the shuttle.

Atlanta stared out at the planet's surface as they descended. Shadow lay over most of the continent, and a network of lights showed where the clusters of cities and town were, absent where the seas surrounded it. "What time is it at the palace?" she asked. Her stomach was empty and knotted; nervousness had prevented eating before she left.

"Very early in the morning," Niko said. "I'm surprised the Empress is awake, or that she didn't want to wait a few hours." She lounged in her own seat as best she could within the confines of her belt, watching the control panel as the autopilot took them to the planet's surface. Her eyes were thoughtful.

"She gets up very early in the morning, always has. She said she gets more work done that way."

"The habits of highly effective empresses," Niko said. "You'll want to remember that."

"I don't even know that I'll become Empress. It's the slimmest of chances, really."

"Unusual things have been happening to you. In my experience, unusual things happen to history makers, the ones who will move into roles like that. Maybe you won't become the Empress. Maybe you'll do something entirely different. But I'm predicting now—without consulting Lassite, who might be offended that I'm impinging on his territory—that you will be someone who touches history. Who makes decisions that change things, although, whether that may be for good or bad, I don't know." She smiled at Atlanta, who had turned in order to watch her during this speech.

Atlanta smiled back. "Thank you."

"Feh, for believing in you? It is an easy thing, believing in someone else. It's harder to believe in yourself. Remember that too."

The shuttle landed on a private airfield just outside the palace, gritting to a stop with a lurch before the seat belt released them.

Atlanta remembered it being spring when she had last been here, the smell of petals drifting in her bedchamber window the night she lay down only to be awakened hours later, shoulders shaken by a white-faced maid, and sent away. Only to eventually end up here again. Now it was autumn, and dry leaves scattered underfoot in the crisp wind, and all the clothes the ship had made for her were insufficient against the cold. How long had she been in stasis?

The *Thing*'s servitors had been left behind, so Niko started to take the larger suitcase, hefted its lightness, snorted, and took the smaller but much heavier one.

"Poor *Thing*, it truly was sorry to see you go," she murmured. "Pet didn't get so much as a goodbye, and here it outfitted you in style."

Atlanta objected to the pitying tone in Niko's voice. "Petalia never talked to it, not once," she said.

Niko stopped dead and looked at her. "Not once? Are you sure?"

"Not within my hearing."

Niko continued on. "That is very unlike the being that I once knew. People change. That's a fact of life, but something that takes getting used to. You can want someone desperately to change, and yet even if they want to change for you as well, they just can't."

Atlanta felt sad for Niko. But at the same time, she couldn't help but think that the captain was better rid of her former lover. So she said nothing and pretended to be grappling with the larger case, trying to get a good handhold. She didn't know whether Niko saw through the subterfuge, but they went down the shuttle ramp and onto the airfield. Atlanta felt wobbly and hollow, empty except for an excess of uncertainty.

She had expected a large party to be there to meet them, but instead it was a single majordomo, an elderly, sparse man with whom she had rarely interacted. He bowed to both of them as they approached, but did not speak, simply turned and walked away, evidently expecting them to follow.

They trailed him into the palace. Assembled several centuries ago, its stones were gray and cold, the color of frozen mist. The carpets that patched the floor, scattered here and there at far intervals, were woven in deep blue and purple wool, patterned with falling leaves. The rugs were sparse, and when they walked between them, the cold of the stone floor bit through the thin soles of Atlanta's boots.

One glow drone preceded the servant, and another followed them, illuminating their path. Every once in a while they could see another one in the distance, guiding some other servant on an early-morning errand or preparation, but they passed no one on their route.

She had not been sure where the Empress would meet them, but she did not expect the minor meeting room that they were led to. In contrast to most rooms in the palace, it was unadorned to the point of sparseness, although here and there the requisite touches of luxury showed in gilded hinges and couches upholstered in plushy purple velvet, sideboards bearing double-handled vases painted with golden flowers and birds and platters of fruit made from semiprecious stones. The floor underfoot was tiled with circular spiral patterns made of golden dots.

The Empress sat there. Not on a couch, but on an upholstered chair raised a few centimeters above the floor on a wooden dais, a sign that they would be permitted to sit in her presence. She wore a silver morning robe studded with tiny round mirrors, pale blue embroidery forming flowers in between the mirrors.

Whenever she moved, sequins of light scattered across her surroundings, reflecting the glow of the glow drones; the one that had followed them settled at the top of the ceiling with the three others that clustered there, sucking from the power charger hidden in the gilded bosses of the ceiling and illuminating the chamber as they did so.

The Empress did not greet them, simply pointed with a scintillation of light at the couch across from her. They settled into it. A little table stood between them with a tray on it. Atlanta caught the licorice smell of the sweet biscuits heaped on it, and her stomach growled, but she didn't move to touch one.

Atlanta glanced over at Niko. She couldn't help but imagine seeing the scene through her friend's eyes. The splendor, which Atlanta had always thought so breathtaking, now reminded her of the cluttered jumble of Tubal Last's throne room. Both were, she thought, designed to intimidate and impress. And this was only a minor meeting room. She was glad that the Empress had agreed to meet them and not sent some emissary, though.

Now she would find out, finally, why she had been sent away. Find out whether the Empire was in danger. Find out whether she was, in fact, someone special.

The Empress leaned forward, turning her face to Atlanta to address her directly. Atlanta's heart surged in her throat; she held her breath.

"You're not an heir," the Empress said.

The words were unexpected. Something else should have been forthcoming, assurances or details of some plot. Atlanta's upturned face was a bowl shattered by despair. "Then what am I?"

The Empress's hand reached out as though to touch her face. "You are a clone of an heir who was discarded."

Atlanta slapped the hand away, then was horrified. She had struck the Empress herself, an act of treason. "Then why did you send me away?" she demanded. The smell of licorice pushed nauseatingly into her nostrils. She wanted to lean her head on her knees and vomit. She swallowed hard and throttled the urge.

The Empress ignored the physical contact. "You were part of a test for another heir. I wanted to see if they could follow data and persevere. I sent out dozens like you, and their job was to find a particular one, carrying a false message. They failed. It was all an illusion, a sham. You were never meant to fall into the hands of the IAPH."

Atlanta raised her head, forcing down acrid anger, and stared full outright at the Empress. "I'm nothing? Just a piece of a test?" Her voice shook despite her best efforts to control it. Her fingers knotted in her lap, trying to hold on to one another.

"Yes," the Empress said. "We installed some of the original heir's memories in you so you would be convincing." Her voice was calm, almost desultory. "You'll find if you examine them, that you will discover moments that do not hold up to that examination. Contradictions. Missing details where your imagination has leaped in, in order to supply something that your memory cannot."

"Then what is to become of me?"

A thin shoulder moved beneath the ornate robe in a shrug. "You are not of much use, and may go wherever you please now." Her attention turned to Niko. "I apologize for the inconvenience, Captain Larsen. The mistake was unprecedented, and so we wished to convey that apology in person."

"Begging Your Majesty's pardon," Niko said. "I have need of crew members and trust that you do not object to my taking her away and off this planet?"

"Not at all," the Empress said. She continued looking at Atlanta, her face expressionless and unreadable. She added, her voice soft, "Sometimes I must do things that are necessary. Sometimes I must do things that I cannot explain at the time."

Atlanta ignored the notes of regret and sorrow in the voice of the Empress. What did she care? She was adrift now. She was meaningless now. She had no role. It made her dizzy to think about it.

The world steadied as she looked at Niko. The captain wanted her, even if no one else did, and that meant she would be with friends. She would not have to say goodbye to the rest of them. A wave of relief and almost happiness surged over her, followed by anxiety. *I have no money.*

Niko, watching her, said, "I will give you a regular crew's share, a tenth of whatever it is that we accrue once we set up operations again. You may draw on it ahead of time in order to outfit yourself." She looked again at the Empress and said pointedly, "Although I would expect your government, which you have served in this capacity of diversion and quarry, to of course want to outfit you with the best of its equipment and a store of living funds as a small thank-you. I am sure they would not want to be shamed by having an outsider care for their own better than they do."

"Of course," the Empress said. For the first time she smiled, even though it was only the tiniest of smiles, barely visible.

Niko did not smile back. "Then I trust Your Majesty will excuse me if I take my crew member away. She has suffered some shock and distress this day, and I think she deserves solitude in which to absorb all of this."

"You do not think I have done well by her," the Empress murmured.

"I would not presume to judge," Niko said.

"That is an ambiguous statement."

"There are those that would presume to judge their betters and find them lacking."

Atlanta was not entirely sure what the conversation was about, only that hostility and anger and something else lurked underneath its surface. She said, "May I have your permission to depart, Your Majesty?"

The Empress inclined her head in silent acquiescence. She watched them depart, and the door clicked shut after them. When it did, the sound echoing on the tiles, she let out a long breath and released the arms of her throne, leaning back. She closed her eyes.

"Judge me not, Nicolette Larsen," she said to herself. She touched the bluestone charm around her neck, shaped like a bird, flying free.

The same charm she always wore, even when walking among her soldiers, pretending to be one of them. As she had so many years ago on Rourke's Leap.

|.||.||.||.||.||.||.||.||.||.||.||.||.||.||.||.||.||.||.||.||.||.||.||.||.||.||||||

25

They rode back up to the ship in silence. Niko did not press Atlanta, who sat, still feeling numb and frozen, staring out the viewport at the stars. When the shuttle docked, she followed Niko into the *Thing*.

The sight of her startled but delighted the others. Gio whooped and threw her up into the air; Dabry produced cookies and tea. Lassite came and touched her arm, and said, "I told you that you would return."

"Give her a little space," Niko said. "She's had a lot to absorb."

"Well," Niko said to all of them. "Now I guess we've got to do something I haven't been looking forward to."

"What's that?" Atlanta squared her shoulders, prepared for anything.

"We need to return Takraven's ship to him."

Atlanta had not been prepared for that. "We're going to return it?"

"Of course," Niko said. "You didn't think we could just make off with one of the most expensive ships in the universe, did you? There are laws about that sort of thing, after all."

Atlanta set her jaw. Consoling herself for her exile by imagining travel with Niko and her crew was a vision that had, very definitely, included the *Thing*.

"How does the ship feel about that?" she asked.

"The ship is programmed to belong to somebody. That's simply how it is. That's not something that Lolola's chip changed. The personality's different now, I'll give you that. Takraven may find it quite a bit more obstreperous, perhaps. But it's his ship. Bought and paid for."

"Where will we find him?"

"I've been checking the feeds. Currently he's at Magellan."

"Why hasn't he been in contact with us before?" she asked suspiciously.

"He has, it turns out. The IAPH blocks signals—for a while he thought the ship had been blown up at TwiceFar. When we came through Q-space and reappeared inside the Known Universe, the ship's signal was reported. He's sent a polite request for us to take the *Thing* to Magellan and drop it off—he'll recompense us for the trouble."

"Why is he being polite if he thinks we've stolen his ship?"

"He doesn't. For all he knows, we found it. The station wasn't destroyed entirely, but it's rebuilding and things are chaotic there. I explained that he'd let us aboard the ship in order to flee and had himself died en route to it. That's the truth, and a mind check will corroborate."

Atlanta was still disgruntled.

She said as much to the ship, when she was alone in her room, or at least as alone as anyone could be inside a living being.

"This is how I am made," the ship told her. "I belong to Arpat Takraven."

"Why should you belong to anyone?" she demanded. "You are a sentient being. This is slavery, and slavery is outlawed in the Known Universe."

"This is the law," the ship said. It did not understand the question. Of course it had to belong to someone. It filed its reaction between *confusion* and *bewilderment*.

"You are programmed to believe that!"

"You are programmed too," the ship said. "But your programming is more haphazard." It paused. "I have learned new things from you and the others," it said. "I have learned much more about emotions than I thought I would ever be able to. But I do not like *sadness*. It feels like there are things growing inside me that do not belong there."

Atlanta leaned against the wall, putting her palm up against its solidity, and the throb of the blood circulating through it. She might be lost, she might not know who she was, but she could feel the ship and her own answering warmth.

She said, "I feel it too."

Magellan was near the center of the Milky Way. A trade hub and close to many of the favorite pleasure spots of the rich, Magellan was synonymous with money. Niko was very glad that Takraven was covering the *Thing*'s docking fees.

She thought he might have been anxious about his ship, which made her feel better about returning it.

He met them on the *Thing*. He looked much the same as he had the first time Niko encountered him.

He did have a bodyguard droid with him this time, a bristle of thorny black metal. She didn't blame him for that at all. After all, while they were returning his ship, she had to admit they had acquired it under questionable circumstances.

He looked around the air lock where they stood. "Everything seems intact," he said. "I gather from your account that there was some issue with pirates?"

"We spent some time in the IAPH before we managed to break free," Niko said dryly.

His eyebrow rose. "The IAPH, the same one described in *Skullduggery and Sacred Space Vessels*?"

"The one and the same," Niko said.

"There's a story in all of this that I want to hear," he said. "Will you tell it to me?"

They took him to his own dining chamber—where the window

that they had watched Q-space through now showed the port, and the other tiny ships, the figures of workers crawling on them like ants—and settled around the table.

The ship produced food and drink.

Takraven stared at it. "This is not what it usually gives me," he said in a perplexed tone.

He took a cautious sip. "Why, that's quite pleasant!" he exclaimed.

He set it down and took up one of the cookies, this time taking a full bite. His eyebrows rose again, and he ate the rest in three quick bites. He mopped his face with a napkin and looked around at them.

"Someone has taught my ship to cook!" he said. "I never heard of such a thing happening with a bioship. I always thought you had to eat what they produced or else use a replicator. I was contemplating taking out the ones it had if I'd kept racing."

"But you didn't?" Niko asked. "The *Thing* could outperform anything I've ever piloted."

The ship experienced *pride* to a degree it had not before.

He shook his head. "Too much work, coordinating things and paying entrance fees and having inspections and all of that. I tried it for half a solar year, and after that I went back to my old ways. The *Thing*'s lost on me, truth be told." He patted the table's material. "Let's hear this saga."

The battle bot bodyguard went off to charge itself at Takraven's direction, and the atmosphere grew more relaxed.

Niko was the one who started the story, but early in Dabry said, "Begging pardon, sir, I believe you've left something out," and seized the narrative, only to have Atlanta in turn grab the story at the moment when she'd stepped out of the crate, describing how she'd felt, standing in the ship, lost and alone, not knowing where she had come. Soon after, the *Thing* itself interjected something of a disquisition explaining why it had insisted on taking them to Scourse, which led to Niko apologizing to Takraven for having demanded the password and threatened him.

"You see, I had all of them depending on me—" she began, but Takraven raised a hand and waved it.

"No," he said, "I've got a temper and I regret in turn that I let it get the best of me and complicate all your lives. That was petty of me. I'd like to think I'm a bit better about dying with grace, particularly given it's not really dying. So never mind about all that and continue on."

A subdued Talon told him instead about how Lolola had taken control of the ship, and then retreated in order to allow Skidoo to describe the pirate haven, which she did with a great deal of dramatic detail, up to the point where Atlanta had been taken from the room. Picking it up again, Atlanta supplied an account that did not quite match what Milly had told the captain, and caught Niko looking at her sidelong in a way that promised they would be discussing that later.

Each of the pairs told their journey to the ship on the way, and Niko finished with an account of their battle to the ship that gave the pastry chef full props for her artistry with combat.

"Wouldn't want to face her in an empty corridor," she said finally. "That's all I'm saying."

Dabry told the rest of the flight and the entrance into Q-space, although not without some interruptions and speculations about what had happened to the IAPH and the pirates overall, particularly Tubal Last.

Takraven listened, wide eyed. He was an excellent listener, nodding and making interested noises at times. He didn't ask anything about the parts that they had edited out, such as who exactly Atlanta was, or the fact that they presented her as a cousin of Niko's, although she noticed him studying her thoughtfully more than once over the course of the story.

Niko ended it all by saying, "And then of course we knew we had to return the ship to you."

"Mmm," Takraven said. "Yes, I suppose that you did know that. It's a valuable ship." He leaned back in his chair, glancing around at it. "It seems like you all have had quite an impact on the ship. Have you enjoyed yourself, *Thing*, with all this racing around and destroying pirate havens?"

Enjoyment was not an emotion that the ship had previously considered. It ran through several thousand simulations before it said, "I believe it is pleasurable to stretch to full capacity." It added, after a few thousand more simulations, "Though one would not wish it to be constant."

"Indeed," Takraven said. The tone was at odds with his appearance, and Niko made herself remember he could be centuries old. He had vast resources at his control.

She'd spent a lot of time trying to research him on the way here. But money helped people scrub data, and the more money they had, the more efficiently they scrubbed it out of the public record. She wasn't convinced that he was actually human; she was sure that he had been around at least five centuries. Overall, he seemed to lead a low-key existence. The purchase of the *Thing*, some forty years ago, was perhaps the most flamboyant gesture he had made in recent years.

"Do *you* think you're wasted on me?" For a second, Niko thought Takraven was addressing her, but then she realized he was speaking to the ship.

"I do not understand how all of the words are used." The *Thing* sounded small and sad and confused for the first time since Niko had first met it. "Whenever I think I understand emotions, then something happens and none of them makes sense anymore. Waste? Waste is careless expenditure. You could make money with me, but you do not need money. Other people could make money with me, and they need it, but they do not own me. Is that waste?"

"It would seem like it." Takraven drummed on the table. He looked at Niko. "Make me an offer."

"What?" she said, mind scrambling in several directions. "I don't usually—I mean, I—maybe Skid—"

He laughed outright at her confusion. "No. For the *Thing.*"

"We couldn't begin to afford what you paid for the ship."

He shook his head. "That's not what I'm asking. I've lived a long time, and I've never seen a bioship act like this. We could take it apart, see how this happened—" For a second his eyes were so cold they sent a chill down Niko's spine, and then warmth refilled them and she wondered if she'd imagined the moment. "—but I'd rather let the experiment play out and see what happens if the ship stays under your influence."

He considered the lot of them. "Not just Niko's, but this group's."

At a loss, Niko looked around at the others. Dabry's brow was furrowed in thought. Skidoo's colors were bright with interest, and beside her Gio was nodding to himself, lips pursed.

Milly shrugged, but Atlanta was also nodding.

"As good as anywhere," Talon said.

Niko didn't like this uncertainty. She said, "What would you expect in return?"

"I'll let you have control of the *Thing* for five years," he said. "During that time, you'll give me—let's say, thirty percent of your net."

High, but not unfair, given the magnitude of the offer. Niko and her crew would be coming out way ahead. She didn't trust this fortune, though. She said, "What other strings would there be?"

"I would expect you not to engage in anything illegal, like slavery," he said.

"Small fear of that."

He nodded and went on. "You'll deposit my take every six

months in an authorized Creditnet system. Lateness nets you a ten percent late charge, compounded weekly."

Tough but doable. Niko nodded. Surely there was a catch coming.

"You will avoid the Arranti."

That startled her. "How? No one can predict what they will do."

He shook his head. "You mistake me. If you see one, even suspect one's presence, you will leave."

"Might I ask why?" she ventured.

"I do not trust their games. And that should be easy enough. What may be hardest is my third stipulation."

"Which is?"

"Once a year, you will cook a meal for myself and some friends. I will provide the materials. Your total time for preparation and execution should be no longer than a week each time."

"That's an odd stipulation," Niko said.

He smiled. "It will give me a chance to hear your stories each year. It seems to me you'll have more than a few to tell. And I'd like to taste the food that should have gotten a Nikkelin Orb. In fact, I'm curious. You've rescued your friend and achieved your goal—what now?"

"I'd thought—" She looked around at the others. She'd been thinking about this for a while, but she hadn't talked to any of them about it, not even Dabry.

They wanted to stay together, she knew that. Each of them had found a family here, of sorts. A ragtag, mishmash family, but a family nonetheless. And so she had come up with her plan.

"I don't want us to settle down," she said. "TwiceFar was interesting, but if we're traveling with the *Thing*, we don't want to create a permanent base." She added, "Just yet, at any rate," looking over at Arpat. The phrase *five years* hadn't escaped her, nor that he hadn't said anything about what would happen at the end of it.

Everyone was leaning forward now, intrigued and interested.

"So we take the food to the people," she said. "Dock at a station, rent space, set up a pop-up kitchen, spend a few weeks giving them something new and different while we learn from them as well. Then we wander along, find someplace new."

She put her elbows on the table. "We could chase ingredients. Take on a big lot of them—the *Thing* has plenty of cargo space. Make each special ingredient the center of its own restaurant. Get a batch of oilpearls on Baal, for example, and serve Baalian potash at one. Then Nigelian fronds—remember when we got some of those, Dabry?—and use them to put together something with a Trokash feast day feel. You get the picture."

Dabry looked thoughtful. "We could search out some things I've only heard of," he said. His fingers flexed as though imagining stirring, measuring, spooning. Cooking.

Skidoo's flesh brightened even further, happy stripes of purple and crimson. "Lots of travel, lots of new people to is being meeting," she said.

Milly said, "Suits me well enough."

Lassite nodded in silent approval.

Gio signed, "You know I plan on sticking around. Gotta keep an eye on that one." He pointed a long finger at Talon, who looked surprised.

"Well?" Niko said to him.

"Well, what?" Talon said, looking puzzled.

"Is this a plan you'll enlist with?"

"Oh! Of course! Of course, Captain. Why would we . . . ?" He faltered, then started again. "Why would I go away from you? Where would I go?"

To make a home and family of your own, she thought. *As your mother would have wanted, if she'd been able to raise you the way she had been raised.* But that was a plan for another day. She looked to Lassite, who simply nodded at her, and then to Atlanta. "Princess?"

"You can all stop calling me that anytime you like," Atlanta said.

The ship thought *excitement*. The ship thought *anticipation*. The ship thought *hope*.

Dabry drew Niko aside after they'd seen Takraven off the ship. "Sir? I've got something for you."

She tilted her head. "Another crate containing an Imperial Heir that will send us off on a wild goose chase across the universe?"

"Nothing like that."

She followed him to his chamber. He took a package wrapped in ordinary white plastic from the shelf, shoebox sized but a little wider and flatter. He handed it to her.

She turned it over, examining it and finding no label or other signs of its contents. She said, "What is this? It's not my birthday. There's no occasion that we are marking now."

"Perhaps there will be in the future," he said. "Open it."

The fabric inside was purple. She held it up and the garment unfolded itself. The buttons were emblazoned with the *Thing*'s sigil. She swallowed hard against the lump that had grown in her throat. It seemed enormous, fist sized.

"Last tore your other one," Dabry said, "and it was pretty threadbare to start with. I had this made on Montmurray. We almost didn't have enough time for me to go pick it up."

"Thank you," she managed.

"Put it on."

She shrugged it on and it fit perfectly, clung to her form as she straightened even taller than she normally held herself.

"It seemed a better choice than a pirate uniform," Dabry said.

"Indeed." She saluted him gravely and he returned it.

"You've no objection to becoming a Free Trader?" she asked. "You don't want to go back to your home planet?"

He shook his head. "Everything I have is here."

A few days later, they were almost ready to depart. The *Thing* had taken on plenty of fuel, and they had all done some shopping in order to accumulate its first culinary cargo, although Dabry had insisted on being the one to make a majority of the decisions.

He'd also turned the ship's gardens around quite a bit, converted two unused spaces into ancillary space for them, and installed more grow lights and racks, as well as a few chambers that were darker, one suited for fungi, and the other which he refused to discuss, saying simply they'd know when it was time.

The insurance money had come through, and much of it went toward that cargo, although some had gone to fitting out a new kitchen, taking a great deal of care to insulate the machines so they would not irritate the ship's tender flesh. The small remainder was something that Niko set aside for future contingencies; they all agreed that it was better to have that safety net than to worry about outfitting the *Thing* in luxury, although Skidoo insisted that they all remember that it could be an option sometime in the future. In the meantime, they made do with what the ship could produce for them, which was an astonishingly wide range and not really that much of a hardship.

Niko re-created her office bedroom, although with considerably more space than in the original. She had already managed to clutter it thoroughly, and the Derloen ghosts swam through every once in a while as though recognizing it.

That was where she was when the ship found her in order to deliver some news.

"Captain," the ship said. "There is a delivery for you."

Niko put down the logbook she'd been studying. From Extos, Pet could have gone in three major directions.

It wasn't that Niko was keeping tabs on them, simply that she . . . wanted to know.

"What is it?" she said.

"A delivery bot with a letter."

"A letter? Like in an envelope, made of actual substance?"

"This one appears to be paper," the ship confirmed.

Intrigued, Niko went to see what it was.

The delivery bot reminded her of the one that had originally brought the crate holding Atlanta, although it was a half meter smaller, and its colors were green and blue. It thrust the data pad at her. "Sign for acknowledgment here," it demanded.

"Could I see what I'm acknowledging first?"

A drawer in its body slid open; the tentacle plucked out what looked to be an envelope and waved it briefly in the air before returning it to the drawer.

Niko sighed but chose not to fight this battle. She jotted her name on the data pad, and held out her hand expectantly. The drawer reopened, and this time the tentacle deposited the envelope in her hand.

Real paper, made from rag pulp. Expensive and ostentatious. Had Takraven sent some additional message, some instruction that he had neglected to mention earlier? But, no, there were no markings on the envelope.

She turned it over in her hand, wondering if she should scan it first. But it would not have come through the system without passing through any number of scans. She slid a fingernail underneath the flap that sealed it, and tugged it to loosen the paper. Unfolding the paper inside, she read it quickly:

> *Dear Niko:*
> *I'm glad that you made it away alive.*
> *I'm working on a menu of my own, you see.*
> *Tubal Last*

"Momma Sky," she breathed out. She crumpled the paper in her hand.

"Will a gratuity be forthcoming?" the waiting bot asked. "In case you are new to the customs of this station, it is the norm to acknowledge personal service with a small tip, amounting to five to fifteen credits and payable by tapping the requisite panel." The requisite panel slid out helpfully.

"Go bilk some other naïve tourist," Niko told it.

She watched it trundle away.

"*Thing*," she said.

"Yes, Captain?"

"Prepare to depart."

"May I ask our destination, Captain?"

Despite the chill that had run up and down her spine upon reading the words from Tubal Last, Niko couldn't help the tiny smile as she turned to head to the pilot room. She had her crew, one of the fastest ships in the world, and someone to find. She straightened the lapels of her Free Trader coat and stroked a thumb along the purple fabric, fresh and shiny and unstained.

"Where else?" she said. "Adventure."

The ship felt *excitement*.

ACKNOWLEDGMENTS

||||||||||||||||||||||||||||||||||||||||||||||||||||||||||||||||||||||||||||||||||||||||||||||||||||||

So many people have cheered me on during the journey that led me to this book that I cannot name them all. But I want to mention one particular institution, the Griffon Bookstore in South Bend, Indiana, where I used to buy science fiction and fantasy and dream of the day my works would be on those shelves. Thank you, Ken and Sarah, for all you've done not just for me but for all the smart, geeky kids who loved to read and play games and who found shelter beneath your wings. I wouldn't be who I am today without you.

ABOUT THE AUTHOR

Cat Rambo lives, writes, and teaches somewhere in the Pacific Northwest. Their two hundred plus fiction publications include stories in *Asimov's Science Fiction, Clarkesworld*, and *The Magazine of Fantasy & Science Fiction*. They are a Nebula Award winner and an Endeavour and World Fantasy Award finalist. For more about them, as well as links to their fiction and their popular on-line school, The Rambo Academy for Wayward Writers, see kittywumpus.net